"Maybe you'd like to come along."

It wasn't hard to conjure up the picture of Sarah running through the grass, throwing sticks for the dogs to chase, her long tawny hair streaming behind her. Without really intending to, Christopher said, "I'll take you up on it."

Sarah wondered if her impulsive invitation had been a mistake. Without his uniform he seemed very different from the icy-eyed, commanding man who'd confronted her the other evening. He was so alive. Vibrant. Unease fluttered in her stomach.

She was just being a good neighbor, she reminded herself. She needed this time with him to help him understand Puppy Power and the successes the program had brought about. She rummaged in the back of the van for her rubber boots, wanting to hide the silly, unwarranted flush that heated her cheeks.

"Need some help?" Before she could protest, Christopher knelt before her, sliding the boot on. The touch of his strong tanned fingers against her sensitive foot was electrifying, unnerving...

ABOUT THE AUTHOR

The writing team of Mary Scamehorn and Karen Parker has been collaborating on wonderful romances since 1983. Their first eight books, written under the pseudonym Blair Cameron, enchanted readers of Dell Candlelight Supremes. We're thrilled to introduce them, under their new pseudonym Kathryn Blair, to readers of Harlequin American Romance. When not writing, the authors teach school—Mary at the elementary level and Karen junior high. Both Mary and Karen make their homes in Tacoma, Washington, and enjoy sharing their lives and hobbies with their families. The two women, who have a mutual love of the sea, found inspiration for *Home Is the Sailor* in the Seattle area.

Home Is
the Sailor
Kathryn Blair

Harlequin Books

TORONTO • NEW YORK • LONDON
AMSTERDAM • PARIS • SYDNEY • HAMBURG
STOCKHOLM • ATHENS • TOKYO • MILAN

For my mother, Verna,
who makes everything possible
—Karen

Published March 1989

First printing January 1989

ISBN 0-373-16285-5

Chapter One

Of all the port cities Christopher Weaver's container ship put in to, Seattle was the most beautiful. Even though Yokohama and Kobe were more exotic, they were working ports. Taiwan and Hong Kong were overcrowded, swarming with trade, and Singapore... well, Singapore was unarguably spectacular, but it wasn't home.

After turning off the engine and pocketing the keys, he sat for a moment in his black Corvette parked above Lake Union. It was always a little jarring to move from one part of his world to the other. Sometimes he wished he had the equivalent of a decompression chamber to help him make the adjustment. It was easier to go the other direction, he thought, shifting uneasily in his seat. It didn't take much time to find his sea legs, but it was more difficult to become accustomed to having solid ground beneath his feet. Although the vast Pacific could be treacherous, blowing howling winds, sudden gales and even typhoons in the seaman's path, he was far more comfortable handling the unpredictable elements than dealing with the emotional entanglements that waited for him in his home port.

Savoring the quiet moment, he appraised Seattle's skyline, silhouetted against the setting sun. His gaze lowered to the water of the urban lake where he saw the reflections of the city wavering on its broad surface. He thought back to when, as a small boy, he'd rowed his skiff on the lake, and the Smith Tower, rising an imposing twenty stories, had been the highest building in this waterfront city. Later, when he'd neared his teens, the Space Needle's slender height rose into the sky, dwarfing the white, small-windowed landmark. Since that time the Space Needle itself had been dwarfed by the glass-walled skyscrapers that rose tier by tier from the hilly streets above Elliot Bay, competing for a place in the rarefied air of the now throbbing, vibrant northwestern metropolis.

Seattle had come of age with him. There, laid out in concrete and steel, was the graphic evidence of the city's past thirty-seven years' growth. But what about him? His breath came out in a ragged sigh. What had he accomplished in his thirty-seven years?

On the plus side, as a permanently assigned chief mate in the Merchant Marine, he was well on his way to fulfilling his goal of becoming the captain of his own ship, like his father before him. But on the negative side, the demands of his chosen career had cost him his marriage.

Christopher's mind slid away from thoughts of his ex-wife, Virginia, and his teenage son, Adam. As if spurred into action by the unsettling memories, he snapped open the car door, picked up a well-worn overnight bag from the leather seat beside him, and unfolded his tall muscular body from the low-slung sports car.

His feet took the familiar wooden steps two at a time as he descended the unrailed staircase to the floating boardwalk that ran perpendicular to the lakeshore. A few long strides and he was on the barge that held his mother's home.

Abruptly he stopped and looked around. The contrast between the immaculately kept ship on which he'd lived and worked for the past thirty-five days and the shabbiness of his mother's houseboat brought an ache to his heart. Four years of neglect in the damp marine climate had taken their toll. Reaching out to pull off a piece of the peeling paint that curled randomly from the unprotected siding, Christopher swore softly. He crumbled the chip between his fingers and let the pieces fall to the deck. The place was even more dilapidated than he remembered.

Tangled weeds now grew grotesquely in the redwood boxes he'd helped his father to build, replacing the profuse flowers that his mother used to tend with care. He grimaced. If something wasn't done soon, this house would be condemned by the city like the one on the other side of the boardwalk. As he bent to set upright an overturned potted tree, he glanced across the way expecting to see the neighboring eyesore. The run-down structure had been a constant irritant to his father until a sudden heart attack had ended his otherwise contented retirement almost four years before.

Straightening in surprise, Christopher stared instead at a neat bungalow-style boat, shining with fresh gray paint. Yellow-and-white striped awnings and overflowing flower boxes framed its polished windows. The pungent odor of bright geraniums wafted on the cool breeze from where they filled whiskey barrels set neatly at each of the four corners of the painted deck. The newly moored houseboat was as shipshape as his father's high standards would have demanded.

Relieved that the old empty houseboat had been towed away, he turned back to his mother's place and pulled his customary three sharp dings on the ship's bell that hung by the entry. Pushing open the door, he went into the two-story house that had been his childhood home.

"Hi, Mom," he called, dropping his bag on the hardwood floor of the small hall. He hung his visored uniform hat on the brass coatrack before turning to enter the cozy living room.

A strange white dog scampered across the braided rug. Circling and barking, it snapped at Christopher's gabardine pant legs as he approached the padded wheelchair in front of the picture window overlooking the water. The dog, a puppy really, seemed determined to keep Christopher from getting close to his mother. Only after she patted her lap and the mutt jumped into it was Christopher able to take her face between his hands and press his lips against her smooth forehead.

"It's good to have you home," Mary Lou Weaver said quietly, raising her right hand to pat her son's face. Her other hand lay paralyzed and useless in her lap.

Feeling a lump in his throat, Christopher swallowed hard. It was the first time since his mother had suffered her stroke that she'd greeted Christopher with the phrase she'd used every time his father had returned from a voyage.

"Where did you get the mutt?" he asked, straightening to his full height, his hand sliding down to his mother's robed shoulder.

"She's not a mutt. Her name is Amanda."

Looking into his mother's faded blue eyes, remembering how they'd once burned brightly in her youthful face, he imagined he could see a spark of interest lighting their depths. A spark he'd almost given up looking for in the past three years.

"Amanda?" he asked, smiling down at the wiggling ball of fluff.

She nodded. "It's what I'd planned to name you if you'd been a girl." The hint of a twinkle played in her eyes as the puppy stretched its muzzle up to lick her under the chin with its long pink tongue. Christopher's eyes narrowed. There definitely was a change in his mother. He hadn't imagined it.

Before he could question her further, the doleful voice of Jeanette Johnson, his mother's companion/housekeeper, interrupted. "Mr. Weaver, I'd like to see you in the kitchen." Christopher felt his mother's shoulder muscles tense beneath his palm.

"Be right back, Mom. I want to hear more about Amanda," he said. Patting his mother's arm reassuringly, he turned and followed the dour housekeeper into the kitchen.

"Either that dog goes, or I do!" Mrs. Johnson hissed as soon as they were out of earshot of the living room.

The thin-lipped woman's belligerent tone set his nerves on edge. She was a disagreeable individual. There was nothing he'd like better than to send her packing, but his hands were tied. He had only the weekend in port this trip. A good part of one day would have to be spent supervising the unloading of the cargo from the ship, and the rest of the time would be spent answering his mail, checking out his condominium and getting ready for another transpacific run.

"I didn't hire on here to clean up an animal's messes," Mrs. Johnson spit out.

"Where did the dog come from?" Christopher countered coolly. "I thought maybe you'd brought it."

"Humph!" she snorted, missing his sarcasm. "You think I like dog hair all over the place? You think I like listening to that ungodly yapping every time I as much as go near your mother? Why, that dog even bit me!" She flung out a rigid finger for his inspection, then snapped it back before Christopher could assess the damage.

"Then where did it come from?"

"From that creature next door! That Sarah Mitchell. She runs some kind of kennel over there, and Lord knows what else. There's a steady stream of peculiar people coming and going, day and night. What with the dogs barking and the doors slamming and the loud voices, I haven't had a minute's peace and quiet since they hauled away that other place and moved her in.

"She came over, bold as brass, almost as soon as they got her tied up to the pilings. She talked with your mother for quite a while, then the next thing I knew, she went home and came back with that hairy little beast. I told your mother that I had all I could do around here caring for her. I told her I wasn't being paid to feed and care for a thankless dog, as well!" She moved to the sink and twisted on the tap. The gush of water punctuated her curt remarks. Peelings from the potato she attacked flew in all directions.

"I'll see what I can do about it," Christopher answered with reluctance, just managing to suppress a sigh. He hated being dictated to by the obstinate woman, but she knew she had him over a barrel. It was difficult to find anyone who was willing to be a companion to an invalid who lived on a houseboat. There was no way he could find a replacement in two days. He'd spent almost two weeks the last time, and the end result of his efforts, he thought grimly, had been hiring this woman.

Consciously calming his ire, he considered. When his mother had first come out of the convalescent center, he'd thought he might be forced into taking a shore job with the company. But as if she'd anticipated his suggestion, his mother had announced that she wouldn't hear of him putting her needs before his career, saying that she'd check into an old folks' home first. Proud that he was following in his father's footsteps, she'd made it clear that she hadn't raised her son to be a landlubber. His relief had been tinged with guilt, but he'd convinced himself that there really wasn't anything to be gained by his staying ashore. Although the situation wasn't ideal, he'd been able to keep her in the home she loved for nearly three years by employing reliable companions. He'd just have to find some way to placate Mrs. Johnson.

Returning to the living room, he pulled up a needlepoint-covered footstool and sat at his mother's feet. Amanda ventured a low growl as she sat curled on her mistress's lap.

"I suppose she told you to get rid of Amanda," Mrs. Weaver said, contentedly stroking the dog.

"She's not happy about her," Christopher hedged.

"So I've gathered," Mrs. Weaver remarked with quiet serenity, turning her gaze back to the window.

"She's threatening to quit."

"I'm not surprised. She's been muttering that threat for days. But better she goes than my Amanda."

Christopher rolled his eyes. His mother had never been one to argue. She just stubbornly refused to be drawn into a discussion when she'd made up her mind. What should he do now?

Damn. It was a shame. The puppy was a cute little thing, and his mother was obviously already attached to it. Reaching out, he patted the furry head. He was rewarded with a smile from his mother and a wet lick from the pooch that dried on his hand as he stood.

"Mom, I need to check the air in the 'Vette's tires," he lied. "I'll be back in a few minutes and we can talk then." He strode purposefully toward the door. He wasn't going to be the heavy in this piece. The irresponsible woman who'd brought the dog over here was going to have to take her back, or come up with some creative solution that would allow his mother to keep her.

Settling his white hat low on his forehead, he jumped across the five feet of boardwalk that separated the two houseboats and pounded on the immaculate white door. The noise of barking dogs and feminine laughter muffled the sound of his knock. He raised his fist and tried again, but the rowdy sounds inside didn't diminish. When he rashly tried the handle, the door swung open beneath his hand, revealing a pleasingly proportioned young woman in jeans and a peach-colored sweatshirt, down on her knees on the living-room floor. Her fresh-complexioned face sparkled with laughter as she played with a bunch of dogs of assorted sizes, shapes and colors.

Christopher watched, feeling a grin lift the corners of his set lips, as each dog vied for her attention. Tumbling and rolling, they jumped en masse until a particularly forceful lick in the face from the largest sent the tawny-haired woman sprawling. She looked up from her reclining position, and her eyes met his.

Sweeping her gaze down the lines of the brass-buttoned, gold-braid trimmed, black uniform on the male who filled the doorway, Sarah Mitchell jumped to her feet.

"Get out of here," she commanded huskily, her hands stroking and quieting the dogs grouped around her.

In spite of the fact that the intruder's height towered an easy foot over her own five-foot-one frame, she raised her chin in defiance. "Unless you have a warrant, get on the other side of that door!"

"Why would I have a warrant?" Christopher asked, remembering Mrs. Johnson's vague accusations.

She shrugged. "You tell me. I'm a law-abiding citizen. But since I've moved here that old biddy across the way has sent the SPCA, the SPD, and even the EPA to check me out. The only one she's missed is the SFD, so I assume that's you. But unless you can show me a piece of paper that authorizes you to be here, get off my property!" She moved behind the door and began to close it.

"You can relax," Christopher said, planting one foot on the threshold. "I'm not from the fire department. That 'old biddy' happens to be my mother's companion. She claims you're the one causing all the commotion."

"I'm not causing any kind of commotion!"

"Mrs. Johnson says you're running a kennel over here and that people are coming and going at all hours. This area's zoned against that kind of thing."

"I'm not running a kennel," she protested. She saw his eyes pointedly take in the rows of built-in wire cages that lined the wall behind her. Too stubborn to explain, she added, "And Mrs. Johnson can just mind her own damned business."

Amen to that, Christopher thought, a glint of amusement lighting his clear blue eyes. He had to admire this small woman. Without a doubt, she could put almost anyone on the run. But whatever she was doing, it was obvious she took more than a passing interest in animals.

"Maybe—" he stroked his chin, assuming a deliberately thoughtful posture "—what you're running here is a dognapping ring."

The young woman's hazel eyes and full mouth opened wide with shocked innocence. "I think you'd better mind your own damned business, too."

"Well, if you are," Christopher teased, ignoring her strongly worded suggestion, "you could use some advice." He made a show of looking over each of the dogs. Bending, he amiably scratched one dog of particularly questionable ancestry behind a floppy ear. "These mongrels aren't worth a plug nickel on the black market. Maybe you can't be arrested for your unfortunate taste in canines, but there must be some law against harboring this many animals."

"What would you know about dogs?"

Remembering why he'd come, Christopher straightened to his full height. "Enough that I certainly wouldn't be giving one to a woman who can't take care of herself. Since you're the Lady Bountiful who dropped the puppy off on her doorstep, it's up to you to make my mother understand why it's impossible for her to keep it, things being as they are."

Almost speechless with anger, Sarah stared up into the ruggedly attractive man's piercing blue eyes. He'd invaded her home—she wasn't sure, but she thought she'd securely shut the front door—and topped that with having the audacity to attack her way of life. Even the authorities hadn't had his nerve. Clenching her fists, she placed them on her hips and tossed back her long unruly mane of hair. She retaliated with a barrage of questions. "Who do you think you are telling me what to do? I've been in this moorage almost a month, and up till now I haven't seen a sign of you! What kind of son are you and what gives you the right to storm in at your leisure and turn your mother's life upside down?"

Mrs. Weaver had told her about her Merchant Marine son, even shown her a picture. But it must have been taken some time ago. It didn't do him justice. His hair was lighter, sun bleached, Sarah supposed, and his tanned face showed the wear of a lifetime of exposure to the elements. It wasn't a handsome face in the traditional sense, but it was strong-featured and compelling. It was the face of a seafaring man, and unless she missed her bet, it had character etched into every appealing line. His mother had told Sarah how good Christopher was to her, but for the moment she preferred to keep that to herself. It was in Mrs. Weaver's best interests for Sarah to keep this man on the defensive.

"I don't have to explain myself or my actions to you." He sounded annoyed.

"That fact, at least, is mutual," Sarah responded wholeheartedly. "I don't have to account to you, either!"

"When you interfere in my mother's life, you do!"

Ignoring his comment, Sarah went on, "And you should be thanking me for that puppy instead of threatening me with the law. Are you so blind that you can't see the change that's come over your mother since I gave her Amanda?"

Forced to acknowledge that his mother's apathy did seem lessened and that she was at last showing interest in something, even if it was just a little dog, Christopher faltered for a moment before answering. In a softer tone he asked, "Even if I had, why should I attribute the change to a small mutt that could double as a floor mop?"

"Because that's what Puppy Power is all about."

"Puppy Power?"

She nodded. She knew she should ask him in so that they could sit down and discuss the matter civilly, but a streak of stubborn pride kept her from it. "It's a private volunteer organization."

"I've never heard of it."

"I'm sure you haven't. We don't solicit funds or ask for contributions. I founded it myself, and we're still very small. Friends I've made during the years I've worked as a veterinarian's assistant have chipped in to help. There are six of us right now."

"What sort of things do you do?"

"Our only purpose is to retrieve suitable dogs from the pound and place them with shut-ins."

"Are you trying to tell me that you all go around foisting off mongrel strays on old people?" he asked. Realizing how rude he sounded, he hastily amended, "I know it bothers a lot of people to think of unwanted animals being destroyed. I don't like the idea myself. But I don't think the answer to the animal population problem is to give dogs to people who can't care for them."

Sarah let out an exasperated sigh. He was missing the point, deliberately or otherwise, she couldn't decide. "I'm interested in the dogs, sure, but that's not the primary reason I do it. That the dogs are happy is just a nice by-product. What I'm most concerned about is the people."

"I don't follow your drift," Christopher admitted.

"There's been some research done the past few years on the beneficial effects that owning pets has on people who live solitary lives. People out of the mainstream. Especially ones confined to prisons or rest homes."

Sarah was unaware of the light that softened her eyes as she warmed to her subject, but Christopher saw it. This woman was the kind a man might overlook in a crowd, but one-on-one she had a special appealing quality. It was her expressive eyes, he decided, and the mobility of her oval face. He couldn't help thinking that she'd be a disaster as a poker player. Her feelings were too easy to read, and right now, he was sure she didn't care much for him.

"One of the biggest problems is that many of those people lose the will to live. They don't care anymore. Most of the research has been informal and subjective, but all of the studies I've read have reached the same conclusion."

"And what's that?"

Sarah regarded him with suspicion. She wasn't sure he was really interested, but she decided to give him the benefit of the doubt. "The people who were given pets to love showed a marked improvement. Their whole outlook on life changed. They felt useful and alive again, because they had someone to love who loved them back."

"So this is some kind of a crusade with you?"

"You might say that," Sarah acknowledged, brushing a wayward strand of hair back from her forehead. "My friends here—" with a sweep of her hand she indicated the dogs that milled around her "—are my latest acquisitions, rescued from the pound last month. I keep the dogs with me for several weeks to get a feel for their temperaments. For this type of placement, they have to be well trained and gentle-natured. They have to like being held and petted. One of the keys to why Puppy Power works is the body contact. It's a variation on the principle that hugs are healthy."

"I see," Christopher said solemnly, hiding his amusement. He supposed this young woman kept abreast of all the latest fads and theories of pop psychology. Judging from her wholesome, all-American-girl appearance, he suspected, too, that she was the kind who shunned white flour and munched on alfalfa sprouts instead of potato chips. "Your volunteers. What do they do?"

"One of them helps me check the dogs out. Put them through their paces. The rest scout around looking for people who need a pet. There's a tremendous need, but placement is hard since we meet with a great deal of resistance from friends and relatives of shut-ins who don't understand the benefits of our program." She shot him an accusing glance. "After we make a placement and get the dog settled in, we do follow-up visits to make sure things are going all right for the owner, as well as for the dog. I do want my dogs to be as happy as their masters and mistresses."

Crossing his arms, Christopher rested one shoulder against the doorjamb. "So that explains the comings and goings over here of all sorts of people at odd hours, to quote the old biddy next door."

Sarah's fair skin reddened beneath her freckles. "None of that's true! That woman makes me furious! Why do you put up with her? I'm sure your mother would be much happier spending her time with someone else. Anyone else. Why don't you fire her?"

"I'd like to," Christopher conceded, "but I'm afraid it's not that easy. I had a devil of a time finding her. She'll never get any votes for Ms. Congeniality, but my mom can't take care of herself. I'm at sea six months out of every twelve. I have to know that she'll be cared for while I'm gone. What you don't seem to understand is that you've put me in a real bind."

He glanced at his watch. "I have only sixty hours in port before I'll be headed out to sea again, and Mrs. Johnson is threatening to quit unless the puppy goes."

Sarah stood her ground, though she was beginning to feel uneasy. The man had a problem. But, she reasoned, she wasn't the cause of it. She'd only been trying to help. His main problem, the one that should be uppermost in his mind, was his mother's health.

"It would be better for your mother if Mrs. Johnson did quit. Your mother needs that puppy. I'd say the biggest danger to her health is her apathy. She's a perfect example of what I was talking about." Sarah hated the pleading tone in her voice, but this was so important she didn't care what he thought of her. "Your dad's gone. You're away most of the time. I've talked with Mrs. Weaver, and she feels that since she's lost her health she doesn't have anything left to live for. Amanda has given her something to care about. Something that's really hers."

Christopher felt a sharp stab of pain. It hurt to hear his mother analyzed by a woman he'd just met. He'd have liked to come up with a rebuttal, but the hell of it was, everything she said was true.

"When I first met your mother, all she did was sit and stare out that window. She even let Mrs. Johnson do most of her talking for her. I could see there wasn't any time to waste. Fortunately Amanda was all set to go. She's such an adorable dog that I was thinking of keeping her myself, but being small I could see she was perfect for your mother. I took her over the first evening I moved in here. Since your mother's had Amanda, there's been a change in her attitude. She smiles now. She's glad to see me when I visit. We've had some nice talks."

Sarah searched Christopher's tanned face for some sign of weakening. Until he'd appeared in her doorway Christopher Weaver had been only a name—a name she'd asso-

ciated with the bland face of a young man who had stiffly
posed for a photograph years ago. The name had no relationship to this vital man, who gave off the impression of
coiled energy and keen intellect. She knew Christopher
Weaver's life included routine trips to the Orient, and she
wondered if some of that famed Oriental inscrutability had
rubbed off on him. She hadn't a clue to what he was thinking.

After a long moment he spoke. "Even if, and it's a highly
qualified if, having a dog will do all the things you claim,
you have to face the fact that Amanda can't cook, can't
clean, and can't help my mother bathe. If it comes to a
choice between the two, I'm afraid Mrs. Johnson wins." His
voice was cold and flat.

Sarah's spine stiffened defensively. "Look, I'm really
sorry. I can see now that I moved too fast. It never occurred to me that a puppy would cause this much of a
problem for you. But it's too late now. Your mother loves
Amanda and there's no way that I'm going to take her back.
You're just going to have to do what you think is best."

Christopher stared down into the thickly lashed hazel eyes
sparking in the implacable face lifted to his. She was chal-
lenging him to make the next move. But what could he do?
Order her to take back the damned dog? That, he knew,
would get him nowhere. In spite of his total frustration he
couldn't help but notice the sprinkling of coppery flecks
across the bridge of her pert nose, nor the charming way her
disheveled hair framed her tanned face. He suspected the
rosy glow of her high cheekbones reflected her ardent feelings.

Long accustomed to unquestioned authority, Christopher felt the wind go out of his sails. If one of his crew spoke
to him like this, the man would be up on charges of insub-
ordination. Watching the young woman kneel to gather the
dogs within the protective circle of her arms, as though she

expected him to seize them and throw them overboard, he
was the one who felt like a reprimanded seaman.

Suddenly the ideal solution seemed clear. He wondered
why he hadn't thought of it before. Taking his wallet from
his back pocket, he pulled out a few bills. "I'd make it
worth your while to—"

"Forget that!" Sarah exploded, jumping to her feet.
"You can't buy me off! And I won't take a bribe to do your
dirty work!"

He stepped back instinctively in response to her anger,
and she slammed the door in his face.

Chapter Two

"Okay, now you, Fred," Sarah commanded, holding open a framed wire door.

Obediently the part collie, part who-knew-what, jumped up into his carpeted kennel. After a few circlings of the roomy box, he settled down and put his muzzle on the floor, although his eyes danced with mischief.

"Good boy. Now go to sleep. Cushy life," she added with affection. She had a full house, two females and three males. Peering into each box she noted that all of her charges seemed comfortable and drowsy. She doubted her sleep would be disturbed tonight, though if even one started to yelp, the whole group would join in, and she'd have her hands full quieting them. It was one of the hazards of the job. At least she'd learned to fall back to sleep the minute her head hit the pillow.

She secured the latch on the last wire door on the second row of boxes she'd built, floor-to-ceiling, against the short wall of her living room. Some people had oak or mahogany shelves, she reflected, lined with interesting books and interspersed with knickknacks. What did she have? Dogs! And not china dogs, either. Real, live, breathing, warm-blooded dogs, with an occasional flea thrown into the bargain.

Yawning, she arched her back and stretched her arms over her head before letting them fall to her sides. It had been a long demanding day at the clinic. She'd been tired even before Mrs. Weaver's son had made his unexpected appearance, but now she was exhausted. Facing down that commanding man had been emotionally draining. Yet even though she hadn't done anything wrong, she felt a twinge of guilt. Poor Mrs. Weaver was the one who stood to be the loser. It was still hard to believe that Christopher Weaver had thought he could bribe her into taking Amanda back. The man had a streak of arrogance a mile wide.

Aware of a muffled growl coming from her stomach, Sarah placed a hand over her midriff. Her mouth twisted in a wry grimace. Her stomach was as demanding as the dogs. Left to herself, she'd never think of eating, but she could trust her gut to kick in and demand to be fed. Not that anyone would believe that, she thought ruefully, running her hands down the swell of her hips. She was a little too bottom-heavy for her own liking, but she wasn't vain enough to do anything drastic about it. She got plenty of exercise walking the dogs and ate only when hungry. If it all went to her hips? Well, those were the breaks.

"Nighty-night, you sleeping beauties," she said softly to the dogs, snapping off the light.

She was smiling with contentment as she went into the kitchen. The animals had been fed and walked, and now it was her turn. Sweet and sour, she decided as she took a box from a stack in the freezer and placed the plate in the microwave. Humming slightly off-key, she quickly fixed a cottage-cheese salad and arranged it on a stoneware plate, pausing only to give her flash-frozen dinner the required half turn and to reset the dial. Satisfied with the salad's appetizing appearance, she placed it on one of the blue place mats on her small glass-topped table.

Though Sarah ate alone and seldom cooked anything more elaborate than a frozen dinner, she made a ritual of her evening meal. She had decided when she first moved out on her own to resist the temptation to grab a bite and eat it on the run, or to fix a tray in front of the television. She used the time to think over the day, clearing her mind of worries and reliving the moments of joy or satisfaction.

As she lit blue tapers, using her cupped hand to shield the flames from the pleasant breeze that lifted the curtains, the microwave dinged for the second time. Simultaneously she heard a knock at the front door.

"Uh-oh," she breathed, blowing out the match. She had to answer it before the dogs became alarmed.

"Hi, kiddo," Erma Stinson's raspy voice greeted her.

"Thank goodness it's you," Sarah answered with relief, shutting and locking the door behind her eccentric friend.

"What's up? Someone been botherin' ya? Got a Peepin' Tom?" The retired policewoman's voice was hopeful. Striking a karate pose, she held her hands stiffly poised at shoulder height.

"Down, Erma, down," Sarah laughed, leading the way to the kitchen. "Nothing that menacing. At least I don't think so," she amended, conjuring up a disturbing vision of Christopher Weaver in an open-necked kimono, a black belt tied confidently around his waist. His lean body could indicate a dedicated interest in the martial arts. There'd been no evidence of middle-aged thickening in his torso, though she knew the man was in his late thirties. "Only a dissatisfied customer who wants to return the merchandise."

"Who? It couldn't be one of mine," Erma said defensively, sitting down and placing her bony elbows on the table. "I checked with Mr. Brady today, and he and Sissy are gettin' along fine. Mrs. Amherst just loves Puddles. And Henry tells me the Orion Nursing Home wants three more."

"That's great. You and Henry have had more luck than any of us. I hope we can find homes for that bunch bedded down in the living room. They'll be ready to go as soon as you check them out. It seems a pity that it's such an uphill battle to place them, since there are hundreds of shut-ins out there who are starved for love." Sarah gestured toward the houseboat across the way. "Actually, the problem's with one of mine."

Erma's wizened face registered pure disgust. "Is that Mrs. Johnson on her high horse again?"

"It's not her this time. It's Mrs. Weaver's son. He wants me to take Amanda back, and I just can't do that," Sarah said with a heavy sigh.

"Of course you can't! That poor old lady needs that dog. What's the deal?" Erma's snappy black eyes fastened on Sarah.

"I'll tell you all about it. Any chance you want to eat with me?"

"Never turn a meal down, as you well know."

"Chinese?"

"Whatever you're havin'."

While Sarah prepared another meal, she told Erma about Christopher Weaver's visit. She was relieved that, although the older woman recognized that she had a problem, Erma was adamant that Sarah couldn't blame herself. Not wanting to upset their digestion, they postponed deciding what to do—if anything—until they'd eaten.

After pouring them each a goblet of wine, Sarah sat down and placed her napkin on her lap.

"Looks good," Erma commented. "I get so sick of eatin' alone I go to McDonald's just for the company. I keep hopin' that one of those nice old men they show in their commercials will come over and sit with me. But all I ever see are bratty kids spillin' their chocolate shakes or teenagers wolfin' down their burgers like they never ate before. It's downright discouragin'."

"I don't mind eating alone," Sarah said, taking a bite. It was true. But it hadn't always been. It had been hard at first, damned hard. The emptiness, the absence of any sound other than her own chewing had terrified her. She'd turned on the TV in the living room, the radio in the kitchen and put a small load in the washer. The discordant racket had been a poor substitute for company, but it'd been the best she could do. It had taken weeks to get through a full meal without having to stop because the lump in her throat was too large to swallow over. But that was a long time ago. "It's the only peaceful time I have most days."

"When ya get to be my age it's not peaceful," Erma warned, "it's downright lonely. Ya better make sure that ya get some nice young man to sit where I'm sittin' soon, or the good ones'll all be taken."

"Plenty of time for that," Sarah said, turning her attention to her meal in the hope Erma would take the hint. Her lack of male companionship was not a subject she wanted to discuss.

"That's what ya always say, and I always tell ya there's never enough time," Erma said, gesturing with her fork. "A pretty girl like you needs a man. All that love and affection you lavish on those dogs would be better directed at a passel of kids."

"Look who's talking," Sarah muttered, realizing her mistake the moment the words left her mouth.

"Don't remind me." Erma's cheerful face darkened. "Biggest damn mistake I ever made, not havin' kids. That's one of the reasons I like to be with you, kiddo. Ya don't have any pictures."

"Pictures?" Sarah dutifully interjected, knowing Erma wouldn't be able to quit until she got it out of her system.

"Yeah, pictures. I can't stand women my age. Ya can't be with 'em five minutes until it's out with the pictures. Kids, grandkids, even great-grandkids. Holidays are even worse. I stock up my liquor cabinet, put in a supply of juicy best-sellers and hole up from Thanksgiving till the first of the year. Can't even turn on the TV without seein' some little snot-nosed kid's smilin' face."

Sarah put her fork down on her plate and placed her hands in her lap. On the whole she didn't give much thought to Erma's age. Only times like this, when Erma repeated things she'd said before almost word for word, reminded her that Erma was an old woman, with an old woman's tendency to dwell on the past. Though Erma only admitted to seventy-two, Sarah figured she was past eighty.

Erma paused to take a long draft from her wineglass. "Things were different when I was your age. A woman couldn't have it all. We had to make choices. My choice was different from most of the rest of 'em. A lady cop was a rarity. A lady cop with kids woulda been a no-go in the department. They'da claimed it was too dangerous on the beat. But I got to give ya credit for one thing, kiddo."

"What's that?"

"Ya got yourself a home." Erma pushed her chair back a little and glanced around the small kitchen with envy. "I never wanted the hassle of ownin' a house. Bernie tried to talk me into it, but I was a stubborn dame. And now look at me. Bernie's been gone five years and I'm stuck by myself in an apartment where they don't even allow pets. Worked half my life trainin' attack dogs and I can't even have a poodle!"

Sarah chuckled at the idea. The mental picture of the sparse, salt-and-pepper-haired woman in her army surplus fatigues and combat boots, walking a strutting pom-pom-cut dog with a rhinestone collar and a pink ribbon in its hair was ludicrous.

"Don't laugh." Erma scowled. "I'd even stoop that low if I could have a dog. But enough about me. What ya gonna do about this business next door?"

"I don't know," Sarah admitted. "I didn't tell you everything. Christopher Weaver tried to bribe me into taking Amanda back."

"You're not serious!"

"I am," Sarah said soberly. "It made me sick. For a while I hoped I was getting through to him, but when he took out his money, I knew he hadn't understood a thing I'd said."

"He sure as hell hadn't," Erma agreed. "Some of those sailors are pretty tough hard-bitten types."

"Christopher Weaver isn't like that at all." Sarah smiled in spite of her concern, mentally contrasting the polished, sophisticated officer with the burly, tattooed caricature she was sure Erma's overactive imagination had dreamed up.

"But I was so furious I shut the door in his face," Sarah confessed. "I wish now that I hadn't. I have no idea what he's going to do. I swear, if I find Amanda back in the pound tomorrow..."

"Ya don't think he'd deep-six her tonight, do ya?"

Sarah let out a sharp breath. "Oh, Erma, you're too much. I can't imagine him doing anything like that..."

"Human nature bein' what it is, ya never know." Erma shrugged. The movement caused the heavy gold earrings that stretched the thin lobes of her ears to bob erratically. "I was in police work long enough to know that some people won't hesitate to act when someone or somethin' gets in their way. He could always claim Amanda fell overboard."

Feeling a prickle of alarm, Sarah pushed back her chair. Coming from anyone else she would have dismissed the suggestion as preposterous, but despite Erma's tendency to exaggerate and overreact at times, the older woman's basic instincts were sound. Years spent on the police force had given her an almost encyclopedic fund of knowledge of human behavior.

"No—" Sarah emphatically shook her head "—that's just too ridiculous." Yet something compelled her to move to the kitchen window and pull the curtain back a little. Erma joined her, looking over her shoulder. As they peered out, the door to the Weaver home opened and Christopher stepped into the yellow beam of the porch light.

Sarah's eyes followed his tall figure as he left the houseboat deck and ran nimbly up the steps to the street.

"What's he got in that bag?" Erma whispered, her voice laden with suspicion.

"How would I know?" Sarah whispered back. "A change of underwear and toiletries, I suppose."

"Handsome devil," Erma commented under her breath, reaching up to pat her wiry permed hair in a feminine gesture. "Wouldn't I love to have a son like that to parade around with! It'd almost be worth puttin' up with his interferin' nonsense, just to have someone like him give a damn.

"Maybe it'd be best if we took a little walk," Erma suggested. "Very casual, all on the up-and-up. We could stop in to see how Amanda and Mrs. Weaver are gettin' along. Of course, if Amanda was in that bag it may already be too late. You talked to him. What d'ya think? Did he strike ya as a person who could do somethin' like that?"

Sarah considered. Though she and Christopher Weaver had had a strong disagreement, he'd had a valid argument. And he had a nice face...even a memorable face. There hadn't been a hint of cruelty in it. The worst she could say about him was that he was obviously used to getting his own way, and he was not above resorting to bribery to get it. "Take her back to the pound? Maybe. Drown her? No."

"Then we've got another chance at makin' this work. Say—" Erma brightened "—how 'bout you and me offerin' to take some of the burden off that Johnson dame?

We could walk the dog and give Amanda her baths. You can be sure that goody-two-shoes wouldn't wanna dirty her prissy little hands doin' things like that. What do ya say?''

"Sure. Great idea," Sarah agreed. It was disturbing to her that she hadn't been mature and thoughtful enough to have offered to take care of the dog in the first place. It was the obvious answer. Why hadn't she? Because something about that man affected her judgment ... put her on the defensive. It was hard to explain, but she'd been so aware of him. Even trying to put a name to the feelings he'd evoked in her was something she'd rather avoid.

The excited yapping provoked by Sarah's tap on the Weaver door caused both women to exhale in relief. Amanda was still there. But Mrs. Johnson's disgusted command to the dog to quiet down put them back on their guards.

"Oh, it's you. What do you want at this hour?" Mrs. Johnson demanded peevishly, pushing her glasses back on her nose and using one leg ineffectively to try to block Amanda from running out the open door.

"I'd like to talk with Mrs. Weaver," Sarah answered, scooping up the small dog and cuddling her against her breast.

"It's late. Way past her bedtime. She's already had enough excitement this evening. So if there's nothing else ..."

"I wanted to offer to take Amanda for a walk tonight," Sarah said. "I know you have enough to do."

"I can handle it. I'm being paid extra for taking care of her." The housekeeper extended a firm hand for the dog.

"Sarah and I were just goin' for a little walk and we decided to be neighborly. Now, give me the leash and we'll take Amanda with us," Erma directed with the air of a woman who would brook no resistance.

Mrs. Johnson hesitated for a moment before turning to get the leather strap that hung from the brass rack. "I suppose Mr. Weaver wouldn't mind me letting you do it just this once." Stretching her hand around the door frame, she picked up a long-handled shovel and thrust it at Erma. "You'll need to take this with you. Be sure to wash it off before you return it." The door shut before they had time to answer.

"Do you suppose..." Sarah remarked almost to herself, as she snapped the leash on Amanda's leather collar and put the wriggling little ball of fur down on the deck.

"Do I suppose what?"

"Well, it's just that I never let him explain his intentions. Given her abrupt turnaround in attitude toward the pup, Christopher Weaver must be paying Mrs. Johnson plenty to take care of Amanda. Do you suppose that he planned to offer to pay me to do that?"

"I couldn't tell ya," Erma said. "Ya may have jumped to conclusions about the bribery. At least we know he didn't dognap her," she grunted as they stepped onto the boardwalk.

Feeling suddenly lighthearted and relieved to find that Mrs. Weaver's confidence in her son wasn't misplaced, Sarah giggled.

"What's so funny?"

"You came up with that crazy dognapping idea, and you think I jump to conclusions?" Sarah's laughter echoed over the vast expanse of still water.

CHRISTOPHER WEAVER stepped over the scattered envelopes and brochures that littered the floor of his front hall under the mail slot, before turning on the living-room lights of his spacious condominium. Bending down, he searched through the mess for any personal letters. His bills were taken care of by the credit union, so nothing else demanded his immediate attention. Finding two letters from his son, he was about to stand when a third envelope caught his eye. Recognizing his ex-wife Virginia's handwriting, he picked it up and opened it first.

Dear Chris, he read, as he walked toward the kitchen. As you know from Adam's letters, I'm being married in June.

Married. Oddly it didn't come as a shock. Some part of him had been expecting it. Even so, he realized, feeling a strong surge of some indefinable emotion wash over him, this change in the status quo was going to take getting used to. Laying the letters on the counter, he took off his jacket and tie and hung them over the back of a stool at the breakfast bar. Then, undoing the top two buttons of his shirt, he pulled open the refrigerator door and took out a bottle of seltzer before sitting down to read the rest of Virginia's letter.

I'm afraid Adam isn't happy about the change this will bring to our lives. But Greg is a wonderful man and, if Adam will give him a chance, I know that he'll make a fine stepfather...

Stepfather! Absurdly he'd never considered that aspect of Virginia's remarrying. How must his son be feeling? Swiveling the stool, Christopher reached out for the bright yellow wall phone, but glancing at the clock beside it he noticed it was after ten. It would be after twelve in Nebraska—too late to call tonight.

He inhaled deeply through his nostrils and let his breath out through his mouth, considering the words that he'd say to his son. Just what the hell would he say? How about the truth, harsh as it was? Something like, *I know I haven't been the father I should have been, but since I sure don't want to be replaced by someone who'll probably—scratch that—*

undoubtedly be more adequate, I'll make a stab at improving?

He groaned and stared into space for a long moment. Raising the small bottle to his lips, he took a couple of deep swallows, relishing the bite of the carbonation. Picking up the letter, he read on, skimming the page.

Greg and I are going to Europe for our honeymoon. I'll be sending Adam to camp as soon as school is out—right after my wedding, in fact. In July, he'll fly to Seattle to be with you as usual.

Chris, I used to wish that it could have worked for us, but we were wrong for one another. I think if we hadn't been so young, we would have seen that right from the start. Even so, I have no regrets. Adam is a living testament to everything that was good between us.

I've found a man who's there for me. A man who can put our relationship first. Maybe I'm selfish, but I wasn't cut out to share my man with the sea.

I know I can count on your love and understanding to help Adam through this difficult time.

Fondly, Virginia

Christopher waited for another surge of emotion to rush through his body. But nothing happened. At long last, he acknowledged, ten years after their separation, it was over.

The letter was as forthright as the writer. Virginia didn't mince words. When she'd decided that she couldn't stand being what she considered a part-time wife to a man who was gone to sea half the time, and that she didn't want to live half a continent away from her home and family in Nebraska, she'd presented her tearful ultimatum. Either Christopher would resign his position and come to work for her father in Lincoln, or she was leaving and taking Adam with her. The boy, she'd insisted, needed a full-time mother more than he needed a part-time father. His arguments that she'd known he was an academy man who'd spent his life preparing to go to sea, and that he'd just gotten a promotion to a coveted position on a container ship, hadn't moved her. She'd been implacable in her resolve.

Since the divorce, he'd often wondered why she'd married him. Her ties to the midwestern prairies were as strong and enduring as his ties to the sea. Had she hoped to influence him to change his life-style right from the beginning? Or had she genuinely thought she could adjust and adapt? He wasn't sure even *she* knew which it had been.

And over the years, surrounded by the extended family that meant so much to her, Virginia had matured into an admirable woman. She would never be independent, but she had good solid values that she'd tried hard to instill in their son.

Christopher trusted Virginia. If she said that this Greg, whoever he was, would be a good stepfather for Adam, he had to believe it. But he couldn't help but hurt for the boy. If he had experienced shock at Virginia's announcement, how much more had his son felt? Anger? Betrayal? Virginia had lived her life for Adam. Who could blame him for resenting the intrusion of a stepfather into their well-ordered existence?

Draining the bottle of its sparkling contents, he rose from the stool and started toward the bedroom, rapidly tearing open the first of Adam's letters. He'd call the boy first thing in the morning.

AFTER GREETING Mrs. Weaver and patting Amanda, Sarah settled herself into a corner of the high-backed floral-print sofa. The shade had been pulled over the picture window that framed Lake Union, and the diffused light cast a rosy glow over the low-ceilinged room, furnished in Early

American antiques. She'd considered going straight home, but she knew it would have seemed odd to the older woman, since Sarah hadn't missed stopping by to visit a single day in the past month.

"Would you like a cup of tea, dear?" Mrs. Weaver asked, her voice cheerful.

"No, thanks," Sarah smiled. "I can't stay long, because Erma and I have an appointment with the director of the Soundview Nursing Home this evening. We hope to convince him to let us place a couple of pets in the home on a trial basis."

"I certainly hope you're successful. I can't imagine what I did before I had Amanda." Mrs. Weaver's face was serene as she patted the pooch, who seemed content to spend most of her time nesting on her mistress's lap.

"Then everything's going all right?"

"Absolutely." Mrs. Weaver shot her a piercing glance. "Did my son happen to come over to your place last night?"

"Yes, he did," Sarah admitted, reddening. The stroke had done nothing to dim Mrs. Weaver's thought processes. She could put two and two together and come up with four every time.

"I thought so." Mrs. Weaver nodded her head. "I didn't believe for a minute his story about his tires needing air. Christopher's just like his father—meticulous with his possessions. He wouldn't have driven that car out of the lot without checking it over from fender to fender. I was quite sure that he'd gone over to talk with you.

"And I have to thank you. I know he wasn't sold on the idea of my having a pet until after the two of you talked. When he came back, he had the matter settled in no time. I can't tell you how grateful I am."

"You don't have to thank me," Sarah said, feeling uncomfortable. "I don't think I had any influence on him."

"Don't be so modest. I'm sure you made quite an impression."

Quite possibly, Sarah admitted, cringing inwardly. But not the kind his mother thought. She doubted that Christopher Weaver was accustomed to having doors slammed in his face.

"Wasn't it your suggestion to pay Mrs. Johnson a bonus to take care of Amanda?"

"No," Sarah admitted, "it wasn't. If I'd had my wits about me, I'd have offered to do it myself. It really wouldn't be any extra bother."

"I wouldn't hear of it," Mrs. Weaver said firmly. "You have such important work to do, and so little time to do it in." She stopped, then asked, her face beaming with a loving mother's pride, "Well, tell me, what do you think of Christopher?"

Sarah struggled for a noncommittal answer. "He's...uh...I can see why you're so proud of him." At this point, she had no idea what she thought about the man. They'd started off their acquaintance on such a sour note that she doubted they would ever be friends.

"Not many women are as lucky as I am," Mary Lou Weaver confided, her blue eyes misting with nostalgia. "A wonderful husband and a fine son seem almost too much good fortune for one woman.

"Sarah, Charles carried me over this threshold over forty years ago. He promised then that he'd build me a house on land if I ever wanted it, but I never did. I felt that my living on the water, close to the elements that were the essence of his life, kept me close to him during the times we were apart."

Sarah listened quietly. Though they'd talked often in the past Mrs. Weaver had never been so open about her feelings. These confidences were a sign that their relationship had moved beyond the cordial stage to a more intimate level. She knew she was being made privy to a real-life love story.

"I know some women pitied me and imagined me miserable having my husband gone for weeks at a time. But it wasn't like that at all. It made me strong and self-reliant, and sure of myself in a way I would have never been if I'd always had Charles by my side to smooth over the rough spots. I never doubted his love. I always knew he'd come back to me and Christopher," she said, her faith and trust reflected in her eyes. "And he never failed me. What those women couldn't seem to understand was that the separations made the time we spent together more special."

"You are a lucky woman," Sarah agreed, getting up to nuzzle Amanda. Then she murmured into the fur, "And you are a lucky dog."

After Sarah had left the Weaver house a bittersweet smile curled her lips. Amanda had found a good home. Sarah almost envied the pup. How much more assured of being loved was a stray dog who'd been taken in than an abandoned child in the same circumstance, she thought ruefully. But she was no longer a child and Mrs. Weaver was fond of her. Nevertheless, a wistful thought tugged at her heart. She would never belong in the Weaver family as Amanda belonged. She had never really belonged anywhere.

Straightening her shoulders, Sarah let out a humorless laugh. Maybe the next time someone needed a pet she'd offer herself! She could see the pitch—tawny-haired female, twenty-seven, lacks pedigree but needs warm loving home. Her smile softened with genuine amusement as she opened the door to her own houseboat.

IT WAS LATE AFTERNOON before the last container left the hold of the super cargo ship and Christopher could relax his concentration on his duties. Watching the massive steel box sway high above the deck, supported by the cables of the unloading crane, he was struck by the similarities between it and himself. Viewed from the outside, it was impossible to know what was beneath the steel covering. The container had been packed at some port and put on the ship. None of its contents had been sorted through or utilized during its long journey. When it reached its destination it would sit on a dock until it was called for. If it had been misdirected it could sit forever, undisturbed. If one day someone opened it out of mild curiosity, its contents would be musty, dated, dried up, possibly even useless.

He was like that. Packed with experiences, sealed by his facade of strength and silence, and shunted from port to port by the demands of his chosen career; performing his duties, shouldering responsibility for his mother, but never showing to the world the emotions that seethed under the covering of his starched white shirt and well-pressed uniform.

Women had been attracted to him in the years since his divorce. But had it been the uniform and its aura of masculinity, or him? No matter. As ridiculous as it seemed now, he had avoided commitment to another woman because of a vague hope that someday he and Virginia would remarry and together provide a home for their son.

Virginia's and Adam's letters had caused the first dangerous fissure, but talking with Adam this morning had split his life wide open like a dropped container. He felt exposed. Unsure. It was the first time the boy had called on him for more than monetary support, and he hadn't been ready for it.

He squirmed uneasily, recalling the early-morning phone conversation he'd had with his son.

"But why can't I come right now?" the adolescent voice had pleaded.

"Adam, it's not up to me. I told you it's up to your mother."

"Will you ask her if I can live with you and Gram? I can stay with you in your condo when you're home, and with Gram in the houseboat when you're at sea." The boy's request hadn't come as a surprise. His letters had been filled with the same question.

"Sure, I will, son, but won't you give this Greg a chance? Your mom says he's a fine man. Have you tried to get along with him?"

"Ah, geez, Dad. Haven't you heard anything I've been tellin' you? The guy's a nerd. I'm tryin' to tell you, I can't stick it out here much longer."

"You can tough it out for a while, son. As soon as school's out, you'll be going to camp for a few weeks. And after that you'll be flying out here. Maybe we can work something out then. Chin up, fella. It can't be that bad."

"But, Dad—"

"Listen, Adam, I'd love to stand and talk to you, but I'm on cargo watch today and I have to hustle if I'm going to get down to the ship on time."

"Are you going to call Mom today?"

"I'll do it as soon as I can. Now, you settle down and make the best of things in the meantime, y'hear?"

The boy had given a heavy sigh, and there'd been a significant pause before he'd heard the final obedient, "Yes, Dad."

Looking out to the far horizon, Christopher felt a prickle of cold that had nothing to do with the mild wind ruffling the surface of the Sound. He knew the boy was unhappy and dissatisfied, but Adam had to learn that there were lots of things in life that couldn't go just his way. Christopher's ship was setting sail Monday, and under the circumstances there wasn't much he could do to help his son right now. The boy would adjust. He'd have to.

Chapter Three

The Latitude 47 bar was beginning to fill up when Christopher strode across the mirrored room to a window table overlooking Lake Union. Though he hadn't spoken with him, he knew Max Pierson would be along soon. Now beginning the second half of his yearly two-leg home port stay, Pierson would be taking Christopher's place after the next run across the Pacific. Ever since Max had joined the company, they'd met at the 47 for drinks and dinner, to talk shop the evening after the ship had been unloaded.

He glanced at his watch. Max was late. Probably stuck in rush-hour traffic. Relaxing in the comfortable chair, Christopher gazed again across the lake to where the houseboats huddled against the northeastern shore, close to the canal linking Lake Union with Lake Washington.

He'd loved growing up on the lake. No childhood memories were sweeter than those of lying in his ship's bunk at night gazing out over the water through the massive spokes of the wheel of a large sailing vessel that was mounted on the top floor of the house where the windows formed a point like a prow. He'd imagined himself the captain of a whaling ship, standing at the helm, sailing off into the Pacific in search of the great sea creatures. Providing oil for the lamps of China.

But times had changed. There was a worldwide moratorium on the hunting of whales. And rightly so. They were an endangered species. And so was the Merchant Marine. Newer and faster ships were rapidly replacing the old models. No ship's wheel graced the fully automated bridge of Christopher's ship. Instead of feeling the worn grips of a teak wheel beneath his hands, he shuffled enormous amounts of paper, even putting in hours of overtime to have the cargo in order by the time they docked in the first port.

And he was no longer a little boy tucked in bed, dreaming of an adventurous future on the sea. Now his son, Adam, always spent a few nights in his old room whenever he was in Seattle. Though Christopher liked to believe that he was close to his son, he realized that he didn't know what kind of dreams Adam had. Had the boy taken after him? Was there salt water flowing in Adam's veins? Or had Adam taken after Virginia, who preferred the vista of rolling acres of land as far as the eye could see? He searched his mind, but he couldn't remember having had a serious discussion about the future with his son since the boy had been old enough to have thoughts beyond childish ideas of being a fireman or an astronaut.

"Hi, buddy." Max Pierson's hand patted his shoulder. The compact redhead slipped into the chair on the other side of the table. "Hey, you're not looking so good. Trouble on cargo watch?" Max eyed Christopher speculatively.

"No. It went off without a hitch. We were out of there by four."

For a moment their conversation was put on hold while a waitress took their order.

"So what's the problem?" Max asked, as soon as she left. "You been assigned to shore duty? Your car get ripped off?" Then sobering, he asked, "Is your mom all right?"

"She's fine." Christopher smiled, remembering the twinkle in his mother's eye. Sarah Mitchell had been adamant in her claims for puppy therapy. He wished he could believe that owning a small dog was all it would take to restore his mother's health. "In fact, I think she's showing signs of improvement."

"That's great! Then what's up? I can tell something's bothering you, old buddy."

"You can read me that well?"

"After four years of sharing a room with that ugly mug of yours? You bet."

Christopher rewarded his pal with a good-natured grimace. He and Max had become fast friends while plebes at the U.S. Merchant Marine Academy at Kings Point, New York. After graduation, they'd kept in touch, but gone their separate ways. Three years ago Christopher had persuaded his friend to apply for a rare opening on the Oceanic Line. He'd been pleased when Max had gotten the position and had been assigned to his ship, one of five the company owned. Though their personalities differed, they shared a management style that let them slip in and out of one another's shoes easily.

"You want it in a nutshell?"

Max nodded.

Their drinks arrived. Christopher picked his up and swirled the straw through the sparkling Perrier before answering. "Virginia's getting married. Adam wants to come live with me. Some woman gave my mother a dog, and I'm having to pay blackmail to Mrs. Johnson to get her to take care of it."

"Is that all? Welcome aboard." Max raised his vodka Collins in mock salute before bringing it to his lips.

"What's that supposed to mean?" Christopher asked sharply.

Max regarded his friend over the rim of his glass. "Look, I got a wife who wants to fly to Hawaii every time it rains. My kid's mouth is a mess. He'll be wearing railroad tracks on his teeth until he's twenty-one, and our dental insurance doesn't cover orthodontics work. And a whole group of high-rise condos are going up between us and the lake. With our view gone, the bottom has dropped out of our property value. We're going to have to eat our losses and go house hunting again.

"And I was late because the two-year-old threw her toothbrush down the toilet. The last time she pulled that little trick, the family was without plumbing for three days while I was gone. But hey, that's life."

"Sounds pretty grim to me."

"That's because you've always had it easy."

"I wouldn't say that," Christopher said, objection in his deep voice.

"Wouldn't you?" Max asked, unperturbed by his friend's reaction. "Think about it. You've had Adam to play Poppa to whenever you could schedule him in—"

"Hey, now, that's not fair. I have him with me as much as both of our schedules will let me."

"But Virginia takes care of him the bulk of the time, and I've never really heard you complaining."

Christopher had never been a glutton for punishment, and he considered putting an end to this conversation right now, but Max went on undeterred by his friend's scowl.

"I know it was rough when your dad died. But he'd had sixty-eight great years and he went quick. The way we'd all like to. And your mom's stroke was a blow, but she pulled through and you've managed to have her taken care of for you, too. All in all, you've been able to sail off without too much on your mind."

"That's easy for you to say," Christopher interrupted hotly, remembering the awful grief and loneliness he'd felt when his father had died and the terrible helplessness he'd experienced while his mother was hospitalized with an uncertain prognosis. He hadn't wept and wailed and gnashed his teeth like Max might have done, but that didn't mean his feelings had been any less intense.

"Now, in my case," Max said, "every trip I've taken lately, I feel like a rat deserting a sinking ship." His grin was rueful, and he clearly realized his statement sounded absurd since he was the one who sailed away. "It's the only thing I hate about my job. Having to put my life on hold for thirty-five days at a time. Every month my ship-to-shore phone bills are higher than my house payment."

Christopher laughed in spite of his irritation, and the tension between them eased. Max could really paint a picture.

"I mean it, buddy. For once you've got some real troubles. Kids and women'll do that to you every time," Max remarked sagely.

"Why weren't you this smart when we were in school?" Christopher quipped wryly.

"Hey, man, what difference would it have made? I love 'em. I may bitch and moan, but I wouldn't have it any other way. They need me, and that's all that counts. All I'm saying is that it feels good to have you cry on my shoulder for once, instead of it always being the other way around. It makes you more human. More sympathetic. Tonight, when I recited my tale of woes I felt like I was telling them to a guy who might have some idea of what I was talking about."

Christopher snorted. "Always glad to help a buddy out."

"Say." Max held up one hand. "Don't get me wrong. I don't mean I'm glad you've got problems—you know that. I only mean that it's time for you to get your feet wet. Maybe even get in up to your knees like the rest of us. You've been skimming on the surface too long." He paused. "Now about Virginia getting married. That was kind of sudden, wasn't it?"

"I don't know," Christopher said, realizing that his son had never given him a clue that Virginia was having a seri-

ous relationship with a man. Hadn't Adam known he'd be
interested in anything that affected his son? "I haven't really
talked to her since Thanksgiving. I took Adam out of school
early so that we could have a week together skiing at Vail. I
hardly saw Virginia."

"Still got a thing for her?" Max asked, considerately
shifting his gaze from Christopher's face to look out across
the now darkening water.

Letting his gaze follow Max's, Christopher thought for a
long moment. "I don't think so. But I guess I always
thought we'd get back together sooner or later."

"Look," Max said, his expression serious, "I'm going to
tell you something I've been wanting to say for a long time.
I think you've used your ties to your ex-wife as an excuse to
keep from living."

"That's bull!" Christopher shot back.

"No, it's not. Virginia gave you your freedom ten years
ago, but you haven't used it." Max picked up his swizzle
stick and pointed it at Christopher. "If you'd really wanted
her, you'd have fought to keep her then."

"I didn't come here tonight for amateur psychoanaly-
sis," Christopher said through clenched teeth.

"Simmer down. You know there's some truth to what I'm
saying or you wouldn't be getting so hot under the collar.
Virginia should have remarried long before this. I hope she's
found a guy she can live with. The whole happily-ever-after
bit."

"She seems to think she has," Christopher said dryly.

"Great!" Max said with an enthusiasm that grated on his
sullen companion's nerves. "Now it's your turn."

Christopher said nothing, lost in thought. Surprisingly
Max's words evoked a memory of Sarah Mitchell's face, her
eyes shining with conviction. She might be stubborn and
headstrong, but the woman had a sincere quality that made
her hard to forget. He shook his head. He must be losing his

grip to be sitting here thinking about a young woman he'd just met—scratch that, they hadn't even been introduced—with all the pressing problems he had to deal with.

"You've got a second chance here. You can get married again and make a go of it this time."

Christopher's eyes registered shock. "You can't be serious. Wouldn't that just be great for Adam! He wants to come live with me to get away from a stepfather, and I give him a stepmother?"

Max gave a dismissive wave of his hand. "The kid is overreacting. He'll get used to the idea of his mom getting married."

"Yeah, that's what I told him," Christopher said edgily. It'd sounded like good advice when he talked to his son that morning, but remembering the quaver in Adam's voice and hearing Max casually brush the issue facing his kid under the rug, he wasn't so sure anymore.

"It might be a good idea if you took him for a while. Give Virginia some time to herself and her new husband. You can put him in the same school you went to. Then when you meet the right woman, you can make a home for him out here."

"Hey, wait a minute. I haven't even talked to Virginia. I doubt she'd ever let Adam go."

"Oh, you never know. Maybe not, but you need some contingency plans just in case she does."

What Max said made some sense, but things weren't that cut-and-dried. At the moment Christopher's concern was Adam, and only Adam. Or was it? Even though he'd never admit it to Max, having his son come to Seattle to stay would sure as hell complicate his life. Maybe he just needed time to adjust, but the idea scared him. He didn't know anything about being a full-time father to a teenage son. Given the problems one small dog had already caused him, he could only imagine what a fourteen-year-old boy would do to his life.

Still, if his son really wanted to live in Seattle, and he could convince Virginia to let him go, well, like Max said, he'd have to be ready. He stroked his chin thoughtfully, grateful that Max had closed his mouth long enough to let him think. He supposed that in September he could get Adam into the Douglas Denton Academy as a boarder from Monday through Friday. And on the weekends he was at sea the boy could stay with his grandmother. He could see that it might be good for both of them. But there was no way he could take Adam before his regular expected time of arrival in July. With all the commotion that Johnson woman had made over the mutt, there'd be no way she'd take on Adam. He was going to have to find a replacement for the house-keeper as soon as this next leg at sea was over.

"Let's eat," Christopher said tersely, pushing back his chair as he stood.

Max appeared undaunted by his friend's abruptness as they headed for the dining room. "Good idea. I still have to hear about the dog."

EARLY ON SUNDAY MORNING Sarah twisted the five leashes, attached to the collars of five impatient dogs, securely around her wrist.

"Ready, guys?" she asked with a fond smile as she opened the door. The dogs panted in anticipation, eager to be off. A faint mist hovered over the calm lake, but through breaks in the low cloud cover she could see patches of blue. The sun should burn through within the hour, and the day would be as perfect a spring day as the one before.

The dogs were a motley crew, full of boundless energy. Over the past couple of weeks she'd become aware of each animal's distinct characteristics. Traits that set him or her apart from every other dog. Traits that made each one lovable and special. Fred, in particular, was a handful. Erma would help her decide, but Sarah was beginning to think they'd have to find a different sort of placement for him. He might need a home with a sturdy mistress or master to keep him in line. Although he was good-tempered, she couldn't picture him being content as a lapdog.

"Heel, Fred, heel," Sarah commanded the straining dog as she struggled to lock the door, but he continued to lunge toward the shore, pulling her off balance. She tried to dig in her heels, but the rubber soles of her moccasins slipped on the damp surface of the deck. Her one hundred ten pounds were losing the struggle with forty-two pounds of uninhibited muscle. Uncoiling his leash from the other dogs', she switched it to her free hand, but before she could get a grip on it, the leather strap slid through her fingers and Fred ran free.

"Damn," she swore under her breath.

"Here, Fred," called a familiar masculine voice. A strong whistle followed, piercing the early-morning air.

Sarah watched Christopher Weaver jump from his deck onto the boardwalk with surefooted ease. A few long strides and he'd caught up with Fred who'd nonchalantly lifted a leg at a nearby telephone pole.

She should have had the sense to take Fred out last—by himself. It was just her luck that Christopher Weaver had witnessed the scene. He was the last person she'd have expected to come to her rescue. Behaving as though nothing out of the ordinary had happened, she presented what she hoped was a composed demeanor as she opened the back door of her brown van and shooed the other dogs into its stripped-down interior. Turning, she took the leash Christopher offered.

"Good morning," she said pleasantly, her voice even and, she hoped, unaffected by her wandering thoughts, "and thank you."

"You're welcome," he replied, just as pleasantly. He grinned, and the appealing weather-etched laugh lines around his eyes deepened. Anyone hearing the two of them would never guess that the only other time they'd met they'd exchanged silly threats and mild verbal abuse.

She hesitated, wondering if he'd go back into the houseboat. He didn't. Instead he stood looking down at her, and Sarah felt her cheeks go crimson. Sometimes she wondered if any other human being blushed as easily and as often as she did.

"I'm taking the dogs out for a run," she said. "I'd like to take Amanda, too."

"That's very thoughtful. But don't you think five unruly dogs are enough?" He wanted to add, "for a small woman like you." She was small. About the same height as the women of the Orient.

"They're not unruly. Just playful. If you're that concerned about Amanda," Sarah tossed out the teasing challenge, "maybe you'd like to come along."

He looked down at her. The red turtleneck beneath her jean jacket accentuated the rosiness in her makeup-free cheeks and lips. Her shining hair was caught in a neat fall that cascaded down her back. Her round, gold-flecked hazel eyes were guileless, friendly, free from flirtatiousness.

"Where're you going?" he asked, more to keep the conversation alive than for information. It didn't matter where she was going. He had work to do. He intended to repair the sagging awnings and pull the weeds in the flower boxes, replacing them with potted plants from the Pike's Place Market.

"Over in the valley behind Southcenter. There's a small lake in a big field where people train their hunting dogs. If I get there early enough, it should be deserted. These guys will have a great time running around. How about it?"

It wasn't hard to conjure up the picture of Sarah running through the grass, throwing sticks for the dogs to chase, her tawny hair streaming behind her. It had been too long since Christopher had taken time-out to play. These days even his racquetball games at the gym were for the exercise, not for the fun.

Finding himself accepting her invitation without really intending to, he said, "Thanks. I think I'll take you up on it." He turned back to the houseboat to fetch Amanda. Hang the awnings and the plants. They could wait until later. But he'd get the boxes filled if it took him all night.

Sarah started the van's engine while she waited for Christopher and Amanda. Christopher Weaver was a surprise a minute. When she'd tossed out the casual invitation, she hadn't expected him to take her up on it.

She smiled when Christopher appeared at the door with the small white pooch resting in the crook of his elbow. The tall golden-haired man and the fluffy puppy weren't right for each other. A golden retriever would be more like it. A sleek handsome dog whose appearance and long-legged gait would be a perfect match for his. His faded black sweatshirt was stretched over broad shoulders and a muscular torso that tapered to a lean waist. His long legs were encased in a pair of well-worn jeans.

Attractive or not, she didn't intend to become involved with him, or any other man. She had the life she wanted. She was settled into a comfortable routine. There was no longer any need for her to consider risking her hard-won equilibrium on the slim chance she'd find an understanding man.

Christopher lifted Amanda over the tape-patched Naugahyde seat to join the rest of the dogs before swinging himself in beside Sarah. He snapped on his seat belt as she started toward the freeway that ran behind the lake. He couldn't remember the last time he'd been in the passenger seat next to a woman driver. The days were past when a man could chivalrously offer to take the wheel. Most modern women would resent the gesture, and he was sure Sarah Mitchell fell into that category. Though she was young— he'd guess mid-twenties—she gave the impression of competence, of knowing where she was headed, in life, as well as on the road. He smiled at his pun.

As Christopher quieted the restless dogs behind her with humorous threats, Sarah wasn't sure her impulsive invitation hadn't been a mistake. Without his uniform he seemed younger, more approachable. Very different from the icy-eyed commanding man who'd confronted her the other evening. He was so alive, vibrant. Every time she glanced at his rugged profile, unease fluttered in her stomach. She was just being a good neighbor, she reminded herself. There was no need to make a big deal of his coming along.

Traffic was heavy on both sides of the six-lane interstate highway as cars streamed into and out of Seattle. Many people were taking advantage of the warm spring weekend. As they passed Boeing Field the sun broke through, bathing the gray landscape with golden light. Sarah felt an instant warmth penetrate the windshield.

"I've met Fred," Christopher remarked over the clamor behind him. "Do these other mongrels have names?"

"The part cocker is Ginny, the black Lab is Mike, the little gray one is Nancy, and the terrier is Matt."

"Males and females? I thought you called them 'the guys.'"

"A collective term. Unisexual. I use it all the time."

"Aren't you afraid they might get . . . well, frisky?"

"Frisky?" she asked. Glancing at him, she watched a grin spread across his face.

"You know, him-ing and her-ing? Foolin' around? Isn't this the season?"

Sarah kept her eyes on the road. "They've been neutered."

"That's a shame," he said, pity apparent in his tone.

"Population control," she said curtly. Her stomach twisted in an uncomfortable knot, even though his reaction didn't come as a surprise. It was typical of a virile man to feel this way. "These dogs were strays themselves. Nobody wanted them."

Smoothly changing the subject, she added, "I named them after kids I grew up with." She forced a laugh. "The last batch I named after the board of directors at the pound. Cunningham, Hamilton, Anderson... I wonder what they'd think if they knew."

"They'd probably hang you in effigy or name a voodoo doll after you and poke pins in it," Christopher suggested. His wide grin showed a flash of straight white teeth.

"No." Sarah chortled. "Those stuffed shirts would never think of anything so exotic."

"You're right," Christopher agreed. "No imagination." He snapped his fingers. "I've got it! They'd pass an ordinance forbidding any mutt to be called by a city official's name."

"Now you're talking. That'd be just their speed. Seriously, though, I'm never quite sure whose side they're on. They profess to be animal lovers, but some of their policies are not in the animals' best interests. So even though it's just a drop in the bucket, it makes me feel good to know that I'm helping a few dogs lead useful happy lives."

"How many have you placed?"

"Thirty-seven so far."

"And you named them all?"

"Yes, and I keep them until they learn to obey to their names. I started out with flower names like Tulip, Daisy and Iris. But I think I'll use Washington counties for a while.

Nice names—Thurston, Pierce, Mason. I think a dignified name adds class, don't you?''

"A dog by any other name is still a dog," he misquoted, a note of humor in his voice.

Sarah smiled and turned her attention back to the road. It wasn't easy to keep up a running conversation over the wet nose of a curious dog, and that was just as well. She didn't want to come across as being too friendly. She didn't want to give Christopher Weaver any idea that she'd invited him along because she was interested in him. His only importance to her was as Mrs. Weaver's son. She had to convince him that Amanda was important to his mother's well-being. She needed this time with him to help him understand Puppy Power and the successes the program had brought about.

Exiting the freeway, she followed a paved two-lane road for several miles. Then, turning onto a dirt cutoff, she shifted down and bounced along for several yards before pulling to a stop. She jumped out of the van and ran around to open the back. Christopher came from the other side just as her hand reached the latch and swung the door open.

The dogs quivered with excitement, poised for action at the door. As Christopher unleashed each in turn, they dashed from the van into the waiting field where, circling and barking, they cavorted through the tall grass.

Sarah rummaged longer than necessary in the back of the van for her rubber boots, wanting to hide the silly unwarranted flush that heated her cheeks.

She'd been thoughtless. The field was damp with heavy dew, and she knew that before the romp was over Christopher's jeans would be wet to his knees. She should have warned him. "I'm sorry I didn't think to tell you to bring along some boots," she apologized.

"No problem. Getting wet has never bothered me."

Of course, he was a seaman. Did he, she wondered, make the rounds of his ship during a storm to make sure that everything was secure and battened down? Or was that a thing of the past? Did it still take bravery to be a sailor, or were his days at sea as comfortable and uneventful as those of a land-bound executive? Bracing herself against the bumper, she removed a moccasin from her bare foot.

"Need some help?" Before she could protest, Christopher knelt before her, expertly folding her pant leg around her calf and sliding the boot on. The touch of his strong tanned fingers against her bare sensitive foot was electrifying—and unnerving. It took a conscious effort of will for her to remain still while he did the same with her other boot. Afterward she didn't give him time to get to his feet before she took off running in the direction the dogs had gone.

Chapter Four

Sarah ran on and on, her feet pummeling the earth, her leg muscles straining until the pounding of her heart was caused by sheer exertion.

Christopher's long easy strides quickly overtook her. Ignoring the puzzled look on his strong-boned face, Sarah slowed to a jog and called to the dogs. Two or three jumped up on their hind legs, turning their heads toward her, before the pack raced off again, with Fred in the lead, in the same direction Sarah was moving.

Christopher let her set the pace as they jogged along side by side, until they reached the banked-up sides of the man-made lake. His breath came easily, and Sarah knew her first impression of his fitness had been correct. The man was in terrific shape.

Dropping to the newly sprouting grass, Sarah lay face-down on the spring-green cushion as Fred and Amanda circled her, trying to lick her face. The other dogs milled around in the field behind them barking with excitement. When Christopher lowered himself to lie beside her on the sun-dried slope, Fred saw his chance. The irrepressible dog took a slobbery swipe at Christopher's closely shaven chin, before the seaman's deep voice commanded him to stop.

"I need a stick." Christopher's hands searched the new grass. Sarah found one within her reach and gave it to him.

A hefty heave, and the dogs were off on the chase, Amanda making a valiant effort to keep up with Fred's longer legs.

Sitting up, Christopher wiped away the moisture on his face with his sleeve. Sarah rolled onto her back, giggling at the look of disgust that turned down the corners of his mouth.

"Dog spit is cleaner than human," she offered with a cheerful grin, her hazel eyes glinting with humor.

"I doubt that!"

"It's been scientifically proven."

"You and your research," Christopher muttered. "You must get your facts out of a grocery store tabloid. You'll have to show me that study from a more reliable source before I'll believe it."

"There's no point in arguing...when you're right," Sarah added sweetly.

He grinned, refusing to rise to the bait. He was delighted to see signs of the spunk she'd exhibited on Friday night, but didn't want to risk becoming embroiled in another argument over dogs. "By the way, I owe you an apology."

"For doubting the reliability of my research sources?" she asked, her eyes wide with feigned innocence.

His grin broadened. "No, I won't issue a retraction there. I'm apologizing for the other night. I was rude. My mom taught me better manners." In his smiling face Sarah could see traces of the impish little boy he must have been. "When I came home and found Mrs. Johnson threatening to quit, I lost it."

"Apology accepted, if you'll forgive my slamming the door in your face," Sarah said, still having a hard time believing she'd actually done that. Knowing it took a big man to make such an open apology, she felt her respect for Christopher Weaver grow. "When I thought you were trying to bribe me to take Amanda back, I'm afraid I lost it, too. I realized a little later that you'd intended to pay me to care for her. I'm just sorry I didn't think to offer to do it."

"Don't worry about it. The sight of my wallet had the opposite effect on Mrs. Johnson. Money talks in most languages, to most people—present company excepted, of course—" he nodded in her direction "—and there's no doubt that Mrs. Johnson is one of those people." His voice held more than a trace of cynicism.

Sarah looked away. Dressed in simple casual clothing as he was now, it was easy for her to forget what a worldly man Christopher Weaver was. Little wonder he grew impatient when having to deal with, what were to him, such trivial matters as one small dog.

But Amanda was not a trivial issue. Sarah fought this kind of skepticism almost every time she tried to place a dog and explain the benefits of the Puppy Power program. But somehow she sensed that she would never meet a more confirmed skeptic than the sophisticated man who lay beside her.

"You never had a dog, did you?" Sarah asked bluntly.

He frowned. Her question made him feel as if he were to be pitied. "No, I didn't, as a matter of fact. But I wasn't deprived."

"I wasn't suggesting that you were," Sarah said softly, her mouth curving into a conciliatory smile.

After looking around and seeing that all the dogs were occupied chasing a flock of small gray birds at the end of the field, Christopher stretched out on the damp grass beside her.

"I had a happy boyhood," he said, wondering why he felt he owed her an explanation.

"I don't doubt it. Your mother is a wonderful person, so I'm sure your dad was, too. You and your dad are her favorite topics of conversation." Along with her grandson, Adam, Sarah added to herself. Though she suspected it would give Christopher fatherly pleasure to hear that, she didn't want to talk to him about his son.

"Pretty boring, huh?"

"No, it sounds like your dad was an interesting guy," Sarah teased. Lying beside him, she experienced a giddy light-headedness. When he propped himself on an elbow, she watched the strong beat of the pulse in his throat, not trusting herself to meet the wonderful eyes she knew were scanning her face.

"What about me?"

"Um, she thinks you're okay, too." Isolating a single blade of new grass, she pulled it out and sucked on the tender shaft, just as she had as a child.

"What do you think?" he asked, entranced by her aura of girlish innocence.

"I'll take the Fifth. That's pretty popular these days."

Christopher laughed, a deep warm sound. "A cautious woman," he pronounced with mock solemnity.

"I try to be," she answered slowly. Much harder than he could ever imagine. It would be so simple to give in to the temptation to indulge in an exciting flirtation with this man, who was so attractive he could be on the recruitment poster for the Merchant Marine. And what would be the harm? He was leaving the next day. But for the moment, she intended to turn the conversation back to him, before he focused on her and asked too many personal questions.

"Mostly your mom talks about the time when you were a boy. The things you did together. The boat you and your father built. I guess Captain Weaver must have been handy with tools."

"He was."

"And paint?" Her inquiry was pointed.

Christopher looked down at her, his blue eyes blank. One blond brow lifted slightly, providing the only clue that she'd hit her mark.

"Are you implying that I'm the one responsible for the shabby look of Mom's houseboat?"

Sarah broke off a dandelion that had gone to seed, and blew its feathery particles into the air before answering. That *was* what she was implying, but she knew it was none of her business. She chose her words with care, trying to be more tactful. "It is a shame to let such a beautiful place get run-down."

There was a flicker of some unidentifiable emotion in his eyes that she would have missed if she hadn't been looking right at him. "You noticed? Frankly the condition that place is in is driving me up a wall. But I'm not responsible, at least not in the way you seem to think."

He sighed, then continued, "You see, Mom refuses to let me have anything done about it. Since she's been in that wheelchair, I don't think she realizes how bad it looks. My dad was the last person to paint and roof the house, and she won't hear of anyone else touching it. I think she likes to sit there and remember him pottering around on the deck. If she doesn't come around soon, I'm going to have to do something about it regardless. Maybe I should have before this, but I didn't want to risk upsetting her."

Seeing Christopher's genuine concern, Sarah's heart went out to him. As an only child, all the responsibility for his aging mother fell on his shoulders. And even though those shoulders were broad and strong, it was still a load. Sarah knew how difficult it was to have to make important decisions all on your own.

"Would you like me to mention it to her? It wouldn't be hard to work it into one of our conversations."

"I'd be grateful for any help you could give me," he admitted. Breaking into a slow grin, he regarded her with respect.

Basking in the full warmth of his smile, Sarah felt as though the sun had come out from behind one of the few clouds left in the sky, where it had stubbornly hidden moments before.

"Maybe she'll listen to you. You seem to have a great deal of influence on her." He sobered. "I hope you understand. I don't like leaving my mother on the houseboat. I've tried to talk her into selling it and moving into a place near my condo. But she's convinced that she doesn't have much time left and wants to spend it where she is."

"What do her doctors say? Is there any chance that she'll be able to walk again?"

He shrugged as though with indifference, but she could tell it was an effort to mask the depth of his feelings. "They used to insist that physical therapy was the answer. They claimed she could be almost completely rehabilitated. But she wouldn't go along with it."

"And you didn't . . . ?" Seeing again the emotion she'd noticed earlier in his eyes and now recognizing it as pain, Sarah stopped.

"And I didn't insist?" he finished for her. "No, I didn't. My mother was always a strong woman. Hardly sick a day in her life. She's no hypochondriac. I believe that if she thought she could walk again she'd be the first one to try. And I also believe that she knows her own body best. I'm not going to push her into trying something she wouldn't be able to handle. All I want is to make sure that she's happy, well cared for and as comfortable as possible."

"People like your mother are the ones most likely to lose the will to live after a debilitating illness," Sarah persisted quietly. "They're used to being strong, and they don't want to compromise. If they can't jump out of their hospital beds as good as new, they don't think life is worth living.

"I wish you had time to go with me to visit some of our clients. Mr. Roderick is a wonderful example of a person Puppy Power has helped. He suffered a stroke almost as severe as your mother's. He never even left the convalescent center he was put in after he was discharged from the hospital. He just wanted to die. But since he's had his dog, he's lost his apathy and has started to do his exercises. He's already regained more than fifty percent use of his paralyzed arm. And the staff is certain he'll be able to walk again. He may always need a cane or a walker, but at least he'll be up and out of his wheelchair.''

"Good for Mr. Roderick," Christopher said with curt impatience. Raw emotion played across his face, causing a muscle to twitch in his square jaw.

Realizing she'd touched an exposed nerve, Sarah said nothing for a long moment. When Amanda tumbled down the hill and flopped between them, an exhausted pile of wet fur, she suggested quietly, "Let's just see what Amanda can do for your mother."

Christopher's lips parted as though he was going to say something, then shaking his head, he stood and reached down for her hand. "Come on, let's use our legs while we still can."

Once on her feet she removed her hand from his. Then raising it to shield her eyes against the sun that had completely burned away the low cloud cover, she looked toward the far end of the clearing where the dogs were chasing each other like a bunch of kids playing tag. "Recess is over. Time to ring the bell." Her shrill whistle pierced the morning air, and the dogs came bounding toward her.

"Spoilsport," Christopher accused with a laugh, as he reached down to scoop up Amanda and settle her comfortably in the crook of his arm. The small mutt was winded by her romp and content to have taxi service back to the van.

On the way home, talking good-naturedly over the roar of the van's engine and the animals' ceaseless noise, Christopher shared his plans for the day with Sarah.

"After I get the dogs settled down, I'll take you to the Pike's Place Market," she offered, telling herself it was the neighborly thing to do. He didn't have much time left in port, and she approved of his planting the flower boxes. "We can put a lot more into Kanga than you can get into that little car of yours."

"Kanga?" he asked.

"Kanga," she repeated. "A great name for a van that carries a cargo of wiggling animals, don't you think?"

"I do, and you're on," Christopher agreed, "as long as you accept my invitation to dinner. I'm giving Mrs. Johnson the night off and I'm going to grill some thick juicy steaks out on the deck. At least I hope they'll be juicy," he amended. "That's another thing my dad did well. I like to think he passed some of his technique on to me, but I'll let you be the judge."

Her hesitation was almost, but not quite, imperceptible. "I'd like that." It would be all right, she thought. Mrs. Weaver would be there. And when the older woman went to bed, she'd go home.

"Great!" His enthusiasm was genuine. "I could sure use your help at the market. I've been at sea so much of the time for so many years that I'm not sure I can still tell a rhododendron from a fern!"

After Mrs. Weaver and Amanda had retired for the night, Christopher opened a second bottle of wine. He filled Sarah's goblet, then his own, and moved his deck chair close to hers, adjusting it to the same semi-reclining position.

Though in the clear light of day she'd promised herself that she'd return home when the two of them were left alone, Sarah was overcome with a delicious lulling lethargy that kept her where she was. Christopher's solicitous attentions to her all evening had been the sort a man makes to a woman he finds attractive. He'd made her feel interesting and desirable. It had been a long time since she'd felt so... right in the company of a man and, she admitted, so emotionally stimulated. She wasn't ready for it to be over just yet.

"You could use the stars." Christopher's deep voice came out of the darkness, blending with the sound of the gentle waves lapping melodically against the side of the barge, breaking the comfortable silence between them.

"What for? I'm not planning to go anywhere," Sarah replied lazily from the lounger where she lay, her gaze rising to the midnight-blue canopy arching above them, studded with blinking diamonds.

"For naming your dogs."

"There aren't that many dogs in the whole world."

"That's true. But believe it or not, even though there are billions of stars out there, on a clear night like this you can only see about two thousand with the naked eye."

She believed him. A sailor would know all about the stars. And without a doubt he also knew the enchanting power of a starry sky to wreak havoc with a woman's control.

His muscular arm lay barely an inch from hers. When he moved, its rich covering of golden hair brushed her sensitized flesh, sending shivers of pleasure racing through her. When he talked with his face turned toward hers, his warm breath caressed her skin.

"There are some great names up there—Perseus, Andromeda, Hercules. There's even a Dog Star, Sirius."

"Not a bad idea." She laughed. "But I'm afraid in less than two minutes they'd become Percy, Andy and Herky."

"I'm sure you're right," Christopher agreed with a chuckle, "but maybe that's not such a bad fate for earthbound stars." He paused, then, "Why don't we forget all about dogs for a while?"

Taking her hand and twining his fingers in hers, he continued, "You're one up on me, you know. More than one. I'll bet my mother's even told you how old I was when I took my first step. But I know almost nothing about you, other than that you've made my short leave a memorable one. Where did you live, Miss Sarah Mitchell, before your barge was towed here?''

"On the canal," Sarah answered, referring to the waterway between Lake Washington and Lake Union. Wondering whether or not to pull her hand away, she decided against it. She didn't want to make a big deal of it, didn't want him to guess how difficult it was to concentrate with her palm pressed against his.

"My house originally belonged to Dr. Blake, the veterinarian I work for. He lived in it while he was going to the university. When he got married, he sold it to me for a ridiculous price, on the condition that he can always moor his sloop to it. He holds the mortgage and I agreed to never sell out to anyone but him. It's a wonderful deal for me, and he claims he saves enough keeping his boat moored here to be able to give away the house."

"I'm sure that's true," Christopher said. "The cost of good moorage has become exorbitant in the last few years. I wondered if you were the captain of that fine sloop."

"Hardly." Sarah chuckled, knowing she couldn't tell a bow from a stern. "But I assume you're the captain of the one tied up behind this house."

"Yes, I am. And next month when I'm home again, maybe we can take a trip out through the Ballard Locks and go sailing on the Sound. I'll be going out anyway. You might like to come along...."

"I'm not a sailor," Sarah protested, vainly trying to free her hand from his hold. "I was raised in Idaho. I'm a better potato farmer than a first mate. You'd never believe how much I don't know about boats!"

"I'm sure you could learn," Christopher said softly. "I'm a very patient teacher. You wait and see. We'll have fun."

Sarah trembled slightly. His voice was so low and intimate that for a moment she'd been afraid he had something other than sailing on his mind. But no, she was imagining a double meaning to his words. It was logical that he'd want to take her sailing. People liked to share whatever they enjoyed most.

"So, you have family in Idaho?"

"I . . . yes . . . no . . ." She stumbled, searching for a reply. Darn! Why had she ever let that slip? She could handle talking about the present, but the past was something she preferred to forget. "My real parents are dead." She abruptly withdrew her hand, swung her legs over the side of the chaise and stood up.

"I mustn't keep you any longer. You have to get up early tomorrow if your ship's sailing at seven. Thanks for the delicious steak. I'm sure even your father couldn't have done better."

He joined her, his large hands circling her upper arms. "I'm the one who should thank you—for being so kind to my mother. She had a good time tonight. I haven't heard her laugh like that since before Dad died. I'm glad you're our neighbor." His smile was a flash of white in his sun-darkened face. "And thank you, too, for a wonderful day and a fantastic evening."

His masculine scent drugged Sarah into forgetting who she was, where she was. For a brief moment she felt released from the haunting certainty of her stark and lonely future. Then as his face began to lower toward hers, she stiffened. Stepping back, she pulled her arms free. No matter how her lips yearned for the pressure of his, no matter how much her body ached to be held in his strong arms, pressed tightly against the long lean length of him, she knew she couldn't risk the moment.

"I'm glad you're letting Amanda stay. I'll do all I can to help Mrs. Johnson take care of her," Sarah promised, her words strained and stilted as she clutched her slipping cardigan and adjusted it back over her shoulders, feeling for the first time the chill of the spring night.

The party was over. Christopher would be back on his ship tomorrow. There would be no sailing trip on the Sound when he returned, no follow-up to the enchanted day they'd spent together. She'd see to that.

"Good night," she murmured without raising her eyes.

"Good night, Sarah." His answering words held a puzzled tone, but he made no move to stop her.

Tears stung her eyes as she crossed the boardwalk without a backward glance and let herself into the solitary darkness of her own house.

AS SHE SLIPPED ON a silky nightshirt and prepared for bed, Sarah couldn't keep her thoughts off Christopher Weaver. Adding what his mother had said over the past few weeks to the disclosures he'd made about himself during the evening, she felt she could form an opinion of him. He had a keen intellect and a dry sense of humor, and although reserved and confident, he wasn't the least bit standoffish.

Maybe, she thought, pulling a down quilt up to her chin and settling on her side, he was the proverbial sailor with a girl in every port—and content to keep it that way. But she wasn't satisfied with that answer. It was too pat and far too shallow.

Oh, he was charming, but not at all in a slick glib way. She sensed that the man was capable of deep feeling and commitment, that his reserve masked a well of emotion that for some reason had yet to be fully tapped.

Restless, she turned onto her other side and bunched the pillow beneath her head, remembering how readily she'd fallen in with his plans for the day. She'd even gone so far as to suggest some ideas herself that had kept her and the appealing man together.

Spending the day with Christopher had been for Mrs. Weaver's and Amanda's sakes, she tried to rationalize. She'd needed the time to convince him of the seriousness and value of Puppy Power. But the telltale heat flaming her cheeks belied her thoughts.

She let out a deep sigh. A pervasive sadness washed over her, taking with it remembered pleasure. Why had she been fool enough to expose herself to such an overpowering dose of a man like Christopher Weaver? The hours she'd spent with him couldn't be worth the unhappiness she knew she would experience over the next few weeks, as she tried to forget him, tried to regain the tight control she usually kept on her feminine emotions. Men like Christopher Weaver weren't for her. Most of the time she remembered that fact. She should never have let herself forget it today.

Curling up in a tight ball, Sarah let her pent-up frustrations, which had been building since the moment Christopher had tried to take her in his arms, come out in a few rare tears. They rolled hotly down her cheeks until, worn out and emotionally depleted, she drifted into a fitful sleep.

A few hours later she awoke with a start, her body bathed in sweat, her covers in a heap on the floor. Sitting up, she gasped for breath that seemed to be stifled in her constricted chest. After all these years, why had the nightmare come back?

Staggering from the bed, she clutched her abdomen and stumbled into the kitchen. With shaking hands she drew a glass of cold water from the tap. Fighting down panic, she forced herself to take deep even breaths until her heart stopped its wild pounding and her consciousness returned from the dark chasm of desperation into which her nightmare had plunged her. Gripping the edge of the counter, she lived through moments of agony until the glaring yellow of the kitchen walls faded back to the warm cheery color she'd painted them.

Exhausted, she sank to a chair, then buried her face in her hands and wept. As the tears flowed and she choked on her wrenching sobs, Sarah relived the times that despair had overcome her. She saw herself as a foster child shunted from home to home, until, at the age of eight, she'd been adopted by the childless couple who had become her loving parents. Then after four years of being a wanted only child she'd been replaced in their affection by the two children of their own they'd suddenly been able to have, one right after the other.

She experienced anew the alienation that had grown between her and her adoptive family until as a teenager her only dream for happiness had centered around the children she would someday bear—the children and family that would be hers and hers alone. But the sharp blow of a hoof from a skittish horse had ruptured her uterus, and ended that dream, leaving her not only barren, but ultimately estranged from her family.

Terrified of large animals since her accident, she'd known she'd never be able to make it through vet school in spite of her adoptive parents' offer to send her. As soon as she'd been able, she'd packed her suitcase and headed for Seattle, the city where she'd been told she was born. A search for relatives there had proved fruitless. She was alone.

Wiping her tearstained face on a cloth napkin, Sarah rose. *I'm all right,* she told herself. *I made it. I have a full life. A good job. Plenty of friends—all people who are grateful for what I do for them. Nothing can take that from me.*

Returning to her bedroom, Sarah stared at her tumbled bed. Not wanting to chance another nightmare, she decided to shower and dress. A walk along the lakeshore would calm her shaken nerves.

CHRISTOPHER HADN'T SLEPT WELL. Not used to leaving behind unfinished business, he'd tossed and turned until he'd decided to get up and make one more try to get a call through to Virginia. He'd tried off and on all day without success. Either she'd gone away on a weekend trip or was deliberately avoiding his calls. But he'd promised Adam he would talk with her about the possibility of his coming to live here. Glancing at his watch, he doubted he could get through in time to catch her before she left the house. If not, he'd have to call her at her office—not a good place to talk about something so important, but he'd given Adam his word.

As he shaved and dressed in his uniform it occurred to him that maybe he'd been a little short with his son when they'd talked. He'd been in such a hurry to be the first one at the dock on Saturday that he hadn't really paid attention to what the kid had to say. Yet Christopher knew he wasn't indispensable. The experienced crew could have gotten the job under way, even if he'd been a couple of minutes late. He should have taken the time to draw Adam out and to insist on specific examples of what his son objected to in his prospective stepfather. For all he knew there could well be grounds for Adam's discontent.

He'd always supported Virginia in what she thought was good for their son. Because of the divorce they'd agreed it was especially important never to give Adam the idea that he could pit one of his parents against the other. But Virginia must be pretty crazy about this guy to make such a startling change in her and Adam's lives. Given her track record as a devoted mother it seemed unlikely, but he supposed it was possible that her feelings for her fiancé were blinding her to Adam's point of view.

As Christopher looked at himself in the mirror while knotting his black tie, he stopped. How would his own father have handled the situation? He could almost hear the advice his father had always given when Christopher had been troubled about his relationships with other people: put yourself in the other guy's shoes; try to see the situation from his perspective before you get yourself in too deep. Had he done this with Adam? No, he admitted, as he slipped on his jacket. He'd steamrollered the kid, insisting that the boy do it his way. Well, this summer, he promised himself, he was going to take time to really talk to his son. Maybe if he tried, he could learn to be more like his own father. Now there was a damned good role model if ever there was one.

Picking up his packed bag, Christopher quietly let himself out of the houseboat. He didn't want to disturb his mother or Amanda.

He locked the door behind him and glanced across the way. All was quiet in the Mitchell household. Most importantly, he hadn't wakened the dogs. A picture of Sarah, serenely asleep, her long hair fanned across her pillow, flashed through his mind. Ordinarily he looked forward to putting out to sea. But somehow this time was different. He was already anticipating his return home. He realized that, among other less pleasant chores, he wanted to get to know Sarah Mitchell better.

He adjusted his hat and quickly strode up the pier.

Almost at the bottom of the steps that led up to the pavement, he stopped abruptly. His heartbeat quickened. He hadn't expected to encounter anyone this early in the morning... And he certainly hadn't expected to see Sarah again before he left. Her long loose hair seemed to capture and reflect the first glints of the rising sun. And her face— though solemn, even strangely sorrowful—was beautiful. Her wide-eyed innocence and elusive vulnerability touched him deeply. Setting down his bag, he slowly moved toward the steps and the slight woman standing at their top.

Chapter Five

Sarah saw Christopher before he saw her. Her first impulse was to turn and run back down the almost deserted streets she'd wandered the past few hours, trying to rid herself of the dull pain that still throbbed in her soul.

The starry evening she'd spent with him had been a serious mistake. During the day she'd been in control. She'd called the shots. And though she'd known she was treading dangerous water, she'd been on guard, aware of her precarious emotional balance. But crossing the boardwalk and entering his territory, accepting his hospitality under the night sky, had created a swell of feeling that threatened to overflow the dam she'd painstakingly constructed to hold back the demands of her heart.

She knew she wanted this man and that she wanted him to want her. Looking down now at the open delight on his face, she realized the independent course she wanted to travel was threatening to veer in an unexpected direction. The admiration she read on his face frightened her. How long would Christopher's interest last when he learned who and what Sarah Mitchell really was?

She knew he was waiting for her to make the next move. Waiting for her to give him some sign. Her sudden need to be held, to be cherished—yes, even loved—overpowered her reason. Slowly she descended the wooden stairs until

Christopher's eyes were level with hers. Their blue depths held concern.

"Sarah, is there something wrong?"

"No, I just couldn't sleep."

"For a minute I almost thought you'd gotten up to see me off." His voice was light and teasing.

"Well, if that's what you'd like to think, it's all right with me," she teased back, a tentative smile lighting her face.

"I would," he answered. He opened his arms and drew her close—and she let him. She heard him whisper, "It's been a long time since a woman rose from a warm bed to see me off."

Raising her hands to his shoulders, she was unaware that her face revealed her pensive yearning. This was not the time nor the place to tell him why she was up and out so early. The past could wait, so could the future. All that mattered was her present impulse to forget everything other than the immediacy of his nearness...to feel his lips against hers, let the balm of his desire seep into the emptiness within her.

Tangling his fingers in the rich wave of tawny hair cascading down her back, he tilted her head to his. Her lips were moist, parted, inviting. He inhaled her clean fragrant scent as his lips captured hers, his tongue launching a tentative invasion of the sweet recesses of her mouth.

Sarah stiffened as though afraid of letting herself go, her arms pushing against his shoulders. Sensing her reticence, Christopher released her and stood a breath away, still gazing into her eyes.

"What's the matter, Sarah?" he asked, his baritone voice gentle.

"I'm afraid," she whispered, unable to keep her voice steady.

His brow furrowed. "Of what? Of me?"

"No, not you," she answered, knowing it was the truth. It was herself she feared. There was no way she could explain her conflicting emotions. No way she could expect him to understand the importance of this encounter. All at once, she wanted him to finish what she'd encouraged him to start . . . wanted to take her first venture into uncharted waters. Afraid that she'd lose the moment, she pushed aside her crippling inhibitions. She curled her arms around his neck once more and pressed her mouth to his.

Her sudden sureness was all the enticement he needed. He'd meant to keep the kiss as light as their banter had been, but the awareness that it was goodbye as well as hello, moved Christopher beyond his usual bounds of restraint. He was a sailor, ready to set to sea, leaving behind a woman he'd just begun to care about.

Lost in sensation, Sarah clung to him. His kiss seemed to draw away her sense of pain, of loss, of fear, leaving her free to enjoy and respond to the feelings his sensuous mouth elicited.

At last his lips pulled away, but he held her until the beating of their hearts slowed. Sarah gradually regained control of her senses, becoming aware of the early-morning stillness around them. A moment earlier, with Christopher the center and whole of her existence, she had half expected to find her surroundings altered in some lasting way. She was surprised to find not even as much as a ripple on the calm lake.

With gentle hands she pushed herself away in order to look at his face. She needed to know if he had experienced the same wild excitement—if their embrace had had any real meaning for him.

The deep blue of his tender yet unflinching gaze met her scrutiny. The gentle intimate smile that curved his firm lips, and the slight catch in his breathing as he looked at her told Sarah far more than words. The sun-bronzed officer had been as affected as she by the embrace they'd shared.

His arms released her, but his hand came up to cup her chin. "Goodbye, Sarah," he whispered before he leaned forward and let his lips lightly brush hers again.

She stood where she was, her arms crossed over her chest in an effort to hold his warmth as long as she could. She waited while he retrieved his overnight bag and ran up the steps to his car. Then, resting her hips against the railing for support, she returned his wave and smile. She watched as he folded his tall frame into the driver's seat of the sleek car, started the engine and drove out of sight.

As HE DROVE ALONG THE STREETS of the awakening city, Christopher tried to keep his mind on the conversation he planned to have with Virginia, but it was difficult. The fresh sweet scent of Sarah clung to his clothes, making it hard to think of anything but the lovely young woman he had left behind. She'd been disturbed about something, of that he had no doubt. He wondered what could have been troubling her enough to send her out to walk the streets at an hour when she should have been safely tucked in her bed. He wished he'd had more time to talk with her.

A grimace twisted his features. Lack of time seemed to have been the problem with his whole weekend. No time to really settle anything. Just stopgap measures for unfinished business, beginning with Mrs. Johnson and the dog, then Adam, and now he had to add Sarah Mitchell to the growing list.

He glanced at his watch. If he hurried he would just barely have time to get in a call to Virginia before she left for work. He accelerated to slightly above the speed limit and headed for the freeway.

At the shipyard he parked his car, then strode rapidly toward the office, responding briefly to morning greetings as he hurried to his desk and picked up the phone.

Adam's sleepy voice answered on the first ring.

"I thought you weren't going to call," the boy said peevishly. "I was ready to cross you off my list."

"Adam, I'm sorry I didn't have time to talk with you longer on Saturday. I tried calling later, and then on Sunday, but—"

"I tried to get Mom to stay home, but oh no, we had to go out with old Greggy boy to look at houses. I don't want to move out into the boonies, but they won't listen to me."

"Look, son, I hate to cut you off, but the truth is I don't have much time." Christopher rolled his eyes. He was doing it again. But it couldn't be helped. Dammit, he really didn't have much time. "I'll write you a long letter when I'm on board ship and you write me."

"A lot of good that will do," Adam muttered. "You don't get your mail until you get home."

"If anything important comes up, you can cable me. You know that." Adam had always been an easy child to deal with, but this time there was no putting him off with pat answers. He couldn't help but wonder if Virginia's plans for remarriage were behind this disturbing change in the boy. "Is your mother still there?"

"Yeah, just a minute... Mom, it's Dad!" Adam shouted deafeningly.

After a few seconds Virginia was on the line.

"Hello, Chris."

"Hello, Virginia, congratulations. I was happy to hear your news."

"Thank you. That means a lot to me, but I know you didn't call for that. Adam told me he asked to come live with you."

"As a matter of fact he did. He—"

"It's absolutely out of the question," Virginia interrupted in brisk tones. "We've been going round and round that issue, and Greg feels he needs time to get around Adam's impossible attitude. He says that if the three of us spend enough time together we'll be able to form a solid family unit...and I agree with him."

Christopher couldn't argue with that logic, even though it hit somewhat below the belt. His lack of time at home within the "family unit" had been Virginia's reason for wanting a divorce.

"Adam doesn't seem sold on Greg yet..." he said carefully.

"That's not Greg's fault! You have no idea of what we've been going through with your son," she shot back. "Greg has bent over backward to please him. This weekend Adam wouldn't even get out of the car to look at houses the realtor was showing us, even when they had swimming pools!"

"I'd like to have the boy, Virginia."

"And right now, I'd like to give him to you, believe me," she said with a humorless laugh. "But I know it wouldn't be right for Adam. These days he's acting like a spoiled brat, and he has to learn that not everything in life is going to go his way."

"That's what I told him."

Her defensive tone softened. "Thank you for backing me up, Chris. I knew I could count on you."

"Virginia...uh..."

He hesitated, knowing he was treading on dangerous ground. But there was no way around it. He was Adam's father, and he had to ask. "There isn't anything specific that Greg is doing to cause Adam to object to him so strenuously, is there? I mean like...verbal or...physical abuse?"

"Of course not!" she answered indignantly. "Not unless you call exerting a steady masculine firmness on Mr. Smartmouth maltreatment. A firmness he hasn't had for a long time, I might add." Her tone was barbed and Chris winced.

"He seems so different. I can't help thinking that your plans might account for the change," Christopher persevered, unwilling to let go of the important point. "I've never known Adam to be rude or disrespectful in the past."

"He's a teenage boy!" Virginia exploded. "That accounts for the change. I didn't have to pull out my old child-development books to find out that some pretty disagreeable changes take place in a boy when he hits puberty. We've all just got to hold on and try to ride the storm out."

Then, in a slightly lower but still-exasperated voice, she went on, "Greg has never laid a hand on the boy, nor raised his voice to him. He's kind, patient, considerate—all those things—and Adam just won't give him a chance. But Greg's not giving up on him. We both agree that this would be the worst possible time to send Adam away."

The finality in her tone told him there was no use prolonging the conversation. He had to have confidence that Virginia knew what she was doing.

"Then give Greg my best wishes. You know I only want what's best for Adam and you, too. Let me talk to Adam again for a minute. Maybe I can exert some—what did you call it?—masculine firmness," he said with mild sarcasm.

"Goodbye, Chris, I'll get Adam..."

In a moment Adam was asking eagerly, "Did you tell her, Dad? What'd she say?"

"We talked, son, and she said you're not doing your part to form a... family unit." He nearly choked on the words.

"You sound just like Greg," Adam said with disgust.

"Well, that doesn't seem like such a bad idea. All I ask is that you meet him halfway. Now I want you to shape up and give it a try."

"I don't see why I can't have my own dad..." Adam blurted out.

Christopher hated himself for what he had to say. He still wasn't entirely convinced that the boy's attitude wasn't a reaction to his mother's plans. "Adam, you know I love you and I'd love to have you, but if your mother says no there isn't much I can do about it. You understand that, don't you?''

"I guess so," the boy grudgingly agreed.

"I'll write you and you write me..." He tried to get some cheer in his voice.

"Yeah, Dad. Well, have a good trip."

"Thanks, son. Goodbye."

Adam's dejected bye did nothing to lift Christopher's spirits as he went into the captain's office for a final briefing.

"I'M IN LOVE, I'm in love," Erma sang out when Sarah opened the door to her knock. "I just came from the pound where I found the basset hound of my dreams. Her name is Bertha, and it was love at first sight."

Sarah grinned and stuck her head out the door to look down at the deck. No bow-legged, wrinkled, floppy-eared, brown and black and white hound. "So, where is she?"

"I thought I ought to ask you first," Erma hedged. "I left her at the shelter, but I told 'em that if you'd take her in for a few days until I can find a new place to rent, I'd come get her out tomorrow."

Sarah smiled, closing the door. "Of course, I'll take her."

"Thanks, kiddo. I owe ya one."

"Don't be silly. If you didn't come over while I'm at work to take the dogs out for their midday walk, the whole Puppy Power program would go down the drain. Now come on in and tell me all about her."

Sarah sat down at the kitchen table to listen to Erma's story of a large family who, when facing an unexpected transfer to Australia, decided not to put their pet through the ordeal of a six-month quarantine.

"So they gave her to a neighbor," said Erma. "All Bertha's done has been dig up bushes, chew through her rope, come close to hangin' herself on the dog run, and take off every time she manages to get out. The neighbor finally gave up and took her to the pound hopin' somebody'd want her. Spunky little devil.'' Erma cocked her head and grinned as though she were the proud parent of a precocious child. ''I always wanted a basset hound.''

''The last time you said you always wanted a Saint Bernard. And the time before that, it was a boxer,'' Sarah said wryly, standing up.

''Aw, those were just fleetin' infatuations. This time it's for real.''

''Then we better hurry up and place a couple of these guys,'' Sarah said, going over to the cages to calm the impatient dogs who had been barking while she and Erma had talked, ''so there'll be room for Bertha.''

''Got it covered,'' Erma said with a smug grin. ''I spent the afternoon out at Jackson Ranch with the boys. The okay came through from the state supervisor of corrections this mornin'. Every bungalow can have a dog. That'll take care of these five, and we'll need one more.''

''That's great!'' Sarah exclaimed, excitedly. Erma and she had been working for months to obtain permission to place dogs at institutions housing juvenile offenders. At times they'd gotten so bogged down in red tape she'd wondered if they'd ever get a go-ahead.

''This calls for a celebration.'' Jumping up, Sarah took a bottle of champagne out of the fridge. The grateful owner of a Siamese had presented it to her in thanks for the special care she'd given the cat when it had been grazed by a car. Then she reached up and pulled a small box out of the cupboard. ''Champagne and dog biscuits all around!''

After the dogs had been given their treats, and she and Erma were contentedly sipping goblets of champagne, Sarah asked, ''But don't you think we should wait until we have a dog for every cabin?''

"Naw." Erma shook her head. "Those boys are chompin' at the bit to get hold of these dogs. The director said he'd loan the sixth cabin his own dog, Maggie, until we get another. She's been kind of a mascot 'round there anyway." Erma chuckled. "That poor pup just about has her fur petted off.

"I was lookin' for the dog we need when I found Bertha. I know ya just got home from work and that I shoulda given ya a few minutes to unwind before I came over, but I just couldn't wait."

"That's okay." Sarah smiled, enjoying Erma's irrepressible high spirits. "Give me a minute to freshen up, and then we'll take these guys out for a run. You haven't put them through their paces yet."

"Don't any of them look like attack dogs to me. But ya never know," Erma said, going over to the cages and giving each dog a long look. Fred whined and nosed at the door hook. One of Erma's specialties was testing the dogs they took from the pound for any signs of viciousness or tendencies to attack—the result of training or something inborn. Only gentle-natured animals would do for their program.

"And Fred needs a refresher course in obedience training," Sarah said over her shoulder as she went into the bathroom.

"No problem." Erma's strident voice rose to follow Sarah. "I'll put 'em on their leashes and take 'em out to Kanga."

Erma's arrival today had been a godsend, Sarah thought, as she hastily pulled off tailored slacks and blouse, and changed into a pair of jeans. The few minutes she'd spent alone in the house had been unnerving.

Though she'd been so busy at work the past few days that she hadn't had time to think about Christopher, his image was imprinted on the back of her mind—an odd catalyst for a renewed devotion to her daily tasks at the clinic. Besides her customary duties as a veterinarian's assistant, she'd had two serious cases in isolation under her direct supervision—dogs stricken with Parvo virus. For several days their condition had been critical and she'd spent many hours past closing time with them. She'd monitored their intravenous-fluid intake, drawn daily blood samples and used her best bedside manner to keep their spirits up. It had been touch and go, but now that their white blood cell counts were rising and their high fevers abating somewhat, there was hope they'd survive the ordeal. If only people would have their dogs inoculated against the virus, she thought, it could be virtually wiped out and no dogs would have to suffer the way the two under her care had. Maybe in time, Puppy Power could take that on as a new crusade.

At five that afternoon, with the crisis past, Dr. Blake had told her to go home. He'd promised to stay with her patients for a couple of hours longer and then check on them later that night. Exhausted, Sarah had gratefully left the clinic in daylight for the first time that week.

When she'd pulled into the parking lot above the houseboats, she'd been hit with the full impact of her memories of the intriguing sailor. Descending the stairway, she'd recalled the feel of his strong body and the shivering weakness she'd been left with after he'd gone.

Unnerving. That was the only word for it. It was still difficult for her to believe that she could remember the brief encounter with Christopher Weaver as though it had been only that morning. She splashed water on her face before running a brush through her hair. Catching a self-conscious glimpse of herself in the mirror, she realized she was making a terrible mistake thinking this much about him. There was no way he could really care about her—that would be too good to be true. She was building castles in the air. There was no reason to think he'd given her a second thought after he'd driven off. Reaching for a towel, she told herself she had more important things to do than to spend her time fantasizing about an unattainable man.

Moments later, after locking the door to the bungalow, Sarah ran up the boardwalk and helped put the dogs into the van. She waited while Erma got a thick, heavily weighted stick, and a sturdy padded jacket from her car.

"Let's go over to the valley," Erma suggested as Sarah coaxed the van's balky engine to start.

She hesitated. "Kanga's tank is almost empty and I don't feel like filling it up tonight. I thought Gasworks Park would do this evening." She nodded toward the tall tangle of pipes and boilers at the north end of the lake. The factory the things had once been a vital part of had closed down, and rather than dismantle them, the city had chosen to paint them in bright primary colors. The effect was interesting and pleasing to the eye. The surrounding acreage had been planted with trees and sod for public use, and Sarah took the dogs there from time to time when she knew it wouldn't be crowded.

The truth was she didn't want to go to the field where she and Christopher had spent their first pleasant morning together. Not just yet. She needed more time to sort out her jumbled emotions.

"These guys are going to be happy at the ranch," Sarah remarked.

"Yeah. And y'know, that opens up the whole state to us," Erma said, turning in her seat to look at her friend. "We got four more institutions along the Sound here to hit. Now that the state's okayed dogs for one, they'll have to give permission to the others. I been talkin' to Henry and we're not gonna be satisfied till every kid has his own dog. He's gonna make a swing around the state givin' 'em the pitch for Puppy Power."

"That's a pretty big goal," Sarah suggested.

"Not for a minute!" Erma exclaimed, her black eyes sparkling with vehemence. "If those kids'd had a dog to be responsible for and who loved 'em, they might not've gotten in trouble in the first place."

"Got any proof to support that theory?" Sarah teased, thinking of the way Christopher had doubted her own claims about Puppy Power.

"No, but after we see how this works out maybe we can get one of those brains at the U to write a thesis on it." Erma cackled at her joke.

"Before we worry about that, Fred has to learn to heel. He darned near pulled me over the other day."

"I'll work on it right away. I'll get him tomorrow and teach him a few tricks. Y'wanna take the dogs to the ranch this weekend? Maybe by then I'll have found another good one at the shelter and I can start trainin' it, too."

"How about Bertha?"

"No way! She's gonna be all mine!"

Sarah chuckled. "I didn't mean for the ranch. I meant when are you going to get her?"

"First thing in the mornin'. You can bet your life on it. I really appreciate your taking her in until I can find a place. I was thinkin' about gettin' a motor home and parkin' it outside the city somewhere."

"Sounds like a good possibility," Sarah agreed as she pulled the van into a space at the waterside park.

"I always dread this part," Sarah confided, pocketing her keys and opening the door.

"Aw, with this bunch, there'll be nothin' to it," Erma assured her before she jumped out spryly and slipped on the oversized jacket. Then taking her stick, she joined Sarah as she sorted out the leashes and helped the anxious dogs down. As though sensing the seriousness of the moment the animals stayed in a group, nervously prancing at Erma's side.

"Gimme Nancy and Ginny," Erma directed. "I don't think we have much to worry about from those two little bodies. I'll test 'em out, but I'm sure they're okay."

"All right," Sarah agreed, separating the small dogs from the pack and holding their leashes with her left hand. "Which dog do you want to take after them?"

Erma looked over the other three. "I guess Matt. He's not as big as the other two, but with his terrier disposition, ya never know. Then I'll take Mike. Save Fred till last. Now, when I wave the all clear, send 'im up. I'll whistle 'im in." She motioned toward the dog whistle hanging around her neck.

"Be careful." Sarah couldn't keep herself from cautioning the frail-looking woman.

"Don't worry 'bout me. I know my business."

"I know you do, but still . . ." Sarah let her sentence trail off under Erma's frown.

She watched with admiration as the ancient ex-policewoman, dwarfed by the cumbersome coat and accompanied by the two dogs under perfect control, strode on her spindly, khaki-clad legs to the top of the mound that overlooked the lake. So far, none of the dogs they'd gotten from the pound had ever responded to Erma's attack command. But there was always the chance that one would lunge and Erma would have to club it down. What if that happened? Sarah thought, feeling a lump grow in her throat. Would Erma be able to protect herself? And what would happen to the dog?

She shaded her eyes against the low golden rays of the setting sun. Though worried, she knew she had to trust Erma's expertise and stay where she was so as not to interfere with the test. Erma had positioned the two small dogs on the edge of the mosaic sundial that topped the hill and was walking backward toward the opposite side, commanding them to stay.

Holding her breath, Sarah watched as Erma placed her arm in front of her face and charged at the dogs. Neither the part cocker nor the little gray mongrel responded, and Sarah exhaled in relief. She laughed a little nervously as Erma roughed them up and tried to get them to bite at her stick. When no reaction was forthcoming from the smallest dogs, Erma released them from their positions and waved her stick over her head, signaling the all clear.

Sarah separated Matt from the three dogs she held and let him go. He bounded up the hill to Erma, who then positioned him on the sundial and took up her stance. To Sarah's relief, the terrier passed the test as Erma lunged toward him.

Patting Mike on the head, Sarah looked into his golden eyes. Surely this gentle part Lab wouldn't have any idea of what Erma was doing in her funny clothes and with her big stick. She unhooked his leash and crouched down, her arm encircling Fred's neck.

It took a while for Erma to get Mike to stay on the edge of the sundial. As soon as she turned her back, he was up and after her, his long tail wagging. After several tries, he finally held his position long enough for Erma to take up her stance. Then, as Erma lunged toward him, he sprang into the air, landed against her chest and pulled her to the ground.

Sarah jumped to her feet and started running up the hill, her heart in her throat. Erma was still down, the big dog hovering over her. No spindly arm with the heavy stick raised up to club the attacker. She must be hurt, Sarah thought, frantically racing up the steep incline.

But by the time she reached the top of the knoll, Erma was sitting up and laughing hysterically, weakly trying to push the playful dog away.

"He thought I was gonna throw the stick for him to fetch," she cackled. "When I didn't let go of it, he came to get it. He's been lickin' my face tryin' to get me to throw it for him. That's what I call a real spit bath."

"I thought he'd killed you," Sarah exclaimed, pulling the big black dog away.

"Naw," Erma said, getting to her feet and wiping her wet face on her sleeve. "I'm fine. Now put old Fred over there and get out of the way. And mind you hang on to that fool Mike."

Erma's lunge on Fred was anticlimactic for Sarah after the scare Mike had given her. Even though he barked wildly and bounded toward Erma, Sarah could tell it was all in fun. He wanted to play with the funny lady and her stick.

"Not a vicious bone in their bodies." Erma's wrinkled face beamed.

"I'm always so scared when you do that," Sarah confessed, encircling the older woman's shoulders and giving her an affectionate squeeze.

"Don't worry about me. I can still take care of myself," Erma assured her with a gruffness Sarah knew covered the pleasure she felt at having someone concerned about her.

After setting the dogs free, they stood on the mound enjoying the view of the bustling urban lake.

"Did ya ever see that Weaver fellow again?" Erma asked out of the blue.

Sarah's answer was evasive. "He's gone out to sea."

"That's right," Erma said, lightly hitting her forehead with the heel of her hand. "You said he was only in port for two days. Hardly gives a body time to get rid of his sea legs, does it?"

Sarah smiled, thinking how effortlessly Christopher had managed the shift from sea to shore—and how that short span of time had changed her life.

"You should stop in to see his mom when we get back," Erma suggested. "I wonder if she misses him. I'd go with ya, except I have to go give my notice and start packin'."

Later that evening, when Sarah took the half-empty bottle of champagne over to Mrs. Weaver's to share the good news about the placement of the dogs at the boys' ranch with her, she noticed the older woman seemed preoccupied.

After they'd toasted the expansion of Puppy Power into new avenues, Mrs. Weaver remarked, "I'm happy you and my son hit it off so well. He needs a friend right now."

"Oh?" Sarah was as noncommittal as she could manage, feeling a twinge of conscience. She hated to pry into Christopher's life, yet she did want to learn all she could about him.

"I've just had a disturbing letter from him," Mrs. Weaver confided, pulling a white envelope out of the folds of her lap robe. "And I need someone to talk to, dear. I hope you won't mind if I bend your ear."

"Not at all," Sarah said sincerely.

After a pause while she laboriously pulled out the folded sheet of paper covered with a bold masculine script, the older woman began, "It seems my former daughter-in-law is being remarried this summer and my grandson would like to come live with his father, but Virginia won't hear of it." She gave a heavy sigh.

"I knew nothing of any of this. I'm sure my son didn't want to worry me until it was all decided. I don't have to read between the lines to know that Chris is very disappointed, and the fact of the matter is I am, too. I love my grandson and I would have enjoyed having a boy around here again. But I can understand Virginia's not being willing to give Adam up. And I guess that I'm in no condition to take care of him while his dad's at sea. A teenage boy needs someone quick-witted and fast on her feet to keep up with his high jinks." Her voice faded off and she turned her gaze to the window, as if lost in thought.

Sarah sat back and sipped her champagne, not wanting to intrude on Mrs. Weaver's thoughts and knowing nothing she could say would help Adam's grandmother deal with her unhappiness.

Sarah hadn't realized Christopher had had so much on his mind. No wonder he'd snapped at her about the dog. Though she ached with the pain Mrs. Weaver was feeling, she could see that Christopher's ex-wife was probably right. And Christopher was hardly in a position to take on the burden of full-time responsibility for his son. Anyway, it really wasn't any of her business.

The mention of Christopher's son caused Sarah to try to imagine Christopher as he had been while growing up in this comfortable home. The house was as American in flavor as a Norman Rockwell print. When she'd once remarked to Mrs. Weaver about the surprising absence of souvenirs, the woman had told her that her husband had preferred it that way. Captain Weaver hadn't wanted to come home to an Oriental bazaar. Sarah tried to imagine Christopher's condo, wondering if he felt the same way.

"I hate to say this," Mrs. Weaver said, interrupting her reverie, "but I'm sorry my son and Virginia ever met while they were both in college back East. When they got engaged Charles believed it was a mistake, but he didn't even try to tell Christopher. The boy thought he was in love and our disapproval would have done more harm than good.

"But the truth of the matter is that Virginia is flighty, and a bit spoiled, though I'll be the first to say she's been a good mother to Adam. Still, Charles had hoped Christopher would find a woman who was, as he put it, 'made of sterner stuff.'" She turned a piercing gaze on Sarah. "It takes a strong independent woman to be married to a man whose life is the sea."

Sarah welcomed Mrs. Johnson's abrupt appearance to remove the champagne glasses. The housekeeper's interruption effectively ended the conversation that was leading in a direction Sarah hadn't anticipated. She knew Mrs. Weaver had wanted a response to her pointed remark, but she had no idea what she would have said.

"I'd better go."

"Oh dear," Mrs. Weaver said, a small frown wrinkling her brow. "I've been running on so, I almost forgot what I wanted to share with you. Listen to this: 'But on the brighter side, Mom, I have to tell you what a charming person Sarah Mitchell is. I like to think of her running in and out of the house keeping you company. We couldn't have a better neighbor. Don't let Mrs. Johnson get you down. If she gives you any trouble at all, tell Sarah. I'm sure she can handle that woman and will be happy to do it. When you see her, tell her I said hello.'"

Sarah rose to her feet, hoping the older woman wouldn't see the color that flamed in her cheeks. "He's right. I will step in if you need me to. Oh, and that reminds me, I told Christopher that I would mention painting the houseboat to you. I don't like to confess to being such a busybody, but I did blame him for the condition it's in."

"My goodness!" Mrs. Weaver said with a chagrined laugh. "I can imagine how much he appreciated that! He's been after me for the past year to let him do something about it. It must look terrible if you felt you had to mention it to him," she said ruefully. Perking up, she stiffened her spine and took on a resoluteness Sarah had never seen. "Of course he can paint it. Seeing Christopher out there working away will be almost like having Charles back."

Then she added with a sly smile, "And besides being nice having him around, it will give you two a chance to become better acquainted!"

THE TRIP TO THE BOYS' RANCH that weekend was one of the most rewarding experiences Sarah had ever had with Puppy Power.

The dogs, shampooed and brushed to a shine by an unflagging Erma, sensed that something was in the air. Sarah laughed to see the wary sniffs they took of each other's clean fur. Loaded in Kanga, they circled and circled, as if unable to find spots meticulously clean enough for their fine coats.

Bertha sat on Erma's lap, blissfully detached from the commotion in the back. Her wrinkled face, framed by her long ears, had already taken on an expression that duplicated her mistress's. Dog and woman were perfectly matched, as their heads swiveled in concert gazing at one thing, then another.

When they arrived at the ranch, the guard took a quick look in the van before letting them pass. Though it was a minimum-security facility, the barbed-wire fence and the armed guard were reminders that it was not a summer camp. But once through the gate, driving down a tree-shaded gravel road, Sarah had a hard time thinking of the lovely place as a correctional institution.

They drove half a mile until they reached the cluster of buildings that formed the hub of the facility. The van was met by more than fifty excited boys and the directors, George and Nancy Bascombe. Erma had told Sarah about the Bascombes. A vivacious young married couple, they were social workers, specialists in the area of juvenile rehabilitation. Sarah liked them immediately. It took unique people to devote their lives, day and night, to helping a platoon of teenagers.

Once the boys had settled down and had gotten into a loose formation, Sarah introduced each dog and turned it over to the group that had been chosen for it by lot.

"I'm sorry we don't have a dog for you boys yet," she told the last squad, "but we're working on it. In the meantime you can have Maggie for your own."

Complaints rose from the disappointed boys.

"Nah, that'll never work out."

"Maggie just follows Mr. Bascombe around."

"That's right. She'll never stay with us."

"We want our own, like everybody else has."

"We want a big one," a dark-haired adolescent declared, turning his attention from the boys who were leading their dogs away. "Not one of those puny little things."

"A great big one," another boy confirmed.

"But you could take turns letting a smaller dog sleep on your beds," Sarah suggested, knowing that the cost of dog food had been one of the major obstacles to instituting the program at the ranch.

"I want one that will have lots of puppies," a small boy ventured.

"Sorry." Sarah shook her head, reaching out to tousle his blond hair.

A few of the boys crouched and began patting Bertha, who rolled her eyes at Erma as if to ask how long she had to put up with this.

"Then how about her?" the little blond boy asked.

"She already has an owner. Come on," Sarah said to distract him. She'd suspected that it would be a good idea for Erma to leave Bertha behind, but she hadn't had the heart to suggest it after the older woman had remarked how much she was looking forward to taking the basset hound on the outing. After all, none of the dogs would be here if it weren't for Erma, and she knew it wouldn't be very long before this little boy had his. "Show me your house. I've never been here before."

A raucous laugh and a loud wolf whistle greeted her statement, as the group moved toward a log cabin in the trees.

"Watch it," Erma whispered out the side of her mouth. "Remember, these kids are juvenile offenders. Kids too tough to work out in foster homes. Every one of 'em has had more than a minor scrape with the law. You don't get sent here for a vacation.

"I'll head out to the other bungalows to show 'em how to talk to their dogs to make 'em mind. Later on you can make the rounds and talk about their care." She saluted Sarah and walked off in another direction. Sarah smoothed down her hair and pulled her sweatshirt over her blue-jeaned hips, trying to look as matronly as possible, before running to catch up with the boys.

It wasn't long before Sarah had sorted out each of the boys from Bungalow Four by name. Most of them were taller than she was, but she knew they were only children and couldn't help wondering what sort of problems had brought them here. She'd felt an immediate identification with these youngsters; many of them, she was sure, had no more idea of who they were than she did. Though she'd never before placed a whole group of dogs at the same time—and she knew she was going to miss the animals, especially that rascal Fred—she was glad they were going to have homes with these isolated boys who needed something of their own to love.

After showing her their house and introducing her to their house parents, the boys accompanied Sarah on her rounds of the other bungalows.

When it was time to leave, Erma and Bertha waited in the van while the boys gathered around the Dog Lady, as they had dubbed Sarah, extracting from her a promise that she would bring their dog in two weeks. Then, honking in response to their shouts of goodbye, she drove out of the compound.

"I'll get them a good dog if I have to buy one," Sarah told her friend, amazed at how attached she had become to the little crew.

"I'm sure one'll turn up soon," Erma answered, smiling down at the tired dog sleeping in her arms. "I'll alert Henry and Francine and the rest of the bunch to keep their eyes peeled. Terri's been doin' double shift at that nursin' home she works at, 'cause they're so short of help. And Pete's been laid up with his back. They're both mighty concerned that they haven't been able to help much lately, but I told 'em not to worry, they can make up for it later.

"I'll personally check out the pound every day till I come up with somethin'. Besides, we have to fill up those cages of yours again. Never can tell when we'll be able to place a pup."

Chapter Six

At sea Christopher was surprised to find how often his mind drifted from his work and his problems to the sight of Sarah Mitchell standing at the top of the pier. The picture of her, dressed in denim jeans and jacket, the soft wind riffling her long hair, continued to evoke tender emotions that grew stronger as his ship relentlessly pushed on across the Pacific.

During the long hours of the night watch, when he'd lean back in his high-backed leather executive chair to rest his eyes from the endless paperwork, he'd live again the time he'd spent with Sarah, from their first meeting—that he knew he'd always remember as a hilarious comedy of errors—to the morning when they had lain together in the freshness of the green field, to the evening they'd spent together under the stars, and to the kiss they'd shared....

He could almost hear the faraway barks of the frolicking dogs that morning in the field, smell the pungent odor of the warm damp earth, see the delicious curves of Sarah's body. Just thinking of her wide-eyed face and the feminine softness of her lips made his spine tingle. Remembering the graceful way she ran, the sound of her delighted laughter and the touch of her slender fingers entwined in his made time stand still.

Had the kiss they'd shared the next morning really been as perfect as he remembered? How he longed to hold her in his arms again, to recreate the magic. She'd reawakened desires he'd thought were long since lost.

Making his rounds of the ship, he wondered for the first time what occupied the crew's thoughts. Was it possible that they, too, were lucky enough to be thinking of women like Sarah?

Each port brought a new excitement, as he imagined how Sarah would react if she could be there. Far-off ports that had become as prosaic to him as the neighboring ones in Tacoma or Sacramento were exotic again. He deliberately avoided his customary haunts and regular acquaintances, seeking out the new and different, the spots a tourist would enjoy.

Passing a jewelry store in Kobe, he glanced at the items on display wondering what Sarah might like. Unable to resist a pair of amber-colored topaz earrings the exact color of her tawny hair, he purchased them and sent them to her airmail. After all, he owed her something for all she'd done for his mother. Inside the box he enclosed a short note that read simply: "Thanks for watching out for Mom. Hope to see you when I get back. Chris."

THE MORNING OF THE DAY the earrings arrived, Sarah awoke early, determined to prevent her heart from ruling her head. Having made up her mind to put the senseless infatuation with Christopher Weaver behind her, she tried to go over the reasons that a relationship with him could never work. Oh, it would be easy to fall head over heels for a man like him. Wonderful to possess him—body, mind and soul. But that was impossible. He had other claims on his heart—blood ties, which would always come first.

Even though his wonderful kiss had proved to her that she was capable of passion, she couldn't afford to feel that way.

At best her relationship with him, even if he was interested, couldn't last long. She wasn't woman enough for a man like him. After a few weeks or months, he'd move on to another who had more to offer than she did.

But the arrival of the package from Christopher upset her equilibrium and weakened her resolve. She sat on the edge of her bed, reading and rereading the note before standing in front of her mirror and slipping the earrings through her small lobes. Admiring their fine workmanship, she noticed the way they complemented the color of her hair. Though she couldn't help but mentally kick herself for being a wishy-washy fool, she couldn't keep her fingers from caressing them, cherishing this evidence that she'd been on his mind.

She had to keep things in perspective. She had to! The gift was just a thank-you, and certainly not the first she'd received for her efforts with Puppy Power. She mustn't read more into it than he'd intended.

Everything she'd ever wanted in her life had been swept away by a relentless current of misfortune. There was no reason for her to believe that the tide had turned, that her luck had changed. Besides, if she ever found a man who could love her, she didn't want to share him, and Christopher Weaver had other commitments, other loves.

Any woman in his life would have to take a back seat to his invalid mother and his teenage son. And that was the way it should be. Christopher belonged to them. Though it made her feel greedy and selfish to admit it even to herself, she needed someone who was hers and hers alone.

Sadly knowing there was no way she could separate Mrs. Weaver from her son, Sarah knew she had no choice. She'd wear the earrings to show Mrs. Weaver and then begin casually laying the foundation for cutting herself out of the elderly woman's life. She'd have to be careful or the older woman would see right through her and make a shrewd guess at her motivation. If she offered half truths as excuses—the demands of her job, her need to devote more time to Puppy Power—she could be convincing. She already had everything ready for Christopher to paint the houseboat when he got back. There was no need for her to involve herself any further in their lives.

By the time Chief Mate Christopher Weaver arrived back in port, she'd be only an occasional visitor to the Weaver home. It made her sick to think of losing her relationship with the dear woman—Mary Lou Weaver embodied everything Sarah had always dreamed of in a mother—but she couldn't risk encounters with Mrs. Weaver's son. No matter what Sarah had to sacrifice, she couldn't risk being hurt and rejected again by someone she'd come to love.

Just as Sarah took a deep breath and opened the front door, steeling herself to begin the painful ordeal of withdrawing from Christopher's mother, Mrs. Johnson exploded onto the deck of the Weaver houseboat shouting at Sarah hysterically, ''Mrs. Weaver's fallen out of her wheelchair, and it's all your fault!''

Spurred on by Amanda's frantic high-pitched barking, Sarah rushed across the pier, brushed the hysterical housekeeper aside, and ran into the Weaver home. Taking in the scene at a glance, her heart skipped a beat at the sight of Mary Lou Weaver sprawled on the living-room floor, ineffectively trying to raise herself with her one good arm. Amanda was frantically struggling to free her neck from between the spokes of one of the chair's wheels.

Making a snap decision, Sarah ran over and pushed the dog's head down to where the metal tines were spread the farthest apart. Once the whimpering pup was free and had run behind the couch, Sarah turned her full attention to the elderly woman. Gathering Mrs. Weaver into her arms, Sarah lifted the invalid's frail body and placed her back in the wheelchair.

"You shouldn't have done that!" Mrs. Johnson screeched, veins bulging in her thin neck. "She might have a broken back! I already called nine-one-one."

"Nonsense," Mrs. Weaver said sharply, though her breaths were short as if from overexertion or pain. "I just took a little tumble. Come here, Amanda. Let me see if you're all right."

"To hell with Amanda!" Mrs. Johnson shouted, her voice shaking, her glasses barely resting on the end of her nose. "She nearly killed you! I'd like to wring her hairy little neck." Hatred blazed from her eyes as she took a threatening step toward the whimpering pooch, who had jumped onto her mistress's lap. "I'm not going to be held responsible for this!"

"No one's accusing you of anything," Sarah said sternly, stepping between the overwrought housekeeper and the wheelchair. "Get hold of yourself. Where is the doctor's number? I'll call him."

"Over there by the phone." Jeanette Johnson gestured wildly, then began jabbing hairpins back into place in an effort to repair her ordinarily tight knot of graying dishwater-blond hair. "I'm packing my bags. There's no way I'm going to stay in this crazy place another minute, with an old cripple, a puny little looney and that...that killer dog!"

Sarah turned her back on the raving housekeeper, feeling a sinking sensation in the pit of her stomach. Knowing it was possible she had made a grave mistake in lifting Mrs. Weaver back into the chair, she was unable to keep her anxiety out of her voice as she asked, "Do you feel all right?"

"I'm fine," Mrs. Weaver assured her weakly, "and I'm sure we'll all feel better when that maniac leaves."

"I am going to call your doctor."

"Of course," Mrs. Weaver sighed, leaning back and closing her eyes. "At least she's right about one thing. I am nothing but a helpless old cripple."

"You are not! Not any more than I'm a puny little looney, or this—" Sarah patted Amanda "—is a killer dog!"

Mary Lou's immediate smile alleviated some of Sarah's fears. Though she was shaken and pale, she didn't appear to have been seriously injured. However, Sarah knew she wouldn't draw an easy breath until Mrs. Weaver had a medical examination.

While Sarah was explaining the details of the accident to the person handling the doctor's calls—he wasn't in the office at the moment—she heard the sirens. The emergency vehicle Mrs. Johnson had called was pulling into the street above the houseboats. After checking to make sure the person on the other end of the telephone line had all the information straight, Sarah stepped outside to direct the running men to the house.

"Mrs. Weaver's had a fall from her wheelchair," she explained as she led the paramedics into the living room.

"I'm all right," Mary Lou protested.

"Well, now ma'am, let's just get you lying down on the couch and check you out anyway," the taller of the two said, his mustachioed face calm and cheerful.

Sarah took Amanda as the medics expertly lifted Mrs. Weaver from the chair and placed her on the sofa. She watched anxiously as the blue-uniformed men checked the elderly woman's vital signs and bones for any sign of injury.

"I don't see any problem other than you'll be a little bruised and stiff, but it'd be a good idea to see your own doctor as soon as possible," the second medic said as he stood up. "I thought from the call that there was a dog bite involved."

"No, nothing like that," Sarah hastened to assure him.

"You the one who called, ma'am?" the mustachioed man asked, while his partner packed away the medical equipment they'd used in the examination.

"No, the housekeeper did," Sarah replied, trying to keep a straight face. She could imagine how Mrs. Johnson must have sounded when she placed her call. "She's a little excitable."

"To put it mildly," Mary Lou affirmed.

The telephone rang. "I'll answer that," Sarah said, going toward the hall. "With any luck it's the doctor."

It was, and after Sarah explained again what had happened and that the emergency crew was there, the doctor asked to speak to the paramedic. Handing the instrument to the one who had joined her in the hall, Sarah went back to sit with Mrs. Weaver.

She listened as the man reported the results of the tests he'd performed on Mrs. Weaver, talked for a few seconds longer, and then hung up.

"Dr. O'Malley will be coming by soon, ma'am. He wants you to stay on the couch till he gets here."

"Thank you," Mrs. Weaver said, then extended her thin hand in gratitude. "You've been very kind."

"Any time," the smaller man assured her, as he and his partner took her hand in turn.

"Now take care," the tall one said as they let themselves out of the house.

The paramedics' footsteps were still reverberating on the board planks of the pier when Mrs. Johnson stalked into the living room holding two large suitcases.

"I'm going to stay with my sister," she haughtily announced. "Mr. Weaver can contact me there to settle up what he owes me."

"Mrs. Weaver is fine," Sarah said, getting to her feet, continuing to stroke Amanda's fur. "No broken bones. Just in case you wanted to know."

"Mrs. Weaver is never going to be fine until she gets rid of that animal," Mrs. Johnson mimicked Sarah's deliberately cheerful tone with a sarcastic sneer.

Sarah walked to the door and opened it. "Would you like some help with those bags?"

"You and your help—" Jeanette Johnson sniffed, as she went out "—I can do without."

Resisting the impulse to make a less-than-kind response, Sarah pushed the door firmly shut behind her.

"The old witch," she murmured under her breath as she went back to sit with Mrs. Weaver.

"Oh dear," the older woman sighed. "What will Christopher think? Promise me you'll never tell him Amanda's part in this."

"If your doctor says there isn't any serious problem, it won't have to be mentioned," Sarah assured her. She was no more anxious for Christopher to know that Amanda's antics had resulted in a fall than Mrs. Weaver was.

"Perhaps Dr. O'Malley can suggest someone to take Mrs. Johnson's place—a nurse, maybe."

"Don't worry about that now. I'll stay with you tonight. Tomorrow we can put our heads together and come up with some answers. I don't have any dogs right now except Bertha. Oh—" she paused as an idea occurred to her "—I'll bet Erma can stay with you during the day tomorrow."

Mrs. Weaver's slight body seemed to sink lower into the couch cushions. "I'm such a bother. To everyone. A useless old woman—old cripple," she amended.

"How can you say that?" Sarah exclaimed. "I think you're a fascinating person, and your son loves you!"

"I'm nothing but a burden to him. Sometimes I wonder if I'm the reason he's never remarried. He deserves more out of life."

"And so do you," Sarah said softly.

Mary Lou's voice sharpened. "What do you mean by that?"

"Do you have to sit in that wheelchair all day?" Sarah asked, hoping her question wouldn't further agitate the elderly woman, yet feeling that now, when Mrs. Weaver's spirits were at a low ebb, was the right time to press the issue.

"I'm damned sick of sitting in that wheelchair."

Sarah's eyes widened in surprise. Mary Lou's expletive had caught her off guard.

"You see, when I had my stroke I hoped I'd die. It was the end of the world for me. Oh, I consented to a little speech therapy, but I thought if I didn't do anything else to help with my rehabilitation the end would come soon. But look at me." Her tone was disgusted. "Three years later and I'm still here. Why? I wonder."

"Because you're a tough old bird," Sarah said with open admiration. She hesitated a long moment before she added, "Do you think you're tough enough to try rehabilitation now?"

"You don't think it's too late?" the older woman asked, a slight tremble visible on her lips.

"It's never too late." Sarah's voice was strong with conviction. "When Dr. O'Malley comes we'll ask him about setting up a program for you."

EARLY THE NEXT MORNING just as Sarah finished getting ready for work, Erma rapped at the Weaver door.

"Hi, kiddo," she said, as Sarah let her in. "How's that poor old lady doing? Any more excitement since y'called me last night? Did that Johnson dame come back?"

"No, I don't expect to hear from her again. Come on in," Sarah urged. "Don't just stand there."

Erma took a tentative step forward. "First time I ever felt welcome in this place. Can't say I miss ole Pruneface scowlin' at me. And here's Momma's baby," she added, squatting down on the floor to press her face against Bertha's, who'd trotted over to her. "She been out yet this mornin'?"

Sarah nodded. "I took both her and Amanda out for a short walk earlier. Mary Lou's still in bed. I'm just grateful she didn't break anything."

"Me, too. That son of hers wouldna taken too kindly to that. He'da thrown Amanda out for sure. How'd Bertha and Amanda get along?"

"Couldn't have been better. They both spent the night in Mrs. Weaver's room. I slept on the couch and tried to keep Bertha in the living room with me, but she kept going over to the bedroom door and whining. Mary Lou finally said to let her in, and I never heard another peep all night."

"Ah—" Erma fondly stroked Bertha's head "—did you have a slumber party?" Then straightening, she said, "You gotta get off to work and I've gotta get busy." Unbuttoning one of the large pockets on the leg of her fatigues, she pulled out a frilly apron and tied it around her waist. "Nothin' lifts a body's spirits like a nourishin' breakfast. I wanna have somethin' special ready for Mary Lou when she gets up."

"I'm on my way," Sarah said, grabbing her jacket and purse. "I've got to use every minute I can find to find a companion for Mary Lou. I'm going to try the classified ads first. But I'm a little concerned, because Christopher said it was almost impossible to find someone reliable to take this job."

"Don't be in a hurry," Erma advised. "I can spare a few days here. I gotta check out the paper, too. I'll take some time to let my fingers do the walkin'. I still haven't had any luck findin' a place for me an' Bertha."

Sarah paused. She felt a little guilty leaving Erma like this. But when she'd called her the night before to tell her where Bertha was she hadn't had to ask for help. Immediately understanding the need, Erma had volunteered to come over for the day. "The kitchen seems to be well-stocked..."

"Now you just run along and let me take care of this,"
Erma broke in. "I was writin' tickets and makin' collars
before you were ever thought of. There's no way I can't
handle two dogs and one nice old lady."

THOUGH THANKFUL she had such an understanding boss,
Sarah's frustration grew during the long day. No wonder
Christopher had been so upset when Mrs. Johnson had
threatened to quit because of Amanda. By evening, after
placing what seemed like at least fifty calls and following up
every lead she'd been given, she was no closer to finding a
suitable companion for Mrs. Weaver than she'd been before she'd started.

She didn't want Mary Lou to know how difficult it was or
how worried she felt. When it came right down to it, the
bottom line was that Mrs. Johnson had been right. It was
Sarah's fault that Mrs. Weaver had fallen. If she hadn't
given her Amanda, it never would have happened. Feeling
a deep sense of responsibility, and also a little apprehension at what Christopher would think about her taking
matters into her own hands, Sarah was in a quandary. Even
if she could find someone to replace Mrs. Johnson, she
wasn't sure he'd approve of, or want to keep on, anyone she
hired. But really, what choice did she have other than to
keep on trying?

LAUGHTER GREETED HER when she let herself in that evening. Mary Lou and Erma, with perky little Amanda listening as though she understood every word, were so
engrossed in animated conversation that they didn't even
notice her entrance. Only Bertha waddled over to sniff her
shoes and give a welcoming wag of her tail.

As soon as Erma caught sight of Sarah, she jumped up
and asked, "You didn't hire anybody, did ya?"

Sarah shook her head.

"Good, cuz we gotta plan, haven't we, Mary Lou?"

"Indeed we do," Mrs. Weaver responded wholeheartedly.

"What's that?" Sarah asked, wondering if there was any chance they'd come up with the same idea she'd entertained during her drive home. That, she thought, would be too good to be true.

"Erma and I have hit it off so well today," said Mary Lou, "I can't imagine wanting anyone else in my house. She's a marvelous cook and I haven't had so much fun in years. My sides ache from laughing."

"So we figured if I was to move in here, I could take that Johnson dame's place and keep Bertha, too. Kinda like killin' two birds with one stone, so to speak. Actually three. Because this way I'll be able to keep an eye on you, too, kiddo." Erma's wrinkled face beamed at Sarah. "No more TV dinners. We're all three gonna eat together like family."

Sarah smiled and gave a sigh of relief. These two had come to the same conclusion she had. They seemed like an odd pair, but as long as they were congenial it was the obvious solution.

"But I do insist on paying you," Mary Lou said firmly. "Sarah, we've been arguing over this point for quite some time. Will you please step into this and tell this generous woman that I can't accept her offer unless she accepts a reasonable wage? I know Christopher wouldn't like us accepting her charity."

"And you tell this obstinate woman I'm not offerin' charity," Erma argued. "It'd be like scratchin' each other's back. We need each other like local berries need fresh cream! Why, this place is the answer to my dreams! I'm willin' to work for my keep here."

"She'll more than earn her keep just by the tales she has to tell about her years on the police force. She's so entertaining," Mary Lou interjected.

"I can say the same of her tales about bein' a school-marm and the wife of a sea captain. Why, she's openin' a whole new world for me!"

Sarah could see that she'd have to settle the argument if either of the women was to have any peace of mind. "I think you're right, Mary Lou. I don't see any reason why Erma shouldn't accept the amount you were paying Mrs. John-son—"

"Well, you can bet your bottom dollar that I'm not gonna need any payoff money for takin' care of Amanda!" Erma's bright eyes sparked.

"Sarah," Mrs. Weaver said, "since my stroke, no one has given me the care that Erma has today. I feel she really cares—"

"Yer dern tootin' I care," Erma snapped.

"What I was saying—" Mrs. Weaver smiled fondly at Erma "—is that she deserves more than Mrs. Johnson ever got."

"Mrs. Johnson's wages will be enough," Sarah said firmly, hoping to end the friendly argument before Mrs. Weaver became too excited.

"Well," a mollified Erma remarked, "I'm not gonna spend a cent of it. I'm gonna tuck it away until I have enough saved to buy a floatin' place for myself!" She stuck her chin out defiantly.

Sarah put her arm around Erma's thin shoulders and gave her a hug. The eternal optimist had to be well on the road to ninety!

As SOON AS SHE COULD Sarah arranged for a wheelchair ramp to be installed beside the steps at the front of the pier, and with the help of a retired neighbor, Erma pushed Mary

Lou up to her car and drove her to the daily therapy sessions Dr. O'Malley had prescribed. They were all so busy that Sarah and Erma had a tacit agreement to put Puppy Power on hold until they had time to adjust and settle into the new situation.

The evening meals the women shared made Sarah feel she belonged to a loving family for the first time in years. All her plans for distancing herself from the Weaver household had flown out the window with Mary Lou's fall. She was more involved with the older woman than ever before—and she liked it. Shopping for stylish yet comfortable clothes for Mary Lou, helping her choose a becoming hairstyle, and giving her a soft home perm filled many happy hours for both of them.

One evening while Erma was out grocery shopping, Sarah began manicuring Mary Lou's nails, paying special attention to her paralyzed hand. Prompted by the subject Mary Lou never tired of discussing and the closeness growing between them, she asked a question that had been on her mind.

"Don't you miss Christopher when he's gone?"

His mother's reaction was placid. "No, I guess it's habit, but I never think of missing him. I know he'll be gone for just a little over a month, then he'll be back. I just look forward to his return. I learned long ago not to fret about his father's being gone to sea. It's too much of a burden to put on your man—and on yourself."

"Didn't you ever feel lonely?" Sarah persisted.

A shadow clouded Mary Lou's eyes and her smile faded. "After Charles passed away and I knew he wasn't coming back, I found out what loneliness really was. All the years of our marriage, my life was alternately filled with a happy sense of expectancy or a wonderful contentment. I was alone at times, but never lonely. There's a big difference."

"Yes." Sarah let out a soft sigh. "I know what you mean."

"Losing Charles was almost unbearable. Since my stroke I'd just been waiting for it all to be over. Then you came along and introduced that little body into my life—" she nodded affectionately at Amanda sleeping by her side "—and since that time nothing has been the same."

"I'm glad," Sarah said. There were so many people like Mary Lou. If only she had the resources to reach more of them. At times like this she wished she could quit her job and devote full time to Puppy Power. But Puppy Power was not a paying proposition, and she had to eat and keep a roof over her head. She was just grateful that Christopher's mother had been one of those she'd been able to help.

"Despite my more recent unhappiness, I have no regrets for myself," Mary Lou continued, "because I made every day count. I didn't put my life on hold when Charles was at sea. I just wish that Virginia and Christopher had been able to make a go of it and find the same contentment Charles and I had together."

Sarah bent her head closer to Mary Lou's hand. She almost wished she hadn't brought up the subject, yet she wondered what had kept Christopher Weaver from marrying again. He'd been divorced for years. Surely he'd met dozens of women who would have jumped at the chance to be the wife of a highly attractive successful Merchant Marine officer. Whatever, he must have had his reasons. Perhaps he just enjoyed playing the field. With his looks and aura of quiet power, she knew he would never have trouble finding someone to play with. She had certainly fallen into his arms quickly enough.

Mrs. Weaver's words penetrated her thoughts as though the older woman had read her mind. "I worry about my son. I think sometimes that his life is terribly lonely. I know it's not too late for him to start again, if he could just find the right woman. What upsets me is that I don't think he looks very hard.''

Later, thinking over that conversation as she dressed for bed, Sarah knew she had to find some way to let Christopher know that all she wanted from him was a casual yet friendly relationship—a pleasant rapport for the sake of his mother. She was adult enough to pull that off. She didn't have to isolate herself from the man; after all, he wasn't contagious. Maybe all her anxiety was for nothing. The gift of a pair of earrings wasn't exactly evidence of a grand passion. What reason did she have for thinking she was the one woman he was looking for to turn his life around? Why was she worrying about putting out a fire that wasn't even smoldering?

BY THE TIME Christopher was due home his mother had regained a noticeable degree of movement in her paralyzed arm and a permanent sparkle in her eye. Wanting to show off her new clothes and hairdo, Mary Lou suggested that they all go down to the ship to meet him.

On Friday afternoon, exactly thirty-five days after she'd met him, Christopher's ship was back in Elliot Bay. From their position on the company pier in the latticed shadow of a mammoth orange crane where they waited to greet him, Sarah thought what a sight they made—one old lady in a wheelchair, another in army-surplus fatigues and combat boots, a full-blooded basset hound, a fluffy mongrel pup...and her. Nervous as she was, she had to chuckle. Christopher was in for a surprise.

She ran her hands over her hips, smoothing the cotton fabric of her slacks. Mrs. Weaver had wanted Sarah to dress up for his homecoming, but the pale yellow sweater and slacks had been a compromise; they were more suitable than a skirt for helping transport an invalid and her wheelchair.

When his unmistakably tall lean figure swung down the gangplank, her beating heart felt like a drum in her throat. Catching sight of the entourage waiting on the pier, his initial look of astonishment was replaced by one of pure delight as his face broke into a wide grin. Quickening his step, he hurried toward them.

The mist of tears that welled up in Christopher's eyes as he kissed his mother brought a corresponding moisture to Sarah's, which threatened to overflow and run down her cheeks as she watched him talk with the older women.

"Mom, I just can't believe this," Christopher said as he bent to give her yet another hug. Sarah listened while he expressed his pleasure over and over again at seeing his mother dressed and out.

"Who's your friend?" he asked, turning to include Erma in the conversation. Sarah knew how pleased Erma must be when, after Mrs. Weaver finished her carefully revised version of Mrs. Johnson's departure and explanation of Erma's role in her improved condition, Christopher gave Erma a heartfelt hug to show his gratitude.

"And your hair, Mom!" he exclaimed. "It looks great!"

"Do you really like it?" Mary Lou asked girlishly, reaching up to touch the fluff of white waves that framed her still-youthful face. "Sarah cut it and gave me a perm."

"It's very stylish," Christopher grinned, leaning down to give her yet another hug.

Sarah held back from taking part in the conversation, wanting to absorb the impressions she was receiving from watching Christopher interact with his mother and Erma. But her conscience was uneasy about the way Amanda's role in Mrs. Johnson's departure had been glossed over. Sooner or later Christopher would have to know the truth. And when he did, how welcome would the dog be? She couldn't help but remember his first reaction to Amanda!

And, she worried, though he seemed more than pleased right now with Mary Lou's transformation from a listless figure sitting dejectedly in her wheelchair to the perky woman newly interested enough in life to greet his ship, how would he feel when he saw how greatly things had changed on the houseboat? She winced, thinking of the five gallon containers of paint under the tarp on the Weaver deck waiting to be applied to the weatherworn siding. Though he'd agreed with letting her talk his mother into having it done, he hadn't said anything about actually ordering the materials. Would he resent the intrusions she'd made into his life? Maybe she had moved too fast. Maybe even a casual friendship was more than she could expect from Christopher Weaver.

She'd meant to steel herself against the impact she knew his presence would have on her senses, but try as she might to ignore her body's response to his uniformed figure, she had to admit that the man before her was more appealing than ever. Even trying to force herself to hold the image of him as the father of a teenage son did nothing to dim that appeal.

She'd worn the earrings. She liked them so much she hadn't had them off since the day she'd received them. Suddenly self-conscious, she raised her fingers to touch them. If he noticed the topazes, would he think she was wearing them as some sort of sign that she wanted to take up where they'd left off? Should she remove them? There was still time. But something kept her from it. It was only common courtesy to show him that his thank-you gift had been appreciated. Yet, confronted by the reality of Christopher Weaver in the flesh, the part of her ruled by her heart couldn't help but foolishly wish that the earrings had been a token of his personal regard for her as a desirable woman. Caught between the undeniable yearning of her heart and the reality that she was nothing more to him than a neighbor—an interfering neighbor—Sarah stood, a little apart from the group, wishing she were anywhere other than where she was.

With the passing moments, however, her anxiety began to fade. Drugged by his nearness, she felt the inexorable pull of the attraction Christopher Weaver held for her. Resolve weakening, she indulged in the luxury—what did it matter if it was pure fantasy?—of believing she was a whole woman, capable of meeting with courage any overture he might make toward her.

"Come on." Erma's raspy voice addressing Christopher, interrupted Sarah's thoughts. "Help me get yer mom into the van. She's had enough excitement for now. Sarah can ride home with you," she added decisively, turning the wheelchair around.

"But wouldn't you rather ride with Christopher?" Sarah quickly asked Mary Lou.

"No, dear," Mary Lou answered just as quickly. "He won't be ready for a while, will you, son?"

Christopher shook his head, an amused smile forming on his lips.

"Besides, it would be too difficult to get me in and out of that low car. I'll ride back in this chair, just like I did coming over. That safety belt Mr. Beasely had installed works so well that I'm quite comfortable. Then Mr. Beasely can help Erma take me down the ramp when we get home.

"You stay here and be company to Christopher, Sarah dear. I'm sure the two of you will find plenty to talk about."

Sarah hesitated. She hadn't counted on being left alone with Christopher so soon. But, she rationalized, it would be embarrassing to object, and besides, riding home with him would give her a chance to explain privately everything that had happened while he'd been at sea.

After Christopher had helped Erma load his mother and the dogs into the van and the four had driven away, Christopher returned to where Sarah waited.

Taking Sarah's hands in his, they stood facing one another, oblivious to the bustling activity around them.

"Hello, there," he said, his voice intimate and low.

"Hello." She managed little more than a whisper.

With eyes as blue as the sky, he gazed into hers, an endearing smile crinkling the laugh lines surrounding them. She couldn't get enough of looking at his face, marveling at how well she'd been able to remember every detail of his features, from the way his sun-bleached eyebrows tilted up at the ends to the deep indentation below the center of his nose above the curved firm bow of his lips.

He released one hand and lifted a finger to gently touch a glowing topaz earring. "I knew they'd look like that on you. I couldn't resist buying them."

"I love them," Sarah said softly, nestling her cheek against his large palm. "Thank you."

His hand slid under her hair to enclose the nape of her slender neck. His senses filled with wonder at the sight of her oval face with its fine skin, her hazel eyes shimmering like deep mysterious pools, her full mouth opening like a tropical flower just burst into bloom.

"Lord, you are beautiful, Sarah Mitchell," he murmured.

"You are, too," she answered, meaning it.

He laughed, filled with the joy of it all. She was wonderful. Absolutely guileless. Struck by the need to be gentle, protective and tender with her, he wanted to give, as well as to take, the pleasure her lovely lips offered.

"You can't imagine how much I want to kiss you," he said, pulling her close with the hand he still held, then releasing it to circle her with his arm.

Oh, yes I can! Sarah's heart sang.

As his lips slowly descended to meet hers, Sarah closed her eyes and gave herself up to the kiss she'd determined she would never allow to stir her soul again. But the touch of his mouth on hers sparked her desire. She let herself sink against his strength and melt into his arms, as his sensuously moving lips parted hers and his strong tongue claimed her mouth. Her fingers clung to the gabardine of his jacket, her own lips and tongue giving a full response to the deep and driving urgency of his.

When his hand moved down her back, gathering her closer, and her arms curled around his neck in complete surrender, the moment was exquisite. "Welcome home," she murmured against his heated lips.

"I wouldn't have missed this homecoming for anything," he whispered back. "But much as I don't want to, I do have to go in to sign the manifest and check my box for further orders."

"Give me your keys and I'll wait in your car."

"Give me another kiss and I might consider it."

And once more Sarah's world was turned upside down, as her lips clung to his and her willing body was fused with his.

"The manifest can wait," Christopher said huskily. Placing one hand at the small of her back, he propelled her toward the Corvette. "I want to hear what part you played in Mom's transformation. I thought I was seeing things when I came down the gangplank."

"I'll bet you did," Sarah said as she slipped into the passenger seat and he closed the door before walking around to the driver's side to join her.

"I thought I'd seen everything in my time," he said, resting his arm on the seat behind her head, "but I think Erma is an original. Where did you ever come up with her?"

Sarah laughed a little nervously. "I've known Erma almost as long as I've been in Seattle. She carried a dog into the veterinary hospital where I work one day. It had been hit by a car and abandoned at the side of a road. We became friends while she practically lived at the hospital until it recovered. She insisted on paying the bill for the dog. She would have liked to have taken it, but she's never been able to find a decent place to live that will allow pets. She advertised in the nickel want ads until she found it a good home.

"Actually she was the first person I told when I got the idea for Puppy Power. There are other volunteers, but she's been my mainstay. Being an ex-policewoman who used to work with guard dogs—"

"Policewoman? Guard dogs? That little thing?" Christopher interrupted.

"That's right." Sarah nodded. "She's been retired from the force for years, but she still tests all the dogs we bring into the program to see if any of them have been trained to attack."

"You've got to be kidding!"

"No, I'm perfectly serious. And things have worked out very well, having Erma take care of your mother. They've become fond of each other. And since Erma is right next door she can still take Puppy Power's dogs for their midday outing like she's always done. She's in seventh heaven because she can have her own dog now—Bertha, the basset hound."

"We met," Christopher said drolly. "Correct me if I'm wrong, but my guess is that Erma has at least ten years on my mother."

"My guess is more like fifteen," Sarah agreed with a wide grin, "but I can't be sure because neither one of them has confided her age to me. I've had to piece things together from little things they've said. But it's no problem, because Erma has the energy level of a woman half her age."

Christopher laughed. "I don't doubt it. But how did you ever talk Mom into therapy?"

"It was easy," Sarah said cautiously. "She just decided she didn't want to be in that chair for the rest of her life." She hesitated. If only she hadn't played a part in it, the fall would be Mrs. Weaver's secret to keep. But as things stood, she would be less than honest if she didn't tell him everything. She could only hope that he would be understanding and let Amanda stay. Whatever he did, she couldn't make the decision or take the responsibilities that were rightfully his. "Christopher... I have to tell you something you may not be too happy about. Your mother didn't want it mentioned, but she had a fall. Not a serious one. Dr. O'Malley checked her over and said she hadn't been hurt..."

His eyes narrowed as his face sobered. "Why wasn't I notified? Did Mrs. Johnson...? Was she negligent? Is that why you sacked her?"

"No," Sarah said uneasily. "She quit."

"Sarah," he said in a deliberately calm tone, "I want to know exactly what happened, and I want the truth."

Though her cheeks flamed, and she barely ventured an occasional glance at his controlled features, Sarah told the whole story, ending, "Your mother didn't want to worry you. It was after the fall that she became furious with herself for being so helpless and decided to try therapy. She can lift her left arm now and her fingers are regaining dexterity—"

"She didn't want to worry me?" Christopher interjected quietly.

"She was afraid you'd blame Amanda," Sarah answered, a slight tremble in her voice, "and maybe demand that she give her up." She stopped short of adding that she'd been troubled by the same worry.

"And what did you think, Sarah Mitchell? That I'm some kind of monster who wants to keep his mother chained to a wheelchair on a dilapidated houseboat, taken care of by a miserable woman who wants to deny her any happiness? A monster whose own mother is afraid of him? Is that how you think of me?''

"Of course not, Christopher," Sarah said uneasily. "I know you only want what's best for your mother. My only worries were that your ideas might not be the same as hers, and that you'd be so concerned about the possibility of another fall that you'd insist the dog go."

"I see."

Sarah felt herself squirming under his steady gaze and forced herself to go on. "I understand a great deal more about the Weaver household now than I did before you left. I understand why your mother's house hasn't been painted. I also understand why you were so upset about having to replace Mrs. Johnson. I tried all day after she quit to find someone suitable to take care of your mother and I came up with zip. I don't know what I would have done if Erma hadn't been willing to fill in for me while I was at work. You can't imagine how relieved I was when she and your mother had such a wonderful time together they both wanted to make the arrangement permanent." Noticing his raised brow, she stopped. "Then again, I suppose you can.

"I don't blame you for being angry with me. I took an awful lot on myself that I really should have called you about. And, Christopher, I certainly would have let you know if your mother had been injured . . ."

"I'm not angry with you," he said, his eyes softening. "I could never tell you how grateful I am for everything you've done. My mother looks wonderful. I'm afraid that you think I'm not much of a son—"

"Not at all," Sarah protested. "I envy the closeness you have with your mother. And I'm glad you're home so you can take over for a while." She smiled.

"And I'm glad I'm home, too," he said, brushing her pert nose with his lips. "Right now I've got to take care of busi-

ness so we can get out of here. I'll be back as soon as I can."
He opened the door and swung his long legs from the car.

"I'll be here," Sarah answered, taking delight in the simple words. For a few frightening moments she'd thought her butting into the affairs of the Weaver household had caused her to lose the people she'd come to care deeply for. If Christopher had become angry, she didn't know what she would have done. He wasn't a domineering person who had to have everything his own way. He was simply a concerned son, and a very good one at that. Seeing how important family was to him, it bothered her that Christopher had never mentioned anything about his son, especially when he'd been grappling with the possibility of the boy coming to live with him. Of course she realized she hadn't spent all that much time with him, and she didn't really want to bring up the subject of Adam, but until she knew more about Christopher's relationship with the boy, she wouldn't feel entirely free to let whatever was developing between them take its course.

Watching him walk away, Sarah realized for the first time since the massive ship had docked that the pier was filled with other men, the crew as well as the land-support personnel. But none of them stood out like Christopher, his tall white-hatted figure moving with masculine grace toward the one-story structure that was quite dwarfed by the freighter.

The magnitude of his position suddenly struck her. Christopher wasn't just another seaman. He was second in command on a quarter-mile-long, oceangoing container ship, responsible for its crew and multimillion-dollar cargo.

After he'd gone inside, she didn't take her eyes off the door until Christopher emerged once more into the sunshine and headed back to her.

As he climbed into the car, she noticed a frown had replaced the bright smile he'd left her with.

"What's wrong?" Sarah asked, her throat constricting with concern.

"We're not going to have as much time together this month as I'd hoped. The whole crew has been ordered to take a special fire-fighting refresher class. It seems there's a new and dangerous substance arsonists are using—one we haven't been trained to control. It's a two-week course."

"Arsonists?" Icy fear spread through her. Her active imagination pictured the holocaust an act of political vengeance or personal spite could wreak on the huge ship.

"Don't look so worried," he said, cupping her chin and leaning over to give her a gentle kiss. "The few fires we've had on board were all easily contained. What bothers me is the time the course is going to take away from us." He turned the key, and the engine roared to life.

"I've done it again," Sarah groaned, slumping down into the soft leather seat as if to somehow make herself disappear.

"What?" Getting no answer, he repeated, "What have you done?"

She grimaced, gingerly choosing her words. "Put you in another bind. I told your mother you wanted to paint the house. She agreed—"

"That's great!" he interjected.

"Just a minute. Wait until you hear the rest of it," she cautioned. "She agreed, as long as you were going to do it yourself. We've ordered and had delivered everything we thought you might need. It's all piled on the deck...waiting for you," she finished lamely.

"No!" he protested. Bouncing the heel of his hand off the steering wheel, he groaned in frustration. "There goes my whole leg!"

Chapter Seven

"I'll help you," Sarah volunteered, wishing she hadn't made such a mess of things. Christopher was no more upset about this turn of events than she. She should have waited for his approval before having all the materials delivered. But there was nothing to be done about it now. She knew Mrs. Weaver would be disappointed if they put it off, since she'd finally made up her mind to have it done. "If we work nights after we get home, we should still be able to finish in time to spend a few days sailing if you like."

"I don't know." Christopher shook his head, a thoughtful look in his expressive eyes. "The boat needs work, too. I haven't had her out yet this year, but I know the hull is in bad need of paint." He frowned. "I'm not sure how I'll manage to get everything done. But I do want to take you sailing."

"I'll start scraping the siding on the house first thing tomorrow," Sarah offered. "It's the least I can do."

"That's too hard a job for—"

"It is not," she interrupted, certain he was going to say "for a woman." "I did my whole house by myself. At least let me help with your mother's."

Christopher considered. "I might be able to get the boat into the boat yard. Even though this is their busiest season, chances are they'll have an open slot come up in the next week or so. There's always someone who cancels out. If I can there will be no need for you to do any work on the house. I've already let you take over too many of what should have been my responsibilities."

"You're making me feel like an interfering busybody," Sarah flared. "What was I supposed to do when Mrs. Johnson walked out? Leave your mother alone until you could be notified? I only did what any good neighbor would do. And about the paint, I admit I may have overstepped my bounds there, but your mother really got excited about having the house done, and I thought... I guess I thought wrong, huh?" she finished lamely.

Her outburst caused Christopher to burst out laughing. "That's the Sarah Mitchell I remember! I thought she was lost under all those apologies. I've been waiting for you to chew me out for neglecting my mother!" he said, taking his eyes from the road for a brief moment to smile into her startled face.

"I have no intention of chewing you out about anything," Sarah said levelly, relieved to know what had caused his slightly antagonistic manner. "I'm only offering to give you a hand. Wouldn't you do the same for me or any other of your neighbors if you had the time?"

"When you put it that way, of course you win, and I should be gracious enough to accept your offer. But I only want you to scrape as high as you can reach. I don't want you climbing on any ladder. I'll do that part."

Sarah grinned and relaxed, glad the issue was settled. Changing the focus of the conversation from herself she said, "The man at the paint store couldn't believe that we planned to scrape the paint off by hand."

"I can't believe it, either." Christopher let out a mock groan.

"He tried his best to rent us a pressure washer. But after I explained the Environmental Protection Agency ruling about not contaminating the lake, he recommended a special marine paint. It was developed for use on houses that are exposed to salt spray. Even though Lake Union is fresh water, he thought it would hold up better than regular paint.''

''Sounds good to me. What color trim did you get?''

''Your mom chose a beautiful slate blue for the house, and she wants it trimmed in white.''

''That's a change!'' He lifted his brow in surprise. ''How come she didn't want it brown again?''

''I don't know,'' Sarah said. ''It was all her idea.''

''Hmm. The house has been that same shade of brown as long as I can remember. The only thing she ever wanted changed was the trim.''

''Does painting it another color bother you?'' Sarah asked.

''No,'' Christopher replied, ''not at all. In fact, now that I think about it, it may be a good sign. A sign that Mom's finally ready to put the past behind her and get on with her life. What do you think?''

''I think you're right,'' Sarah answered with a smile.

''Well, it'll save time if I spray the paint on. Since we have to cover the brown, it will take at least two coats.''

Sarah let out a relieved breath. Christopher had come around and taken the news with more grace than she'd expected, after his initial dismayed reaction. ''I know it's going to be a big job, but I'll help you all I can.''

''You already have a full-time job. You've got to promise not to exhaust yourself.''

''I promise,'' Sarah said, her voice meek. It felt surprisingly good to have someone care enough to tell her what to do.

''And can you spare the time from Puppy Power? How're old Fred and the rest of the guys?''

"Fred and the others are in their element," Sarah answered, smiling delightedly. "They're settled in, living on a ranch with a bunch of boys." As they pulled onto Eastlake Drive she went on to tell Chris about the correctional institution and her trip there. "And Dr. Blake found the final dog we needed the following Monday—an Irish setter. The boys didn't have to wait. They got their big dog and didn't even ask if it could have puppies when they saw it was a male." She enjoyed Christopher's laughter at her story.

Pulling into a parking spot above the houseboats, Christopher cut the motor. When he turned toward her, Sarah realized that his face had sobered. Perhaps she shouldn't have gone into such detail about the boys. She wondered if he was thinking of his own son. If he was, he didn't say so.

"I know I haven't seemed grateful for your talking Mom into painting the place," Christopher said, looking at her intently, "but I want you to know I am."

"You don't have to say that," Sarah said, just able to resist an impulse to reach out to soothingly caress the strong lines of his jaw. "I never thought that you weren't."

"It's just that painting the house and fixing up everything that's been neglected for so long—on top of going to fire-fighting school—is going to take a big chunk out of the time I'd hoped to spend with you. And I'll admit I'm disappointed." He sighed. "I know we only had a couple of days together—just a few hours, really. But it meant a lot to me. I've thought about you, Sarah. In fact—" he gave a short laugh, feeling like an adolescent boy pursuing his first girl "—I've had a hard time thinking about anything else."

"I've thought about you, too," Sarah admitted shyly, wondering what about her could be so appealing to this worldly man.

"I haven't had a meaningful relationship with a woman for a long time," he confided, somewhat embarrassed to be expressing his feelings so candidly. "Too long. I guess without realizing it I'd shut a door on that part of my life...on those kinds of feelings. But being with you has made me remember what I've been missing, and frankly I was looking forward to spending every minute I could with you. Now it looks like I'll be working most of the time."

"We'll be spending plenty of time together," she said, knowing that she would do anything if it meant a chance to be with him. "Every evening and every weekend until we get the job done. It's going to be fun," she finished gamely.

"But I wanted to take you places," Christopher said, resting his head against the high back of the leather seat. "I'd planned to wine and dine you at the best restaurants. And for us to go dancing, sailing—"

"Next time," she told him, an excitement tinged by nervous apprehension mounting within her.

Next time, he thought, his mind echoing her words. Next time, he knew, Adam would be here for their yearly father-son camping-sailing trip. If things went as he hoped between them, he'd have to tell Sarah about that. But now wasn't the time. He still wondered what Sarah's feelings were about the boy. He'd considered mentioning Adam when she'd been talking about the boys at the ranch, but had thought better of it. He had the troubling notion that Sarah was avoiding the topic of his son, but he could be way off base. It was just as logical to assume she hadn't mentioned Adam because he'd never introduced his son into one of their conversations. He made a mental note to ask his mother what, if anything, she'd told Sarah about the boy.

Avoiding a direct response, reaching over to wind a silky strand of her tawny hair around his index finger, he said, "At least tomorrow night, after I finish my cargo watch, we'll go out on the town. I'll call Max Pierson and ask him to bring Alani along. They're my oldest and best friends, and I want you to meet them."

"I'd like that," Sarah said, wondering how far back their friendship went. Had the four of them been friends when Christopher had been married to Virginia? If they'd been Virginia's friends, would they be hostile to her? Surely not, she told herself. Christopher and Virginia had been divorced far too long for the Piersons to resent anyone he dated.

"Great. I'll call the Space Needle Restaurant and get reservations for tomorrow, but what would you like to do tonight?"

"I think we'd better stay right here. Your mom would be disappointed if we took off somewhere, and Erma would really be put out. But I'm warning you," Sarah said with a grin, "you'd better be prepared for the unusual."

"How so?"

"It seems cooking is one of Erma's hidden talents. We had to clear off one whole shelf in the kitchen for all the cookbooks she hauled in. She claims she's never cooked the same thing twice, and after eating quite a few meals over there, I believe her. She has some creative ideas of what goes together to make a meal. It may not always be well balanced, but it's colorful and your mom loves a surprise after Mrs. Johnson's steady diet of meat and potatoes. Tonight Erma's cooking up something top secret for your homecoming."

Christopher's roar of laughter warmed Sarah's heart.

A few hours later, while Sarah helped Erma put the finishing touches on the dinner, Christopher sat with his mother in the living room. He could tell there was something on her mind other than the regular conversation they were having, catching up on one another's news. He didn't want to hurry her. It was a real joy to see her so actively interested in her life again. Watching his mother sitting contentedly stroking her puppy, bubbling over with stories about all that had happened while he was away, he listened with amusement, especially enjoying the parts of her recital that concerned Sarah. He couldn't help thinking that if by some miracle his mother ever walked again, he wouldn't give the credit to the doctors or to Amanda. He knew he'd have to thank the warm, sincere and generous young woman who'd come into his mother's life.

"Virginia called yesterday," Mary Lou said, effectively bringing Christopher's attention back to her. "She's always been careful to check up on me while you were gone."

Christopher said nothing.

"She didn't mention that Adam had asked to come live with you."

"I suppose she thinks that's a closed book."

"You don't?" Mrs. Weaver asked, looking at her son intently.

"I don't know. Adam is dead set against living with a stepfather."

"Too bad I'm not up and on my feet. Between us, we could offer him a good home."

"I'm sure that he has that now, Mom. But when I talked with him the day I sailed I could tell he had changed a lot from the boy we had here last summer. I suppose he was growing up right under my nose when we took our ski trip together last fall, but he seemed the same Adam then, except for being a few inches taller. I'm afraid you're in for a shock when he comes at the end of July."

"Soup's on," Erma's voice rasped out as she came into the living room to push Mary Lou's wheelchair over to the table.

Christopher was ready for the interruption. He knew the conversation would veer to Virginia's remarriage, and that was a subject he didn't want to get into with his mother. He knew she thought it was well past time for him to be thinking of remarrying, and this was not the time to hold that discussion.

The meal, featuring a whole salmon poached in orange juice, seemed rather strange to his palate, but he manfully ate a generous helping.

"Where did you get that unusual recipe?" he asked Erma as she cleared the table for the next course.

"Just a little somethin' I made up. Vitamin C is good for sailors, otherwise they git scurvy," she remarked sagely.

"Oh, they give us an orange every day on board ship to take care of that," he managed to answer with a straight face, causing Sarah to choke behind her napkin. "There hasn't been a case of scurvy on our line since we changed over from sails to diesel."

For a moment Sarah was fearful that Christopher would look at her with a wink, leading Erma to think that Christopher was pulling her leg. But the sincerity with which he made the outrageous statement matched Erma's own, and led to his divulging culinary secrets he'd picked up over the years about Oriental cooking. He kept Erma fascinated throughout the rest of the meal while he ate Erma's second course, stuffed artichokes dipped in hot jalapeño sauce.

Erma watched with apparent rapt interest as Christopher wiped his brimming eyes on his napkin.

"Hot enough for you?"

"Yes, thank you," he answered in a strangled voice, sniffing loudly.

"Your mom said you liked things kind of spicy. I thought the hot-pepper sauce would sorta jazz things up after the bland salmon."

"You thought right," he assured her, after taking a long draft of ice water. "Aren't any of you trying this unique combination?" he asked, noticing that his mother and Sarah were dipping their leaves in what looked to be melted butter.

"No, thanks," Sarah said innocently, having decided weeks ago that Erma had a cast-iron stomach. "I just love this buttery flavor."

"They're sissies," Erma said disparagingly, scooping up more of the fiery concoction and popping it into her mouth. "I just knew you were man enough to enjoy somethin' a little spectacular!"

Fortunately, the dessert was a muddy-green iced sherbet. Erma divulged that it was flavored with kiwi and avocado, and it effectively soothed Christopher's mouth—enough that he felt he wouldn't have blisters on his tongue. But just to make sure, he asked for a second helping, a request that, Sarah knew, endeared him to Erma forever.

THE NEXT MORNING Sarah stood on the pier, dressed in her oldest jeans and sweatshirt, waiting for Christopher.

He caught sight of her as he came through the doorway of the Weaver home, and his rugged face broke into a wide smile.

"This is getting to be a habit of yours," he murmured, nestling his face in her fragrant hair as his arm went around her shoulders. "And it's one that I'm not having any trouble getting used to."

Walking him up to his car, Sarah slipped her arm around his waist, marveling at how natural it seemed to be this close to him. The evening before had been wonderful. His delightful bantering with Erma and Mary Lou had shown her a side of him she would always cherish having known, no matter the outcome of their relationship. His enjoyment of old ladies did nothing to detract from his masculinity, though. If anything it served to enhance his charm.

When the older women had tactfully gone to bed, she and Christopher had stayed on in the cozy kitchen, doing the dishes and talking. Discussing all sorts of preferences over steaming cups of mocha, they'd expressed mutual delight whenever they found they agreed on something, even if it was as trivial as liking their pepperoni pizza topped with pineapple and black olives.

And as they'd talked, Sarah had been acutely aware of a disturbing but compelling undercurrent of sexual tension flowing beneath their words. When Christopher had suggested a walk, she'd quickly agreed, telling him that both Amanda and Bertha needed to be taken out.

With each of them holding a leash, they'd walked a long way beside the lake. When she'd stepped into a depression beside the road, he'd steadied her. His arm had stayed around her shoulders then, as it was now.

He'd kissed her good-night at her door. And though his embrace had been tender, she had known by the way his taut muscles had rippled under her palms that he'd been holding back, consciously controlling himself. Perhaps he'd sensed that she was still a little fearful, unsure of herself in this new role, even though that light touch of his lips had kindled a desire that had smoldered deep within her for hours after he'd gone. Sleep had been a long time coming, yet she had awakened early, feeling refreshed and ready for the new day.

Her impulsive decision to greet him as he left for fire-fighting class was born of her surety that Christopher Weaver was genuinely interested in her, that something real and wonderful was happening between them.

When they reached the car Christopher put both of his hands on her shoulders and gazed for a long moment down into her eyes.

"Lord, I hate to think of you working all day while I sit on my duff in class."

"I don't mind," she answered honestly. "I've been itching to get at this place. I like making things look new again."

"Well, don't scrape the skin off your beautiful knuckles," he said, sliding his large hands down her arms to take her hands.

"I'll wear gloves," she promised, amused and touched by his solicitousness. Expecting a kiss, she raised her face, but was disappointed when he stopped just inches from her lips.

"I can't kiss you now," he whispered. "If I did I wouldn't be able to stop." Raising her hands he kissed them instead. "See you tonight," he said, giving her tingling fingers a squeeze.

Then he was gone.

Sarah worked hard all day, stopping only to eat the meat loaf-and-sweet-pickle pita pocket sandwich and slice of rhubarb-and-cream-cheese pie Erma brought out to her on a tray.

"Hey, kiddo, you don't have to get it all done in a day. Why don't you take a break?" Erma suggested.

"I'll go home pretty soon for a long soak in the tub," Sarah answered. "Christopher is taking me out to dinner tonight."

"That's nice." Erma beamed happily. "Mary Lou said he wouldn't be home. Said he usually eats out with some fellow named Max who takes over the ship for him when he's on leave."

"That's right," Sarah said, barely suppressing a giggle. To hear Erma tell it, the captain of the ship was nonexistent and Christopher ran the whole operation by himself. "But tonight Max is bringing his wife along and we're making it a foursome."

She would have liked to have had a little advice on what to wear for the evening, but Erma, who she'd discovered wore flowered muumuus and chenille mules for leisure wear, was not the one to ask.

"Well, you're sure earnin' your supper," Erma added with a cackle. "But as I said, you'd better knock off pretty soon for a little R&R. If you keep this up you'll fall asleep in your soup.''

Sarah worked on into the afternoon, moving with the shade, careful not to let the May sun catch up with her. Though she enjoyed its warm rays, she burned easily, and she didn't want to look as though she were second cousin to the lobster Chris had promised for dinner. She was grateful for the tiresome job. She needed a physical challenge to fill the hours until she would see him again. Each time she thought of the long evening they'd spend together, an unsettling twinge of panic butterflied in her stomach, stimulating her to apply the scraper at twice her normal speed. When at last she decided to call it a day, she was pleased that she'd scraped two sides of the weatherworn houseboat up as far as she was able to reach.

Squatting down to secure a lid on the large container of paint scrapings she'd swept up from the deck, Sarah realized to her surprise that she wanted to be with him every minute he could spare. Although she'd told the truth about enjoying working on renovations, the larger part of her motivation in offering to help with the painting had been to free him up to spend more time with her. She loved the sound of his voice, his ready wit and his engaging personality. She was ready to throw caution to the wind for the pleasure of being held in his arms. But did he feel the same way? And even if he did, given the demands of his commitments, did she want more than he was free to give?

It was a different Christopher who knocked at her door that evening. Dressed in a well-tailored navy-blue sport coat and knife-pleated khaki-colored slacks, a burgundy tie neatly knotted at the neck of an impeccable white dress shirt, he could have been a young corporate executive calling for his date.

"You're gorgeous," he exclaimed, giving a whistle. "I've never seen you in a dress before. Turn around and let me look."

Sarah's color deepened as she turned before his appreciative gaze. She gave wordless thanks to the dress shop that had put the designer dress she wore on sale for a fraction of its original cost. The understatedly elegant, white silk dress clung to her curves and plunged to a discreet vee above an overlapped waist. Its above-the-knee skirt was light and frothy, making a faint whispering sound as she walked.

When she'd bought it, she hadn't had any idea of when she'd ever wear it. But she'd been glad to see it hanging in her closet this afternoon when she'd looked for something to wear for tonight.

"You've got the kind of legs short skirts were made for," he commented, his eyes lighting with genuine appreciation. "First time I've seen them, but they're everything I could have hoped for."

"You're not so bad yourself," she answered in an effort to hide her embarrassment. She gathered up her purse.

Taking her elbow, Christopher steadied her as she walked carefully up the boardwalk, trying not to catch her narrow heels in the spaces between the boards.

"What would you have done if I'd have asked you to pirouette for me?" she asked, smiling up into his sun-darkened face.

He grinned. "I'd have done it, of course, and have felt as flattered as I hope you did."

Pleased with his answer, she linked her arm with his, resting her hand on his lower arm for support. "You have an answer for everything, don't you?" she teased.

"There was a time not too long ago when I thought so," he admitted with an easy smile, "but life has a way of deflating our sails when they get too puffed up with self-importance."

"And you've learned that lesson so young?" Sarah asked, her full mouth curved in a mischievous smile as he helped her into the car.

"Not entirely," he admitted as he joined her and started the engine. "I'm confident you could still find more than a few who'd testify to my being an arrogant bastard."

"Well, most of us have our little failings," she said with a mock solemnity that broke them both up.

"And just what are yours?" he asked.

"Mine?" Giddy with the joy of going out on the town with the most attractive man she'd ever met, Sarah's round eyes held a provocative flirtatious look. "You'll just have to find out for yourself."

"I think I'm going to enjoy that very much," Christopher said with a wink, as he pulled onto the thoroughfare. "You know," he said thoughtfully, "since her stroke I've felt guilty every night I've gone out to eat and left Mom alone with her companion. But with Erma there I don't think she even misses me. Those two really have a great time together, don't they?"

"They do. I don't think they'll ever run out of things to talk about. They're both interesting women," Sarah answered.

"And so are you, Sarah Mitchell," he countered sincerely.

"About tonight. I should fill you in a little. Max and I went to the academy together..."

Sarah listened, enjoying the sound of his rich melodic voice. "So it will be mostly shoptalk tonight?" she asked, when he had finished.

Chris shook his head. "Not with Alani there. The rest of us will be lucky to get a word in edgewise."

Moments after meeting the beautiful but strangely tense woman, Sarah knew what Christopher had meant. Alani Pierson wasn't the kind to be upstaged by anyone. Seeing how the deep jade of Alani's halter-necked dinner dress complemented the bronzed tone of her skin and the dark fall of her lustrous black hair, Sarah remembered Christopher saying that Alani was a mixture of the races that made the native Hawaiian women so beautiful.

After smothering them with a gushy greeting, Alani made a show of taking in Sarah's outfit with an appraising eye. "Love your dress," she threw out, before hooking her arm with Christopher's and leading him toward the glass-enclosed elevator in the base of the Space Needle.

Red-haired Max earned Sarah's eternal fondness by taking her arm and remarking, "So you're the lovely Sarah. Christopher told me you were special, but I had no idea you were so beautiful."

The women stood in front of the men so they could all enjoy the breathtakingly lovely ride up to the restaurant. The whitecapped Cascades, dominated by majestic Mount Rainier, provided a spectacular background for Seattle—the Emerald City on the Sound.

After they were seated at a window table in the revolving restaurant, Alani launched into an entertaining monologue about her problems trying to keep the house immaculate for realtors to show to prospective buyers, with two children and their friends running through and mussing up faster than she could clean up after them. She finished by saying, "But of course, Christopher, you have no idea what I'm talking about. After all, you've never had to put up with having Adam underfoot at every turn."

Though she remained outwardly composed, something twisted inside Sarah. She knew that no matter what happened between her and Christopher there would never be children they'd have together under their feet or enriching their lives. She supposed Alani's words were typical of an exasperated mother and housewife; yet she wondered how

Alani would feel if there were not, and could never be, any children of her own filling her house with childish laughter.

Then, as if unaware of the awkward silence that followed her remark, Alani went on to address Sarah. "You know, Max and I, and Chris and Virginia were married on the same day at the academy chapel. It seems like an eternity ago." She favored both uncomfortable men with a charming smile. "If we'd known then what we know now I'm sure it would have been a different story. Virginia threw in the towel and went back to her family after just a few years of trying to raise Adam with only a part-time husband. But," she added with an elaborate sigh, "I've stuck it out. It hasn't been easy, I can tell you that."

Christopher caught Sarah's eye as Alani paused to take a sip of her cocktail. She knew from the faint roll of his eyes and the slight lift of his brow that he was telling her not to mind Alani. Virginia and Alani must have been close friends, Sarah decided, and Alani must feel a little of the hostility Sarah had feared, or else she surely wouldn't have introduced Christopher's ex-wife into their conversation on so short an acquaintance.

Seemingly oblivious to her dinner partners' discomfort, Alani turned to her husband and prompted, "Max has an announcement he wants to make."

Max's fair skin reddened under his freckles as all eyes expectantly turned toward him.

"Not now, Alani," he said, clearing his throat with embarrassment.

"Yes, now." Her sweet tone took on a hard edge. "You wouldn't want your best friend to hear it from someone else, would you?"

"Hear what?" Christopher asked warily. Though Alani looked smug and self-satisfied, the expression on Max's face was a dead giveaway that he wasn't going to enjoy whatever was coming.

"I'm resigning," Max said. "After my next leg. Alani's father is ill and she—" he quickly amended his slip of the tongue "—we want to go back to the islands. I'm going back to my old job."

Christopher sat as though stunned by Max's news. Sarah took his hand under the table and stroked his thumb with hers, trying to offer what little support she could. She wasn't sure why Christopher was so disturbed by Max's announcement, but it was obvious he was.

Recovering, he spoke. "But I thought you liked working on the big ships. I thought the island hopping had gotten you down."

"Island hopping, as you put it, is a lot easier than house hopping," Alani broke in, her tone disdainful. "It's too hard on the children. They need stability. And they need both a father and a mother," she added pointedly. "Especially now that the older two are reaching that impossible adolescent stage. I've often wondered how Virginia could handle Adam all by herself. Oh, by the way, I hear she's getting married again. Are we supposed to congratulate you or something?"

Meeting Alani's unflinching eyes, Christopher saw the resentment glittering in their onyx depths. He'd known that Alani had never been happy in Seattle, but until this moment he hadn't realized how much she blamed him. She had to be terribly bitter to take such cheap shots at him in front of Sarah.

Refusing to be drawn into a senseless argument that had the potential to turn nasty, Christopher forced a broad grin and gave Sarah's hand a light squeeze.

"Alani, I think congratulations are in order for you and Max," he said expansively. Raising his glass to her, he took a sip before going on. "It was a mistake to try to transplant a lovely island flower like you to the mainland. I'm going to miss you, but I know you'll be happier, and that's all that counts." He paused. "I'm also happy for Virginia." Christopher's tone was even as he looked the brown-skinned beauty straight in the eye. "Now, shall we order?"

His cool question called for no answer, bringing the conversation to an abrupt halt. When he turned his full attention to the menu and began making suggestions to Sarah, Alani angrily settled her shoulders back into the upholstered chair.

The rest of the evening was strained, in spite of Max's and Christopher's sporadic attempts at jocularity. Alani had evidently come prepared to say her piece and was primed for an argument. But when Christopher failed to rise to the bait, she spent most of the dinner hour in sullen silence.

Although Sarah felt ill at ease among the others, who knew each other so well and were obviously very upset beneath their urbane veneers, she did her best to hold up her end of the conversation. Realizing how much she cared for Christopher, she wanted to defend him against Alani's gibes. He'd been hit with one verbal blow after another, and had been too much a gentleman to retaliate. She became more and more vivacious and animated, hoping her efforts to be entertaining would take some of the strain off him.

Christopher sat back admiring his petite companion and her witty conversation, though his thoughts were in turmoil. Another rift had opened and was widening between himself and his past. Although he and Max would always remain friends, he knew nothing would ever be the same again after this night. Having given up his berth on the container ship, Max would never have a chance at promotion to captain. He was throwing away his career to satisfy his wife's whim. The idea was unsettling and incomprehensible. Try as he might, Christopher couldn't understand how Max could give in to Alani on something so important.

Though the two couples parted amicably outside the Space Needle when the valets brought their cars around, neither asked the other home for a nightcap.

"I'm sorry about tonight," Christopher said, pulling the car out into the flow of Saturday-night traffic. "That whole scene was pretty grim. If I'd had any idea what was coming I'd have never dragged you into the middle of it. Alani wasn't herself. She's usually very charming and likable." When she isn't on the attack, he added to himself.

"I wanted to defend you," Sarah admitted. "She wasn't being fair."

Christopher gave a humorless laugh, reaching up to adjust the rearview mirror to ward off the glare of headlights from the stream of cars behind. "I don't think Alani would agree with you. Tonight she was after revenge." He smiled darkly and put one hand inside his jacket, resting it against his chest for a moment before bringing it out for inspection. "See any blood?"

Sarah shook her head, an amused expression in her eyes.

"I'm surprised. Alani's words were so barbed that I can't believe I withstood the attack without at least a little damage to my fuselage."

"So she *was* deliberately trying to hurt you," Sarah said. "You didn't say she was a vicious person."

"No." He shook his head. "Ordinarily she's not. In fact, I don't believe that's what she thought she was being tonight."

"I still don't understand," Sarah confessed.

Christopher let out a heavy sigh. After the evening she'd spent, he owed Sarah an explanation. "You see, I'm the one who persuaded Max to leave Hawaii. Alani was making it clear that she holds me to blame."

"But she's persuaded Max to go back to Hawaii. I wouldn't think there'd be any problem now from her point of view. But you seemed upset about his decision. Is there something wrong with what he's doing?" Sarah asked.

Christopher snorted. "It's the worst thing he could do for his career. He'll never make captain now."

"Oh," Sarah commented in a small voice. "But you said they'd be happier there. Didn't you mean it?"

"I only hope they will be," he answered, his expression grim. "There's been plenty of friction in their marriage over all this, and now both of them will have to live with the knowledge of what he gave up for her."

"Is it so bad if he doesn't make captain? Maybe Alani being happy is more important to Max than his career," Sarah suggested. But from the hard set of Christopher's jaw she could tell he couldn't bring himself to believe that.

"I sure as hell hope so," he muttered. "Let's drop the subject, shall we? I've had enough of Max and Alani for tonight. Where would you like to go? Dancing?"

As down as he was, the idea appealed to him. The rift with Max and Alani had left him feeling oddly estranged from his surroundings. Holding Sarah in his arms, having her warmth and vitality pressed to him—physically connecting him to the promise of a new and better future—seemed the only way to blot out the haunting shadows of the past.

She smiled. "I'd love to go dancing, only let's make it some other night. I hate to admit it, but I'm beginning to feel a little stiff. What I'd really like to do is relax, maybe go see your condo."

Without taking his eyes from the road, he reached over and rubbed her shoulder and the side of her neck with strong yet sensitive fingers. "I forgot for a moment what a hard day you put in. Tell you what," he said, suddenly decisive. "We'll go to my condo for a nightcap and I'll give you the massage you've earned."

Chapter Eight

"It's absolutely breathtaking!" Sarah announced in awed tones as she stood looking out the living-room window of Christopher's high-rise condominium. The drive from the shores of Lake Union to where the building stood on the densely populated bluff separating Lake Washington, and the glacier-dug valley it filled, from the city that lay below her had taken less than ten minutes. During that short drive she'd been filled with an exquisite nervous excitement that had made it difficult for her to sit quietly in her seat. More than once the words to tell him that she'd reconsidered and wanted him to take her home had been on the tip of her tongue, but at the last moment she'd suppressed them.

The truth was she hadn't really wanted to go home. She'd wanted to be right where she was now, gazing down at the irregularly shaped urban sea of sparkling lights, blotted here and there by dark splotches she knew must be the several lakes incorporated in Seattle's boundaries. Beyond the lights of the metropolis stretched the blackness of the Sound, the inland waterway that led north to where it merged with the vast waters of the Pacific. It seemed incredible to think that Christopher was as much at home there as he was here.

Her extreme nervousness had lessened while going up in the building's elevator with him. He'd seen to that. Overcome with shyness, she'd kept her distance and avoided his eyes when they'd stepped into the small compartment and begun their ascent to the twelfth floor. Though they'd been alone in the intimate cocoon of the two-seater Corvette, the darkness and his very nearness there had lulled her into a sense of security that had bolstered her courage. But the impersonal atmosphere of the closed elevator had served to heighten her anxiety, and she'd kept her eyes fixed on the pattern of the carpet beneath her feet. She'd become almost unbearably tense when without warning they'd come to an abrupt stop halfway between the sixth and seventh floors.

Sarah smiled, remembering their conversation.

"What's wrong?" she'd asked, raising questioning eyes to his.

"It's this darn elevator," he'd said with a frown. "It has a reputation for being unpredictable. If you want to be sure of getting someplace on time it's best to take the stairs."

Her eyes widened. "How long will it stay like this? Minutes? Hours?" Though she wasn't claustrophobic and ordinarily wasn't bothered by an elevator ride no matter how high the building, the prospect of being suspended indefinitely six and a half floors above ground in a cubicle supported only by cables hadn't thrilled her.

He'd shrugged and offered an enigmatic reply. "That depends."

"Oh, Christopher," she'd said, putting her arms around him, resting her cheek against his solid chest. "What are we going to do?"

"Don't worry, honey," he reassured her, "this old elevator might be persuaded to continue on its way, if it was sure its lady occupant was relaxed and ready to make the trip."

"What?" Suddenly realizing he was holding her with only one arm, she pushed away and looked around him to where she could see his finger was firmly pressed against what she was sure was the Stop button on the control panel.

"You devil!" she'd accused. Looking into his eyes she saw the mischief dancing there. "You really had me worried!"

"You had me worried, too," he confessed, as he drew her back against him. "You were getting so stiff and tense I was afraid you might keel over any minute. This was the only way I could think of to get you where I want you," he drawled. As he lowered his face to hers and both arms came around her, Sarah was dimly aware that once more the elevator was moving upward.

Locked in a loving embrace, it had taken them a moment or two to realize that the doors had silently slid open at the twelfth floor. It had been a novel approach to dispelling the awkwardness that had threatened to ruin the remainder of their evening, but it had worked, Sarah thought now, enjoying the sound of Christopher's whistling coming from the kitchen.

He'd kept his arm around her, as though not willing to chance her withdrawing from him again, and unlocked the door to his condo and switched on the lights. There'd been a note of pride in his voice when he'd said, "I had my own ideas, so I decorated this place myself. Take a look around while I fix us a drink."

The sophistication of the off-white leather-upholstered furniture on light beige plush carpeting had been intimidating at first. But catching sight of herself in the smoke-gray mirrored panels that lined the walls, she'd been reassured. In her white designer dress she looked as though the spacious room had been decorated to show off her elegance. She'd slowly realized that the effect was not accidental, but rather a carefully calculated one. The decor provided a dramatic backdrop for the tastefully selected and placed pieces of ornamentation Christopher must have picked up over the years on his trips to the Orient. She approved, as she'd somehow been sure she would, of the way he lived.

Before she'd had the chance to really look at and appreciate each of the vases, statues and pictures, the view had caught her attention.

"It's beautiful," she remarked, raising her voice so that Christopher could hear her. "You must be able to see the Olympic Mountains in the daylight."

"And the islands," Christopher said, coming into the living room. Sarah watched his reflection as he set two glasses on the brass-rimmed coffee table and came over to join her at the floor-to-ceiling window. The graceful fluidity of his movements, unusual in so large a man, never failed to amaze and please her.

"Does the traffic ever slow down on the freeway?" she asked, letting her gaze fall on the red and white ribbons of light streaming on the raised six-lane viaduct partway down the steep hill.

"It gets heavier during rush hours but stays pretty steady the rest of the time, day and night, since it's the only freeway in the state running north and south." Moving behind her, he raised his hands to her shoulders, his thumbs expertly rubbing the tight cords running down the back of her neck.

"Mmm, that feels good," she said with a sigh. "Oh, I see a ferry!" She started to lean forward, but his hands restrained her with gentle pressure, pulling her back until her body rested against his. Her heart seemed to leap into her throat, and she was sure he must feel the wild pounding of her pulse.

"That one's a commuter, bound for Bainbridge Island. And there at the mouth of the Duwamish Waterway on Harbor Island is my ship." Christopher pointed far to the left with one hand, the other continuing to knead her tense neck muscles.

Visually following the flow of traffic exiting the freeway toward the West Seattle Bridge, Sarah's gaze came to rest on the huge ship, lit up like a horizontal skyscraper.

"Are they working tonight?" she asked, her voice husky and low.

"Around the clock," he affirmed. "Have to lift all the containers off and load the others on before it sails Monday morning. I don't like to think of it being Max's last trip as chief mate."

"Then don't," Sarah advised softly. "I've been thinking about it, and I don't care what you say. Alani was wrong to say those things to you. She didn't have the right. Max wouldn't have taken this job if he hadn't wanted to. You didn't force him. And as for the rest of it, all I know is that then was then and now is now. People change. Circumstances change."

After a pause, she added, "But like you said, let's forget about them. Let's just remember that the rest of the evening is going to be ours." The gentle squeeze he gave her shoulder in reply convinced her of the rightness of her decision to come home with him. He didn't need to be alone with his thoughts tonight.

"You know," she said, "I still have a hard time making myself believe that those rows of containers I saw stacked high on your ship are the same compartments loaded on the chassis of those eighteen-wheelers rolling along the highways. I'm petrified when I have to pass one of them in rainy windy weather. Kanga is about as stable as an empty pickup, and the wake from one of those loaded rigs is almost enough to blow me off the road. But the size of your ship dwarfs those containers so that they look like little matchbox toys."

"They're not toys," Christopher assured her. "They're portable warehouses that have revolutionized the export-import trade. They've changed the face of every harbor I know. Traditional warehouses that used to line the piers have become obsolete, replaced by multimillion-dollar cranes and acres of paved lots. The crane operators that load and unload those babies have a real job to do. Some of those fellows are so highly skilled they could center a container on a dime.''

"I'd like to see that," Sarah said.

"I'll take you down there sometime, show you around the ship," he promised, "and explain the whole operation. But not while I'm on cargo watch. You'd be too much of a distraction, and I don't want to be written up for dereliction of duty!" His tone was intimate and teasing.

Once more Sarah was fleetingly impressed with the magnitude of Christopher's job, but as they'd talked he'd continued his massage. The sensations his deft fingers were causing on her shoulders and upper arms were not ones of relaxation, nor were they conducive to concentration. Each nerve ending he touched seemed to branch into hundreds, sending disturbing impulses all through her nervous system.

"That feels wonderful," she murmured. "How is it you know just the right places to touch?"

"I've had at least one massage on every trip I've ever taken," he confided. "You can learn a great deal while being worked on by a good masseur or masseuse. I'm just doing to you what I like to have done to me. Small wonder you're so tense," he observed. "I couldn't believe the amount of area you scraped today. You shouldn't do so much at a time."

"I want to do as much as I can so you won't have so much left," she admitted. "You promised me a sailing trip, remember?"

"I could never forget that. In class today, I'm afraid I was a disinterested student. All I could think of was how you'll look sitting on the bow of my boat."

"I'm going to need lessons," she reminded him. "You may get a little exasperated with me."

"Never," he promised, turning her around to face him. As he pressed her close, his hands still working their magic down her spine, she became frightened at the intensity of her feelings. Was his seduction deliberate? Or were the sensations he was arousing an unintentional by-product of his efforts to ease the tension in her muscles?

Perhaps she was overreacting. Christopher had said he liked to have these things done to himself. Would she be this light-headed and giddy in the hands of a professional? No, she was certain she would not. Only these hands and this man could stir her in this way.

Fearful of emotional entanglements, she'd taken pains to construct a life that allowed her to lavish the affections of her loving nature upon animals and people from whom she expected nothing in return. But the tall man who held her in his arms, caring enough for her to try to ease the soreness of her tightened muscles, was just as surely rubbing smooth the jagged edges of her fear.

"Feel better?" he asked.

"Much." She fought to keep the tremor of desire from her voice.

"I'm glad." His hands stopped their sensuous massaging, and his supple fingers came up to stroke her throat, raising her chin to trace the outline of her lips with his forefinger. Her breath caught in her throat at his gentle touch.

"I'd forgotten anyone could have such soft luscious lips until I met you," he murmured, desire smoldering in the depths of his compelling eyes. For a long moment he held her gaze, and she made no effort to veil the message of yearning her own eyes conveyed.

Circling his waist with her arms, she held him tight, suddenly sure, all apprehension gone.

His moist pliant lips covered hers in a slow kiss, patiently arousing her awakening sexuality. Receiving her sweetly satisfying response, his body trembled. Sarah, with her aura of innocence, touched him as no other woman had ever done.

He wanted to see her eyes alight with the pleasure he longed to give. Though he sensed a deep passion burning within her, she was so tentative and openly vulnerable that he feared driving her away with the force of his ardor.

Her hand ran through the thick thatch of his sun-bleached hair, as her arm went around his neck and her fingers traced the outline of his jaw. A wild heat raced through her body, kindling her excitement to a red-hot flame. As one soul-stirring kiss blended into another, her body strained against his, begging for release from the sweet torment.

Burying his face in the fragrant mass of her hair, he let out a low groan. "Sarah, I shouldn't have brought you here."

"I asked to come," she breathed. "Don't stop. Kiss me again." Her hands reached up to pull against the steel of his neck, bringing his mouth back to hers.

Urged on by her willing invitation, his kiss became more and more demanding as he gave free rein to the urgency that drove him. Her need matched his as she allowed him to draw her tongue into his mouth, intoxicated by the sensation.

In one movement, without taking his heated mouth from hers, he lifted her off her feet and held her close. As Sarah pressed against him, she felt the throbbing force of his masculinity and reveled in her delicious feminine power as a deep groan rose up in his throat.

Lowering her to her feet again, he began a thorough exploration of the soft contours of her figure. As his fingers slipped beneath the silky fabric of her neckline to knowingly caress her taut nipples, Sarah knew she wanted to be in his arms forever. She wanted his eyes, his hands, his mouth, to discover every intimate secret of her body, and in turn, she wanted to know every secret of his.

When he drew his lips from hers to catch a ragged breath, she heard her tremulous voice say, "I want you." Ecstatic in her newfound freedom, feeling like nothing more than a gull with a broken wing who had tenderly been nurtured back to health by this sailor, she was ready to soar to dazzling new heights. Tears of joy filled her eyes and trickled down her flushed cheeks.

Seeing them, Christopher's heart welled with an emotion stronger than mere protectiveness. Sarah aroused in him indescribable feelings he couldn't remember ever having felt before. His touch was tender as his fingers found the fastener of her dress and the material fell in a silken pile on the plush carpet, exposing her lush breasts, cupped in a wispy lace bra that barely covered her high rosy nipples. A lacy garter belt secured the creamy nylons that encased her shapely thighs and calves. A thin ankle strap held her high-heeled sandals to her slender feet. Standing, shy but unashamed, Sarah heard his sharp intake of breath when he took a step back to run his eyes over her beauty.

The tentative smile that touched her lips curved sensuously when she raised his openly entranced gaze to hers.

"You are beautiful, Sarah," he breathed. "Even more than I'd imagined."

Desire rose in her heart, a desire so compelling she wasn't sure she could bear it. "Christopher," she whispered. "Oh, Christopher, hold me. Hold me."

His arms went around her, caressing her back, freeing her breasts from their lacy constraints. She shivered when his hands moved lower and he bent his head to take the tip of one breast then the other into his mouth. Then he knelt before her, his moist tongue circling her navel, while his hands cupped and then gently kneaded the rounded swell of her buttocks, and the sensations rocking her body were so great that she had difficulty staying on her feet.

The lights of the city far below blurred and her fingers buried themselves in his hair as she instinctively thrust her hips forward. Her bones threatened to dissolve as he unfastened her garters and ran his fingers down the sensitive flesh of her inner thighs and calves, stripping the stockings from her legs and taking the shoes from her feet.

Dimly, Sarah realized, that though she'd imagined lovemaking would be wonderful, she hadn't in her wildest dreams believed her lover would arouse every nerve in her body and every emotion in her heart like this. Was this what separated human beings from the rest of the animal kingdom, this act of giving and expressing love? This merger of mind, body and soul? Giving oneself out of love, she decided, was the ultimate freedom, the ultimate right. Though she had no true way to judge, Sarah was sure Christopher was an incredibly giving sensitive lover. She was filled with an insatiable yearning to share an intimacy with him so absolute that she would be his, and he, hers—body and soul.

When he rose to his feet and took her naked body in his arms once more, she was fully aware of his tense masculine hunger. Her arms encircled his neck as she raised her face to meet his.

"Are you sure about this?" His deep voice was laden with passion.

"I've never been more sure of anything in my life," Sarah answered, reaching out to loosen his tie. She'd never undressed a man before, and her fingers trembled with the effort of not letting her inexperience show. She felt his gaze on her face as she stripped off his tie and unbuttoned his shirt. Her fingers burned each time she touched his skin, but his face was controlled, a careful mask; only his eyes gave a clue to the intensity of his feelings. He cooperated, assisting when she pushed the shirt from his broad shoulders, then from his muscular arms. She could hardly take her gaze from his torso, burnished bronze with a furring of blond hair across the chest that feathered down to a narrow line that disappeared into his pants. Her hand tingled at the feel of his lean hard belly as she slipped her fingers beneath the waistband of his slacks to undo the button.

His control cracking, he visibly tensed at her touch, and a muscle worked in his jaw as he took her hand away. "I can manage now," he said, lifting her off her feet and cradling her again in his arms. Catching a glimpse of the two of them in the mirrored wall, Sarah saw how the soft white of her skin contrasted starkly with the bronze of his. Feeling her naked flesh against his, she knew, at long last, what it was to be a woman. Her toes curled as she clung to his neck, burying her face against his shoulder. She savored his scent, while an exquisite emotion, at once complex and whole, surged through her.

In the bedroom he gently placed her on the king-size bed before stripping off the rest of his clothing. In a moment he was beside her, stretching his length along hers. Captivated by her beauty, he was awed by the depth of his need for her. He reverently ran his fingers down her slender neck and over the fullness of her breasts to the concave flatness of her abdomen, then sought the pulse hidden in the moist tangle of hair between her thighs.

When he found and knowingly began to stroke the nub of sensitized flesh, Sarah gasped, shuddering in disbelief, arching toward him and writhing in uncontrollable response to the sweet waves of sensation that assailed her. She cried out his name over and over, wondering how his mouth and hands could be everywhere at once.

He paused. "Do you want me to use protection?" he asked.

She shook her head. "Just love me," she begged. "Just love me."

In response, he lowered his head and placed a fiery trail of kisses down her belly that went lower and still lower, until she gasped in astonishment when his tongue resumed the tender torture of her womanly flesh.

"Christopher," she moaned, tossing from side to side. "Christopher, I can't..." She bit her lip to keep from crying out.

"Not yet, honey," he murmured, positioning himself above her. "Wait for me. Just hold on and wait for me."

Turning her head, she couldn't meet his eyes at the moment of penetration. She was his. Nothing could stop their union now. A brief shattering stab of pain caused her fingernails to bite into the flesh of his muscular back.

He turned her face toward his, the look in his eyes demanding a response.

"Yes," she murmured, feeling as though her life was in the balance ... wondering how she could bear it if he pulled away from her now.

Poised above her, he was speechless. Knowing anything he might say would be inadequate to convey the enormity of his feelings, he had only his body to express his gratitude for her gift.

Though it was agony for him to wait, his movements were gentle and slow as he gave her body time to adjust to his invasion. When she began to meet his thrusts, a rumbling groan escaped his lips, as his control gave way. Sarah responded in wild abandonment, instinctively matching his rhythm, losing herself in the primitive joy of their union. When he stiffened and cried out, she shared his release, finding at last the complete fulfillment that had eluded her for so long.

As they lay together afterward, wrapped in a warm afghan he had pulled around them, Sarah listened to the thud of Christopher's strong heart. Experiencing an indescribable sense of inner peace, she realized that the woman who had entered the apartment was not the same one who would leave. The other Sarah had been sealed up in walls of her own making for many long terrible years, unwilling to break out of the emotional prison she had built for herself. How long would she have gone on like that, she wondered, if the compassionate man who held her now had not come into her life to free her?

"Thank you," she murmured, pressing tender kisses on his neck and shoulder.

"Thank you," he whispered back, caressing her hair with his lips. "I know I could never explain this, but you made it all brand-new for me, too."

He lifted the afghan from Sarah's languorous body and couldn't keep his lips from the peaks of her firm full breasts. When he spoke again he chose his words with care, asking the question to which he couldn't hazard a guess. "Why have you kept this beauty untouched?" he asked, his tongue again savoring first one then the other of her hardening nipples.

"I never cared enough before," Sarah answered dreamily, feeling the delicious stirrings of desire pulse anew between her thighs. "I've been saving myself for you." She smiled, planting a long kiss on her inquisitor's mouth.

Correctly assuming that further questions would be futile, only serving to intrude on their wonderful closeness, Christopher went back to the delicious pastime of kissing her breasts. When his warm tongue feathered down to her abdomen, a quick intake of breath shuddered through her body.

"You have a scar," he whispered, still another question in his voice. His moist tongue traced the fine line of raised flesh.

"My appendix," she lied, her fingers twining themselves in his thick hair.

His tongue continued its downward quest until it found the source of her pleasure, and sent wave after wave of convulsive joy washing over her weakening frame.

She gasped. "Can we . . . ?" Feeling her cheeks flush, she amended, "I mean, are you ready again so soon?"

Christopher grinned. "We can, and I am."

Hours later they slept, satiated and exhausted, nestled in each other's arms.

Chapter Nine

When Sarah awoke she experienced a moment of loss. Sunlight streamed through the window and she was alone in the large bed, the sheet securely tucked over her breasts. Sitting up, she listened for any sound of the man who'd given her her first night of ecstasy. Hearing his footsteps in the kitchen and the rattle of crockery, she lay back, her lips curving in a contented smile.

"Coffee, madam?" Christopher asked with a roguish grin as he entered the room carrying a bamboo tray.

"Great room service," she quipped, sitting up and holding the sheet under her arms.

"I do my best," he answered. He placed the tray across her thighs, then sat on the side of the bed looking at her, his face a mirror of her own contentment.

"Umm," she said, after sipping the fresh brew, "it tastes as good as it smells."

Suddenly the telephone rang, its shrill tones shattering the intimate moment. Grimacing, Christopher remarked, "Wouldn't you know it? I think I just might let it ring."

"No," Sarah said. "Don't do that. It might be Erma or your mother."

"You're right." Christopher picked up the phone on the bedside table. After he had spoken only a few words into the receiver, she knew it was his son on the other end of the line.

"Adam," Christopher said, "we've gone over all of this before. You are not being disloyal to me by taking part in your mother's wedding. It would not only be impolite for you not to be there—it would be a real insult to your mother."

After a pause during which Sarah could hear Adam's voice speaking rapidly but could not make out the words, Christopher said, "Camp is not Mickey Mouse. Last year you didn't even want to come home. How about those friends you only see once a year? Don't you want to see them again?"

Christopher listened for a few more seconds then stood up, turning his back to Sarah. "Now, Adam," he said, his voice rising, "I've had enough of this. You will participate in the wedding and you will go to camp. That's all there is to it!" Regaining his composure, he sat back down on the bed. "I'll be at sea while you're at camp and after we've both done our duty there'll be plenty of time for us to loaf around together. You'd better sharpen up your cribbage game. I don't want to win your allowance from you too easily.... I know you can do it, fella.... There'll be a new fly rod and reel in it for you if you do.... Okay, and a new pair of waders, too.... Just hang in there, son...goodbye."

Putting down her cup Sarah lifted the framed photo that stood by the phone. A lanky freckled-face boy with curly auburn hair grinned back at her.

"Adam?" she asked, looking in vain for a resemblance to Christopher's face on the unformed features of the adolescent.

"My son," he confirmed, taking the frame from her and looking at the picture for a long moment before placing it back on the table. "That's his school picture. He's changed so much. Looks more like his mother every year."

"Do you see him often?" Sarah forced herself to ask. It was past time she found out how important Adam was in Christopher's life.

"Not as often as I'd like, and certainly not as often as I should." The undisguised note of regret in his voice stabbed at Sarah's heart.

"Your mother told me that he wants to come live with you," Sarah persisted.

"Just a pipe dream, on both our parts," he said disparagingly, jamming his hands into the pockets of his short robe as he walked toward the window. "He's very upset with the idea of his mother marrying again. For a little while I got carried away with the idea of being a real father." Running his hand through his hair, he turned and came back to sit beside her. "Hell, what do I know about being a father? Virginia was quick to point that out. The kid ran a little scared when she told him he was going to have a stepfather. He's had his mother all to himself for a long time. I guess he doesn't like to think of sharing her.

"I got my nose a little out of joint at the idea, too—the stepfather bit, not Virginia's marriage," he admitted with a slight sideways motion of his head. "But as my ex-wife said, the boy needs a father, and since I'm away at sea so much I'm not the best candidate for the job."

"Then he's not coming?"

"Not to stay. But he'll be here for a couple of months in the summer and you'll meet him then. I usually take him sailing and camping when I'm off for my two-leg stint. This time there'll be the three of us." He smiled and lifted the coffee tray from between them.

Sarah hesitated a moment, wondering how Adam would feel about her coming along. She'd have to meet the boy before she could make any plans. If he seemed to like her, she could ask Dr. Blake for some extra time off. If not, she'd make excuses to stay in Seattle until Adam was gone. She didn't want to make an enemy of Christopher's son.

"I might be able to manage a few weekends if you're not going too far. I'm a working woman." She handed him her empty mug.

Taking it, he set the mug on the tray and said, "We have a small cabin on Whidbey Island. That's only a couple of hours' drive, so you won't have any trouble being a weekend commuter. I did a lot of thinking about Adam while I was gone," he went on. "About myself, too. It's not that I don't love him. I do. I care very much about everything he does and about all that happens to him. But I guess I just wasn't cut out to be the kind of doting father Max is. Does that make sense?" he asked.

"Yes." Just like some women aren't cut out to be mothers, Sarah thought, opening her arms to him.

THE NEXT TWO WEEKS Sarah and Chris worked side by side on the houseboat every hour of evening daylight. The time flew by, filled with their conversation and laughter. Neither of them had had a true confidant for so long that the pleasure they had in sharing their thoughts and feelings overshadowed the burden of their task. Only the daily nagging soreness of her muscles reminded Sarah that she had spent the previous evening doing anything more taxing than being thoroughly entertained. And even that was easing as she grew stronger from the exertion.

Sarah found it hard to believe that she and the accomplished naval officer had so much in common, but they found they agreed on almost everything, from their views on the world to such small matters as flavors of ice cream and colors of cars. And they also agreed on their need for each other. As soon as darkness made further work unproductive, they'd hurry to his condo where they'd shower and make love as though they'd invented it. The pace she was keeping should have left her exhausted, making her hours at the clinic drag, but instead her workday seemed shorter, filled as she was with anticipation of the evening to come.

As they worked and Christopher discovered that Sarah had a week's vacation coming to her, their plans for the proposed sail on Christopher's boat grew until it was decided that if they finished the houseboat in time they'd take the sailboat out onto the Sound and cruise the San Juan Islands. Christopher never seemed to tire of elaborating on his plans for her enjoyment—describing the meals he'd prepare, the wines he'd serve, the places they'd tie up to for the night—until Sarah could hardly wait for them to sail away together.

The sly smile that lifted Erma's wrinkled face every evening when she'd bring dinner trays out to them on the deck told Sarah that the older woman knew what was going on between Christopher and her, and that she not only approved of the situation but was willing to help it along any way she could.

The day finally came when the last of the trim was repaired and painted, and Mrs. Weaver was brought out to inspect the finished job. Fearing the moment might prove traumatic for the widow, Sarah had conspired with Erma to serve a celebratory dinner on the deck in order to divert Mrs. Weaver from memories that might prove painful. But as Mary Lou was pushed around the deck, years seemed erased from her time-etched face, and at every corner she found something new to admire about the job they'd done. The sight of Christopher kneeling to receive his mother's grateful hugs and kisses brought tears to Sarah's eyes.

The next day Christopher took Sarah over to the Ballard Locks to show her the role she would play when they took his sailboat out through the locks onto the Sound. Although she'd been to the lock area before to see where the man-made canal made its passage from Lake Washington to the Sound, she'd never really looked at how the boat entering and leaving the waterway were handled as they were lifted or lowered to the different levels.

White gulls screeched raucously over their heads, and a fine spray of water blew into the breeze, as she stood with Christopher on the narrow folding metal walkway above the filled lock. She watched with interest as a wide variety of pleasure boats were taken in and secured. Then listening to Christopher's explanations while observing the procedure she learned how the securing lines were thrown from the boats to the men working onshore, who wrapped them around large cast-iron cleats. As the water was lowered in the lock, two crewmen on each boat let out the line until the vessel had reached the level of the salt water leading out to the Sound.

Christopher and Sarah then watched as the procedure was reversed on the opposite lock, bringing other boats up to the level of the fresh water.

After Christopher was convinced Sarah understood her part in the maneuver as first mate on his boat, which they planned to clean and provision that afternoon, they turned their attention to the foaming gray waters of the sluice. Pesky sea lions, rolling like fat black inner tubes, dived and surfaced, pursuing the sleek silver-colored salmon that were making a valiant effort to enter the nearby fish ladder in order to swim upstream to the mountain rivers of their birth.

Feeling sorry for the hopelessly trapped salmon, Sarah asked, "Can't they do anything to get rid of those poachers?"

Christopher shook his head. "Not with the Marine Mammal Act written the way it is. The Department of Fisheries has tried everything from setting off underwater firecrackers to towing the blubbery gluttons away, but nothing works. The sea lions are always back the next day."

"It just doesn't seem right," Sarah said in a small voice, immediately identifying with the underdogs. "Those poor fish have a terrible uphill battle without having to try to escape from those monsters."

"They're not monsters," Christopher said, slipping his arm around her shoulders. "You're just seeing up close how the food chain works. It may look cruel from this vantage point, but what about all those fishing trawlers out there with their nets? How many salmon do you think they take in a single haul?"

Looking up at him with troubled eyes, Sarah didn't answer. He was right, of course. The few salmon the sea lions managed to catch and eat in a day were far less than a day's catch on a single trawler. But the sight was disturbing, nonetheless.

THE WEEK-LONG TRIP to the San Juan Islands was the idyll Christopher had promised. Cut off from the world and its cares, immersed in the full wonder of the natural elements, life took on a leisurely pace governed only by the wind, the sun, their love and their empty stomachs.

Sarah soon developed her latent talents as a sailor, quickly catching on to which side of the sloop was port and which starboard, discovering that a rope was a line, and that the jib was the red, white and blue front sail. She learned to trim and to tack at Christopher's command, enjoying the exhilaration of a full-sailed run before a fresh breeze. Christopher's seemingly limitless knowledge of the creatures who lived in the sea added a fascinating dimension to her life.

It was with sincere regret that Sarah, suntanned from head to toe and sporting a peeling nose, put out the bumpers and expertly threw the painter up to a waiting shoreman at the incoming lock, as Christopher eased the sailboat into place. It was the Saturday before he was scheduled to put out to sea, so they'd cut their trip short by a day so that

Christopher could keep his final date with Max. Standing at the wheel, arms around each other, they motored into Lake Union thoroughly at peace with the world and themselves.

No sooner had they finished tying up at the back of the freshly painted houseboat than Erma shattered that peace.

"Adam has run away and his mother's scared spitless!"

Christopher jumped from the boat to the dock. After quickly fastening the bowline, he asked Sarah to secure the stern.

"When did he leave?" he demanded.

"Two days ago, I guess," Erma answered. "Virginia wants you to call her."

Running into the house, he was met by Amanda, wiggling her whole back half, then lying down for her usual belly scratch. But Christopher had no time for the dog.

"What happened?" he asked his mother.

"I'm so glad you're home. Virginia's been calling every hour since this morning. I just haven't known what to do."

"Mother, please, just tell me about Adam," Christopher said. He kept the impatience he felt out of his voice, seeing how pale and drawn she appeared.

"Well, son, Virginia said Adam took his backpack and camping gear Thursday night, and told her that he and several of his friends were going camping for a couple of days to celebrate the end of school. I guess they've done that sort of thing before. He promised her he'd be back before the wedding rehearsal this afternoon. But he hasn't shown up. Virginia called around and none of the boys he was supposed to be with have even seen him for the last two days. I've been frantic wondering what to do."

"You could have radioed. You have my call number."

"What good would that have done?" she asked reasonably. "We knew you were coming in today anyway, and if I had called I knew you couldn't get here any faster. Erma wanted to call out the coast guard, but I told her you'd be ome before they ever located you. They have more to do han chase down the countless sailboats out on the Sound ooking for your boat.''

"You're right, Mom," he said, calming down. "I'm just glad we came in when we did."

Going to the phone, Christopher punched Virginia's number. She answered on the first ring. After she'd repeated the information his mother had already told him Christopher asked, "Then you think he's run away?"

"I'm sure of it," she replied.

"Dammit, Virginia, why didn't you check to make sure he was where he said he was going to be?"

"Don't you swear at me, *Mister* Weaver," Virginia shot back. "You have no right to accuse me of any failings as a parent. All the time he's been missing you've been out cruising around in your sailboat without a care in the world. I'm being married tomorrow and I've had more than a few things on my mind."

"I'm not swearing at you," he apologized, lowering his voice. "I guess I'm too upset to be rational. Do you have any idea of where he's gone?"

"To live with you, of course!" she shouted. "Ever since he got that bee in his bonnet, he's made my life miserable. I guess he thought since I wouldn't give him permission to go, he'd do it his way. I've been out of my mind the past two months trying to deal with him," she continued, so loudly Christopher had to hold the phone away from his ear, "and I've had it! I'm not going to change my wedding plans at this late date because of this little stunt he's pulling. I've devoted fourteen years of my life to that boy, and if this is the gratitude I get because he resents my having a husband, he can just damn well stay with you."

"I told you two months ago that I'd take him," Christopher irritably reminded her.

"Ha! You don't have any idea of what it means to raise a teenage hellion," she scoffed, "or you'd never have made that offer. But you're going to get your chance now, because I'm getting married and I'm going on my honeymoon. I know that sounds selfish, but it's about time I enjoyed some of the freedom you've taken for granted for the last ten years!

"When he shows up, and I've no doubt he will, you can send him off to camp for the next six weeks while you're gone to sea. It's all arranged and paid for. Then you can finally find out what being a parent's all about!"

"Have you called the police?"

"Of course I have, but there's a lot of territory between here and Seattle, and he's been gone for two days. I've found they won't do much about runaways." Her voice broke as she began sobbing. "Find him, Christopher," she begged. "I'm so frightened."

"I will," he promised, his voice cracking as he suddenly remembered the day Adam was born.

"Does he have any money?"

"He has his allowance and what he's saved in his bank. I suspect he's been planning this for quite some time."

"I'll get on it right away, Virginia. I'll keep you posted."

After he hung up the phone he went into the living room where the three women sat, anxiously waiting for word. "You heard?"

They nodded.

"Virginia's sure he's coming here."

"And so am I," Mary Lou Weaver put in, looking a little better since she no longer had to bear the burden of worry alone. "I just wish he had the good sense to know how worried we'd be about him and give us a call. But knowing teenagers as I do, he probably thinks that no one in the world cares a thing about him."

Christopher shook his head, a perplexed expression on his face. "I just don't get it. Virginia's so upset with our son that she's ready to give him to me. How can a woman who's been such a protective mother make such a complete turnabout?" Without waiting for an answer, he went on, "With Adam missing, how can she go on with her plans for her wedding? I'll never understand her."

"I imagine my grandson's been a royal pain in the neck ever since she started dating," Mary Lou said calmly. "Her attitude's not that hard to understand. Teaching junior high school for thirty years taught me a little bit about teenagers. Many women who raise sons by themselves are ready to hand them back to their fathers when the boys reach their teens. It's a very difficult time of life for the children, as well as for the parents."

Sarah nodded, remembering how often she'd been ready to pack her bags if there'd been anywhere she could have run to.

"I never was like that," Christopher declared, looking to his mother for confirmation.

Mrs. Weaver huffed. "Oh, you weren't, were you? I think the only reason I kept my sanity during your adolescence, and the reason that we got along as well as we did, was that you went to boarding school during the week. I knew you were in good hands Monday morning through Friday afternoon. You had your sports and friends, and the school saw to it that you did your homework. That didn't leave us much to quarrel over.

"Adam is a smart boy," she went on sagely. "And he's had the benefits of a stable home with an extended family. Virginia's folks are fine people, and he's grown up surrounded by aunts and uncles, as well as grandparents. He's not being driven out onto the streets like some truly unfortunate teenager. But he's not a child anymore, and it's normal for him to feel that something's missing in his life. If I know anything about that grandson of mine, he's on his way here right now. A boy his age needs to be with his own father.''

Somewhat reassured by his mother's reasoning, Christopher considered for a long moment. If Adam did arrive here, there was no way he could take off on a leg at sea Monday morning and leave the boy with his mother and Erma, any more than he could leave if the boy hadn't been found.

He should have paid more attention to Adam's pleas, should have questioned him more thoroughly, should have anticipated what a headstrong boy would do when thwarted by every adult in authority over him, and done something to avert his running away. Suddenly Christopher wasn't so sure his mother was right. Suppose the boy had met with foul play? Suppose...? Panic made his throat dry, and a cold sweat broke out on his forehead.

''I'll call company headquarters and ask to be relieved from the next run.''

''You'd better leave a message for Max, too,'' Sarah reminded him. ''Or he'll be expecting you at the 47.''

Christopher ran a hand through his hair and sighed in frustration. He'd needed this night with Max. He couldn't stand the idea of his best friend's leaving for the Hawaiian islands without clearing the air between them. But this was not the time to think about that.

''You're right. I'll have to let him know that I won't be there and why. Then I'll start calling the local and state police in every town between here and Lincoln,'' he said, going back to the phone in the hall.

Christopher's decisive action broke the tension that had kept Sarah and Erma sitting side by side on the couch.

Sarah started to say that she'd unload the boat, when she suddenly realized she wanted to spend every second at Christopher's side giving him all the support she could.

Going out to join him in the hall she heard him say, "Look, I don't think Thompson's problem can be as pressing as mine."

He leaned down to allow her to put her ear next to his. Sarah listened as the dispatcher explained that since Mr. Thompson's request for relief on the next run had been made two days ago and already been processed, Mr. Weaver's request could not be honored.

"I know the ship can't leave with two replacements in ranking positions," Christopher responded, his face darkening with anger.

"Sorry, sir, it's not up to me to arbitrate the matter."

"Then take a message for Chief Mate Pierson."

"Yes, sir."

"Tell him..." Christopher hesitated, caught in a quandary. If Max knew what was going on, he'd come right over. But Max had just spent five weeks at sea, and Alani needed Max more than he did. There was nothing his friend could do. Yet if he didn't level with Max, his friend would be left to believe that Christopher was nursing a grudge against Alani.

"Just tell him I can't make it tonight. I've run into a little problem with my son. He'll understand that."

"Certainly, sir."

"I guess resigning from my crew and applying for a position with another one later is my only choice," Christopher said dispiritedly after he'd hung up. "God only knows where I'll end up. Stuck on land chasing down misdirected containers, or chief mate on a damned ferry between here and Bremerton!"

"Not yet," Sarah begged. "We'll find Adam. We have to." Panic rose in her throat at the thought of the young boy out there alone, undoubtedly scared to death, possibly in real danger.

"My...my father is a truck driver," she volunteered haltingly. "I think if we went to several truck stops outside of town we could get them to help us—you know, in case he's hitchhiking. They have their CBs and they can cover a broad area in a matter of hours."

"Good thinkin', kiddo," Erma chipped in from the kitchen where she hadn't missed a word of what was going on in the hall. "You do that and I'll get on the phone and take care of the police calls. I still got an in with the department."

The rest of the afternoon and night seemed endless, as Christopher and Sarah drove to all the truck stops within a sixty-mile radius of Seattle, showing Adam's picture and giving his description to every trucker they could find. But their efforts, and their hourly calls to check on Erma's progress, failed to turn up any clues.

As dawn paled the night sky, a dejected and tired Christopher announced, "I'll take you home now, Sarah. I've done some thinking and I may have an out—" he ran his fingers through his disheveled hair "—Max. After I shower and get into uniform, I'll go talk to him. I hate to ask him to sign on for another leg, but I can't see any way around it. If he agrees, I'll go see the captain. I want to give him twenty-four hours' notice that I won't be sailing with the ship tomorrow."

"I'm sure Max will do it for you," Sarah said.

His quiet nod kept her from saying anything further. Watching a muscle work at the side of his broad jaw, a day's growth of stubble softening the angles of his rugged face, Sarah thought of how much Christopher must love the boy. And, though she knew it was wrong to be thinking of herself at this moment, she couldn't help but reflect that when Adam was found there would no longer be any room in Christopher's life for her. She turned to stare out of the window, tears of regret stinging her tired eyes.

This was to be Virginia's wedding day, too, Sarah thought. Could Adam's mother go on with her plans to marry not knowing where the boy was?

After Christopher had dropped her off at the pier leading down to the houseboats and she had explained his plans to Mary Lou and Erma, Sarah went out to the sailboat to begin the job of unloading. She needed to be busy. More than that, she needed to spend some time alone in the place where she'd been the happiest in her life, wanting to engrave on her memory every moment she and Christopher had spent there.

Through a haze of tears she picked up Christopher's orange flotation jacket from the deck. Hugging it close, she stumbled down the ladder to the hold. Dropping down onto the padded bench and burying her face in the folds of the garment, she inhaled the scent of his body still lingering in the slick material. She loved him. Loved him as she had never loved another person. But the events of the past few hours had turned that love into an agonizing pain, paralyzing her emotions, leaving her in limbo with the ache of uncertainty. Exhausted to the bone and unable to cope with the fear of losing him, she closed her eyes.

A second later she came to with a start. The door to the forward cabin opened, revealing a tall and lanky disheveled teenager.

"Adam," she gasped, jumping up to grasp the boy's arms as though to make sure he wasn't an illusion.

"Who are you?" he asked, raising his arms out of her reach and backing away.

"I'm Sarah . . . Sarah Mitchell . . . a neighbor. We've been looking all night for you."

"Where's my dad?" he asked, with a sleepy yawn.

"He's gone to find someone to take his place when his ship leaves tomorrow," she answered, a sharp edge to her voice.

"What does he want to do that for?" Adam asked, his face taking on sullen lines.

"He doesn't want to. He thinks he has no other choice. He's worried about you. A lot of people are worried about you. There's no way he can set sail until he knows that you're all right."

"I'm all right. You can see that for yourself. He doesn't need to do a thing like that." The boy's voice sounded worried.

"Where have you been all night?" Sarah asked, suspicion narrowing her hazel eyes.

"Right here. Sleeping. Got any food aboard besides those crackers? I'm hungry."

It took the last measure of her control to ask evenly, "Why didn't you go inside when you got here? Let someone know you were safe?"

"I saw my dad's car was gone and I didn't want to bother Gram."

"Bother her!" Sarah exploded. "Given her some peace of mind, would be more like it! She's been up all night worrying about you!"

The young boy hung his head sheepishly, and despite her irritation, Sarah felt an overwhelming rush of tenderness for the awkward child.

"Come on," she said softly. "Let's go in and spread the news that you're here. I'm sure that Erma will be only too glad to feed you."

Picking up his backpack, he followed her up the few steps to the deck. Then, jumping down, he ran ahead to open the door.

Sarah was right behind him as he called out, "Hi, Gram?" in the direction of Amanda's shrill barking.

"Shhh," Erma admonished, scooping up Amanda and closing her muzzle with her hand. "I take it you're the runaway. Your gram's asleep. She didn't get any shut-eye last night on account of you know why."

"This is Erma," Sarah said, trying to keep from smiling as the boy took in the older woman's fatigues and combat boots. "He's very hungry," she added, "but I'm sure you can take care of that. I'm going to call Christopher."

"Hey, cool rags," she heard Adam say in approval as he followed Erma into the kitchen.

She dialed Christopher's number, and it rang several times before he finally answered.

"Christopher..."

"I was in the shower," he hastily explained. "What's up?"

"Adam is here."

She heard his ragged sigh of relief. "Thank God! Where's he been? How'd he get here?"

"I'm not sure. All I know is he spent the night on the boat. I found him when I went aboard to unload."

"How is he?"

"Fine. Hungry, he says. That's a good sign."

"I'll call Virginia. Then I'll dress and come right over."

After waiting for Christopher to arrive and staying long enough to see him take his nervous son into his arms for a hug, Sarah left the Weaver house and went for a long walk. She needed to get Puppy Power back into full swing. Not having any dogs to walk increased her sense of loneliness. Returning home much later, looking over toward the Weaver houseboat, she knew she wasn't ready to think about the implications of what was going on there. Fearful of the waves Adam's appearance would make in her life, Sarah showered and collapsed on her bed, falling into an exhausted sleep.

URGED BY ERMA to share the hearty breakfast of bacon and eggs she'd cooked for Adam, Christopher sat down beside the boy.

"How did you get here?" he asked.

"By bus."

"But we checked all the major stations and they couldn't remember you."

"I went up through Canada," the boy said with a wide grin, chewing a heavily buttered piece of toast. "Fooled you, didn't I?"

"Not funny," Christopher said. Watching the boy slumped over his plate, shoveling in large mouthfuls of food, he was tempted to tell him to sit up straight and to stop wolfing down his breakfast. But he decided that now wasn't the time to correct his son's table manners.

"When was the last time you ate?" he asked, watching Adam drown the home-fried potatoes Erma had added to his plate in ketchup and begin attacking them with vigor.

"Ran out of money before supper last night. I found some stuff on the boat, but I guess I was just too tired to eat."

"I imagine you know you caused a lot of people a lot of worry. Darn near ruined your mother's wedding day."

"Big deal," the boy growled.

Christopher decided to let that remark pass. "She's agreed to give me full custody of you."

"Hey, Dad, that's radical!" Adam grinned before he washed down the last of the potatoes with a full glass of milk. Wiping his mouth on the sleeve of his filthy sweatshirt he said, "I've been telling her to do that for the past year. That wimp she's marrying gives me a pain in the you-know-what."

Christopher frowned. He and his son would have to come to a quick understanding of what was and was not acceptable for Adam to say concerning his elders—including his mother's choice of a husband. But he wanted to get the full picture from Adam's point of view before he put a lid on his son's adolescent candor. "Can you tell me, son, exactly what it is that you object to about Greg?"

"That guy thinks he can boss me around. He makes me make my bed and help with the dishes. And every time me and Mom get into it he steps in and sends me to my room. I'm not a baby. I got a right to say what I think."

Christopher was beginning to get a glimmer of what Virginia had tried to tell him, and why she was ready to give up custody of their son. This gawky teenager was not the little boy she'd been so crazy about. This kid was balky, unruly and more than a little rebellious.

Adam rose from the table without asking to be excused, and knelt down beside Bertha. Sharing his last piece of bacon with the dog who hadn't moved from his side since he'd entered the house, Adam buried his face in the skin of her wrinkled head and flapped her ears up around his own.

"Neat dog."

"Quit wiping your face on Bertha," Erma objected. "Git upstairs and take a shower. Y'got any clean clothes with ya?"

"Naw, all my good stuff is packed for camp," Adam said, standing. "I couldn't take any of it with me without tippin' Mom off."

"Then go peel off that gitup and leave it outside the bathroom door. I'll put it in the washer." Erma sighed with resignation.

Christopher looked at his son with an appraising eye. "You've grown at least two inches since Thanksgiving."

"Two and a half," Adam said proudly. "Just two more to go, and I'll catch up with you."

Christopher smiled. What his son lacked in maturity, he made up for in height. Too bad it wasn't a trade-off. "It's a good thing you showed up before I got hold of Max or the captain.

"Tomorrow you're getting on a bus for camp and I'm heading out to sea. We don't have much time to spend together now, so let's make the most of it."

"If you make me go to that lousy camp tomorrow after all the trouble I went through to get here, I'll never forgive you," Adam shouted.

"Simmer down, fella," Erma cautioned. "Your gram needs her rest."

"Sorry," Adam said contritely.

"Listen, son, and listen well." There was steel in Christopher's voice as he took the boy by the shoulders and turned him to face him. "You don't make threats around here. Is that understood?"

"Yes, sir," Adam mumbled. "It's just that—"

"It's just that nothing!"

"Yes, sir."

"I want you here, son, I really do. And I'm going to do my best to make it work. But if you're not willing to meet me halfway, I'll ship you off to the most highly disciplined military school in the country so fast your head will spin. Is that understood?"

"Yes, sir."

"Good. Now go in and call your mother." Christopher consulted his watch. "If you hurry you can still catch her before she leaves for the church. We want her going off on her honeymoon without a care on her mind, and knowing how much you appreciate all she's done for you, don't we, boy?"

"Yes, sir," Adam mumbled, refusing to meet his father's eyes.

Christopher waited in silence, catching enough of Adam's conversation to know the boy was doing as he'd asked.

When Adam returned to the kitchen, Erma instructed, "Now, git out of those dirty duds. I don't know whether to wash 'em or dig a hole and bury 'em." She sniffed with disdain. "Root around in the drawers up there. You might find somethin' left over from your dad you could put on."

"I'm not wearing any old fifties' stuff," Adam muttered, going up the stairs, Bertha at his side.

"Fifties' stuff!" Christopher snorted when the boy was out of earshot. "The kid must think his old man's a relic."

"Got yer hands full, there, I'd say." Erma shook her head in commiseration.

After Erma followed Adam up to take care of his clothes, Christopher quietly let himself out and walked across the boardwalk to Sarah's. He stopped for a moment and took in a few deep breaths of fresh air, feeling as though the trip they'd taken together was a lifetime ago. Max had warned him, he remembered with a rueful grin, that kids would do that to you every time.

Did Sarah want kids? he wondered. He couldn't remember them ever discussing her feelings on the matter. She had the right to make the decision, but for his part the thought of trying to mix a couple of tiny tykes in a household with an adolescent sent shudders of apprehension up his spine. He'd seen an occasional announcement for parenting classes in the public-service section of the local paper. If Sarah decided he was going to be poppa to a couple more, he'd have to enroll in as many as he could.

Whatever, it would have to wait until his life was more settled. While they'd been moored at Friday Harbor, he'd been tempted to ask her to marry him. But the knowledge that he needed to see how Virginia's "family unit" worked out had kept him from it. It had been a wise choice. As Max had predicted, the boy was his to keep. Now when he asked Sarah to be his wife, she'd have to agree to take not only a husband, but a full-time teenage son. Knowing what an adjustment this was going to be for him, how much more would it be for the woman he loved?

Opening her door, he softly called her name. When he got no response he walked into the bedroom.

Asleep on her side with her lovely bare legs bent at the knee, her short-robed form was enticing. Sitting on the edge of the bed he gently loosened the tie at her waist. Then, opening her robe, he exposed her beautiful body. His sharp intake of breath awakened her. Answering her sleepy smile, he buried his face in the sweet fullness of her firm breasts.

Cradling his head with her hands, she put her worries out of her mind, letting him nuzzle and nip, enjoying the delicious sensations his tongue and teeth were sending throughout her system.

"For two cents, I'd climb into that bed with you."

"Cheap enough," she said with a grin. "Hand me my purse."

"Can't," he said, sitting up. "I've got things to do."

"Did you get hold of Max?" she asked, suddenly worried again.

"I don't have to now. I have to go down to the bus station."

Sarah's eyes widened. "They've made you first mate on a Greyhound?" she asked with a giggle.

"Not yet." Christopher grinned, playing along with her silliness. "I have to get Adam a ticket for camp. If you'll see that he makes his bus tomorrow, I can still ship out on schedule."

"Are you sure that's such a good idea? He just got here. Is he ready to be sent off again?"

"He doesn't think so," Christopher admitted. "But my son has to learn that we all have duties. And right now, his responsibility is to follow through with the plans his mother made for him. Since he's none the worse for his experience he has to see that my immediate responsibility is to my crew.''

Surprised at his hard line, Sarah realized that Christopher was reacting more like a commanding officer than a father. Was his duty to his ship that important? She guessed it was to him. She knew he didn't want to ask Max to fill in for him unless it was a matter of life-and-death, and now that Adam had been found safe and sound there was no question of dire need. To be fair to Christopher, he wasn't accustomed to making important decisions concerning his son. But she would have thought, seeing his true concern for the boy just hours before, that he would have done anything to spend the next weeks with him. But then, what experience had she ever had to give her any insight into how parents really feel about their children?

Maybe for both Adam's and Christopher's sakes, it would be best for Christopher to be at sea until he had time to accept his new responsibilities. In thirty-five days he could do a lot of thinking about his son, and before he came home she was sure he would have adjusted to the idea that he was now a full-time father. After all, Adam had been thinking this move over for quite some time, but Christopher's new role had been dropped on him cold turkey.

"Okay,'' she said thoughtfully. "You board that ship tomorrow morning, and I'll see that Adam boards the bus.''

Christopher grinned. Sarah would make a great mother and a fantastic wife. How wonderful to have someone else to bounce his ideas off, especially someone who knew just what he needed to hear. "I'll have to go back to my condo and get this monkey suit off. Come with me and we'll finish what we started. First I'll run over to my mother's.''

After pulling on a hip-hugging pair of acid-washed jeans and a pink polo shirt, Sarah slowly walked up to the street and got into the car. She would finish what they'd started. She'd give Christopher this one last night and she'd take all the joy it could hold before she bowed out of his life. Somehow, even as she waited, she felt no urge to cry.

Their parting had been inevitable. She'd always known deep in her heart, even though she'd tried to tell herself it wasn't so, that it would come to this sooner or later. But she had no real regrets. She wouldn't change anything that had happened between them. It had been so sweet while it lasted, but as life had shown her over and over again, she'd been dealt a hand with no winning cards. She would have been foolish to think that anything had changed for her. These past weeks with Christopher had been more wonderful than any she could have imagined. She could give him up to his son now. She had to and she would. There would be no emotional goodbyes. She had more than enough priceless memories stored to keep her going for a long time.

While Sarah waited, Christopher explained to Erma that he was going back to his condo to change his clothes, but that he would come back to take Adam shopping.

"Virginia's having Adam's trunk sent on to camp, but the boy needs some clothes to wear until it gets there."

"I won't argue with that," Erma chuckled. "I think you oughta catch forty winks while you're at it. Your eyes look like burnt holes in a blanket. I can take care of Junior for a while. We need to get acquainted."

"What about you?"

"I catnapped off and on during the night. I'll stretch out later while yer mother takes her afternoon rest."

"Erma, you're a real jewel," Christopher said with conviction.

"Yeah, I know," she said with a grin. "I've heard that line before—a diamond in the rough."

THE NEXT MORNING Adam and Sarah were on the pier to see Christopher off. Before he boarded ship, Christopher felt he should have one last talk with his son. Taking him aside for a few minutes, he put his hands on the boy's shoulders and looked him straight in the eyes. "I know that you're not happy about going off to camp, Adam, but going there is one of your responsibilities. You've already not fulfilled one by missing your mother's wedding. We won't go into that since it's water over the dam. But I'm counting on you to make the best of the next few weeks."

"Yeah, Dad, I hear you," Adam answered, meeting his father's gaze without flinching.

"I'm not happy about going off and leaving you, either," Christopher went on, "but I have to see this trip through. The company is counting on me to meet my responsibilities, like I'm counting on you."

"I'll be all right, don't worry," Adam said. "And Dad, you better practice your cribbage playing because I intend to take you to the cleaners. I'm saving up to buy a car when I'm sixteen."

Christopher drew his son to him and gave him a hug. He didn't know if he'd gotten his message through to him or not. Hell, who was he to be lecturing anyone else on meeting their responsibilities when he was running out on his?

Turning to Sarah, he took her in his arms for a final kiss. Seeing the tears glistening on her lashes, he was moved to murmur, "Don't cry, darling. I'll be back soon. Always remember that I love you."

Christopher's departing ship had barely reached the channel between Bainbridge Island and the mainland when Adam announced to Sarah, "Forget the bus ticket, I'm not going to camp."

Chapter Ten

"Adam! You agreed to go. You're breaking your word to your father."

"I didn't cross my heart, did I?"

"That's childish!" Sarah exclaimed, but looking at the gangly teenager, she knew that at fourteen he was still little more than a child.

"Gram's getting better. A whole lot better. There's no reason why I can't stay with her just like I used to before Grandpop died and she got sick."

The innocent appeal on the boy's open face caused her to reconsider. Undoubtedly he was remembering days that had been precious to him, days that had been special to all the Weaver family. But those days were gone.

"That's out of the question," she said firmly. "Even though your grandmother's health is improving, she's still far too ill to be responsible for you."

Adam turned his back and kicked at an imaginary stone, his thin shoulders hunched in dejection.

Sarah was at a loss. What was she supposed to do now? She couldn't bodily pick him up and put him on the bus.

"Why didn't you tell your father you had no intention of going?"

"That's a dumb question," the boy retorted. Though his dark eyes filled with tears, he unblinkingly held her gaze. "What he doesn't know won't hurt him."

The flippant tone was too much. "You will be on that eleven-thirty bus," she insisted, "if I have to hire a security guard to get you there!"

"How's that going to keep me from running away again?"

"I think you're fresh out of places to run to," she answered coolly, turning her back on him and starting for the parking lot.

The sullen boy followed her to the van and slammed the door shut. Then, changing stations and turning up the volume on the radio, he leaned his head back and pulled his baseball cap over his face.

Though irritated almost to exasperation, Sarah tried to put herself in Adam's place. She knew his bravado was covering up a troubled soul. Unhappy enough with his mother's plans to actually run away, he'd come to his father—a man he loved—only to have that man ship him off to camp the very next day. The boy had memories of his grandmother's home and the welcoming comfort he'd always experienced there. Naturally he couldn't understand why anything had changed. Would shipping him off to camp alleviate or heighten his insecurity? Though she'd rationalized in order to support Christopher's decision at the time, she'd ignored her gut feeling. Now that Christopher's ship was gone, she was suddenly sure he hadn't made the right choice in leaving his son at this crucial point in the boy's life.

"Look," she said, turning down the radio, "if your grandmother approves—and it all hinges on that—I'll give you a choice. Either you go off to camp as your father expects you to, or you spend the next five weeks with me. You can sleep in your own room at your gram's and Erma will feed you, but the rest of the time you'll take care of the dogs and help me with Puppy Power.''

"Puppy Power?" he sneered. "What's that?"

"I'll explain later," she said, letting her breath out through clenched teeth. "Just make up your mind and make it up fast."

After mumbling, "Some choice," and making a great show of trying to come to a decision, Adam finally declared that he'd rather stay in Seattle, even on her terms.

"Then if your grandmother agrees, we'll have to get a cable off to your dad."

"Do you have to tell him?"

Sarah hesitated. She couldn't let the boy know, but she was quickly coming around to share the notion that in this case, what Christopher didn't know wouldn't hurt him. But she hated giving Adam the idea that she was going behind his father's back. Sighing, she said, "Maybe we could just tell him that everything's taken care of without going into the details."

"Right on!"

Wanting to dampen his enthusiasm over what she knew he took to be a personal victory, she added, "Cool it, kid. It's not up to me. Remember, your grandmother has to make the final decision. And I want you to cross your heart on our agreement right now—and none of your other tricks, either."

"What for?"

"You've got to promise not to even threaten to run away until this is settled, young man. And promise that you're going to mind me if your gram agrees to let you stay here. Now get those arms up there and promise."

"Aw, you make me feel like a little kid," he protested, making a show of slapping his arms across his chest.

But when Sarah pulled the van over to the side of the road and slammed on the brakes, forcing a confrontation that was to be the first of many in the weeks ahead, he quickly crossed his heart and gave her his solemn oath.

Rolling her eyes, Sarah eased back into the early-morning traffic. "The first thing we'll do when we get home is take Amanda and Bertha out for a walk. You'll carry the shovel!"

After the dogs had been walked, Sarah took Adam in for a conference with his grandmother. She let Adam have his say first, biting her tongue to keep from interrupting his exaggerated tale of woe about the cruelties he'd suffered since Greg Anders had entered his mother's life.

Adam finished by whining, "And the only reason I ran away was to be with you, Gram. I knew Dad was going to be gone. I didn't want to go to camp. None of this would have happened if Mom had let me come here in the first place."

Reassured by the bright twinkle in Mary Lou's eyes and her suppressed smile, Sarah knew Adam's grandmother had taken every word with a grain of salt. But Erma, frustrated mother that she was, was taken in hook, line and sinker, her facial expressions running the gamut from disgust to pure horror.

With a covert wink, Sarah reassured Mrs. Weaver that they were on the same wavelength where Adam was concerned. She presented her proposals, adding that if Adam stayed she would make out a list of his daily responsibilities and see that they were performed.

Mary Lou listened, regarding the boy in grave silence as he fidgeted under her thoughtful gaze. At last she spoke. "I agree with you, Sarah. There's no need for Adam to go away to camp when he has this opportunity to become used to his new home. I also agree that he should have regular chores that he'll be expected to do cheerfully and on time. I agree with Adam that there will be no need to inform his father of the change of plans...just yet." Sarah caught the supercil-

ious smirk Adam made in her direction before turning a
bland face back to his gram.

"Adam, I'm delighted to have you here, although your
way of coming was a bit irregular. I trust you won't put us
through that sort of anxiety ever again." Her kind smile
softened the severity of her words.

"Cross my heart, I won't," Adam vowed solemnly.

Erma looked as relieved as the subdued boy. Her whoop
of joy and the accompanying bear hug she gave Adam broke
the tension-filled moment.

Standing and adjusting the wide waistband of her white
cotton sweater, Sarah said, "I'm going to work now. I'll be
home around five. I'll stop at the bus station to cash in the
ticket. Then I'll see what arrangements I can make to have
Adam's trunk sent on here."

"Take my car," said Erma, her heavy earrings dancing
with joy, "and leave the van. That way Adam and I can go
to the dog pound while Mary Lou is in therapy."

"The dog pound?" Adam repeated with distaste. "What
for?"

"To see if we can pick up any more strays." Erma cackled at her own joke, flinging her thin arm around the tall
boy's waist.

IT WASN'T LONG before Sarah wondered if she'd bitten off
more than she could chew. A few days had passed since
Erma and Adam had come home with a van full of dogs and
Sarah's cages were full. Instead of tending to his duties,
Adam had sought out and become reacquainted with boys
he'd known in his early years on the lake, and he was rarely
home during the day. His chores were done slapdash at best,
and she knew Erma had covered for him on several occasions. The times she'd confronted him, she'd met with such
surliness she'd backed down before he'd had a chance to
openly rebel.

Her nights hadn't been any better. The five weeks with Christopher had been heaven; seeing him every day and lying in his arms every night; he'd been the center of her existence. But what they'd shared they'd never have again. Adam had come to demand his birthright, and her claim on Christopher would be eclipsed by the boy's.

By Saturday her nerves were on edge. After sweeping spilled dog food off the kitchen floor for the fifth time that week and throwing away the empty pop cans that littered her ledges and table tops, she reached the conclusion that Adam Weaver was a spoiled brat, used to being waited on hand and foot.

Seeing him on the Weaver deck playing with an adoring Bertha, Sarah marched out her door. Today was the day she and Adam were going to come to a workable understanding, or he was going to find himself on a bus headed for Camp Oswego! As she walked toward him she noticed that the hair that curled so attractively on his forehead had a strong red tint she hadn't noticed before. The sun wasn't yet strong enough to have bleached his hair in so short a time; he must have done it himself. My Lord, what would Christopher have to say about that! But hair dyeing wasn't the issue now. She had more important fish to fry with this young man.

"Adam," she called.

The boy paid no attention.

"Adam," she repeated, walking over to him.

"Yeah?" he answered, not bothering to turn to look at her.

She positioned her five-foot frame directly in front of his towering height. "I want to talk to you."

"Well, make it fast," he said, openly impudent. "John's coming by in his boat to pick me up, and we're going over to the big lake to mess around for a while."

Sarah felt the color rise in her cheeks. "You didn't ask me if you could go."

"So?" He laughed down at her.

"When I agreed to let you stay here against your father's express command, I also agreed to take responsibility for you."

"So?"

"So leaving here without telling me where you're going, or better yet, asking me if you may go, is out!"

"Says who?"

"Get over to my house, now!" she shouted, "and I'll tell you who says." Then lowering her voice, she added between clenched teeth, "You're not going anywhere until we get some things straight around here."

For a long moment they stood face-to-face, each one trying to stare the other down. Finally Adam reached down to give Bertha's ears an affectionate pull before ramming his hands down into his pockets. Then with slouching shoulders he ambled toward Sarah's door.

Once they were both inside and the door was shut against any possibility that Grandmother Weaver might overhear what Sarah suspected would soon become a heated discussion, she motioned the boy into the kitchen. She closed that door behind them, too, just to make sure.

"Now," she barked, placing her hands on her hips, "pick up that phone! Call John! Tell him you're not going anywhere today! Tell him something important has come up!"

"Aw—"

"Do it!"

She held her breath, wondering whether or not he'd obey. When he threw himself into a chair and began jabbing out a number, she let out a silent sigh of relief. If he chose to openly rebel and run wild, she'd have no choice but to wire his father. The next few moments were going to tell who had the upper hand—she or Adam—and she couldn't afford to make an error in judgment. How she wished she had more experience handling kids Adam's age!

She waited while he made his call and winced as he angrily slammed down the receiver.

"Now," she said, sitting down at the table opposite him, "I want to know what the problem is."

"What are you talking about?" he snarled.

"I want to know what's wrong between us. With Erma and your grandmother you're wonderful. With me you're a pain in the neck. When I go over there to find out how things have been going during the day, it's as if we were talking about two different boys. They say you're happy, cheerful, cooperative. Yet over here, I clean up your messes and get talked to as if I were scum beneath your feet."

She waited, but he made no response.

"I wanted to spend some time with you today so we could get better acquainted. I thought we could drive out to the boys' ranch to see how the dogs are working out. I want you to see how Puppy Power works."

"You and your dumb Puppy Power," he shouted, his voice cracking. "In fact, you and your dumb everything!" Tears sprang into his eyes as he buried his head in his arms and broke into racking sobs.

Sarah jumped up and went to the stricken boy. She put her hands on his shoulders, but he jerked away from her gentle touch.

"What is it, Adam?" she asked quietly. "What have I done to make you feel like this?"

"You're sleeping around with my father, aren't you?" His muffled sob-choked voice demanded an answer.

Sarah knew she couldn't deny the obvious. Adam was well aware she and his father had spent a week together on the boat. But she certainly wouldn't call what she and Christopher had shared "sleeping around." Before she could decide what to tell the boy, he raised his red-blotched face.

"That's what happened with my mom and Greg. First they started sleeping around and then they decided to get married. That gave him the idea he could boss me around. I don't want my dad to marry you. I don't want him to marry anybody. I just want him to be mine! So why don't you go take a big jump in the lake?"

Seeing the naked anguish in the boy's eyes, Sarah fell to her knees in front of him and took his hands in hers. Remembering the day the bottom had dropped out of her world when she'd been replaced in her adoptive family's loving affection, she answered the suffering boy from her heart.

"Adam, I'm not taking your father from you. I have no intention of marrying him."

Chapter Eleven

On his first watch-free evening, Christopher received a message requesting his presence in the captain's cabin.

"Good evening, sir," he said, when the small graying man opened the door to the spacious sitting room.

"Good evening, Mr. Weaver," Captain Loftus answered, a pleasant smile on his weathered face. "Come in, come in. I'd like to talk with you, if you can spare the time."

"Certainly, sir," Christopher said, taking off his hat and tucking it under his arm as he entered the room.

"Have a seat." The captain gestured toward one of two leather wing chairs. "Would you care for a glass of wine?" He pointed with his pipe to a tray holding a bottle of topaz-colored liquid. Immediately the picture of Sarah's face set off by the sparkling earrings rose in Christopher's mind. "I was just going to have my usual nightcap."

"That sounds good, sir." Christopher stood before his chair, waiting until the captain had seated himself.

"Then I'll get another glass and we'll see how you like this chardonnay. Gift from my wife," he chuckled, opening a cabinet and taking a crystal goblet from the slotted rack built to hold the glasses secure no matter what weather the ship encountered. "Thirtieth wedding anniversary. She had it sent on board without my knowledge. Thirty bottles of the stuff. Some woman. She knows my tastes."

Then, settling in his upholstered chair, he removed the cork and poured them each a glass. Christopher sat down, placing his hat under his chair.

"Very nice, sir," he said after taking a sip of the smooth cool vintage from the glass the captain handed him. "Almost like a dry Moselle."

Captain Loftus nodded his approval of Christopher's palate. "Not the regular table wine served in the mess, is it?"

"No, sir." Christopher smiled. "I'm afraid not."

"I know you must be wondering why I asked to see you," the captain said, "so I'll come right to the point, Christopher. I'm concerned about you. You haven't been yourself on this trip. Oh, you still handle your job well—you're too professional to ever let down there. But you seem distracted and preoccupied. Would you like to tell me about it? Something pretty serious is on your mind."

"I don't want to trouble you with my personal problems," Christopher said quickly.

"Nonsense," the captain interjected. "Anything that concerns you concerns me, too. Always interested in my men. And I'm a pretty good listener. Been told I have a sympathetic ear," the older man offered graciously. "I hope it has nothing to do with your health or the health of your loved ones."

"No, sir," Christopher said. "In fact, my mother is improving greatly. She's in therapy and is learning to walk again."

"Glad to hear that, glad to hear that." The captain beamed, taking a draw on his short pipe before exhaling a small cloud of smoke. "Well, in my experience, if it's not a medical problem, then it's a problem woman who can set a man on his ear, and not necessarily in that order, either," he said with a wink.

"How about a teenage son?" Christopher asked with a grin. "Where would he fit into your scheme of things?"

"Right at the top of the list." The captain laughed. "I remember those days only too well, now that you mention it. In fact, I claim that each one of these gray hairs is directly attributable to some antic any one of my four sons pulled during their teens. All turned out to be fine young men though," he said with satisfaction. "Maybe I can give you a tip or two..."

Settling back into his chair, Christopher considered the captain's friendly offer. He needed someone to talk to about Adam. The more he mulled over the actuality of the boy's physical presence in his life, the more inadequate he felt as a father, and the larger the problem of what to do with the boy became.

"I have only one son, sir, but right now that seems to be more than I can handle. You see, he has just come to live with me. In fact, he ran away from his mother and appeared on my doorstep the day before we sailed."

"Ah, this sounds like we need a second glass," Captain Loftus interrupted, lifting the wine bottle and refilling their goblets. "Now, start at the beginning, Christopher."

The captain nodded with understanding and interjected a comment now and then, as Christopher briefly recounted his life with Virginia and the part her remarriage had played in Adam's decision to come to Seattle.

"And you've not remarried?" the captain asked, when Christopher had finished.

"No, sir. But I've finally met the woman I want to marry," Christopher confided, a frown wrinkling his brow.

"Ah, I'm beginning to see the picture. A little soon to give the boy a new mother, and a little too soon to give the little lady a teenage son."

"That's about it, sir. This woman—her name is Sarah, Sarah Mitchell—came into my life like a bombshell and changed everything. For the better."

"Ah, yes," the captain chuckled, "they do have the power to do that, don't they?"

Christopher nodded. "But she's young. She deserves to have a family of her own." He let out a heavy sigh. "I'm afraid that I may be too old to start a new family now. Especially since I didn't do such a great job with the one I had. And I just hope that I won't do anything to ruin the second chance I'm getting with my son."

He shifted uneasily, putting down his glass, afraid that in his agitation he might snap its thin stem.

"And by marrying me, Sarah would not only get Adam in the bargain, but she'll also have to share my commitment to my invalid mother."

The captain nodded, taking a long draw on his pipe. "You have a couple of mighty weighty problems there, Christopher. A real two-horned dilemma. I can understand your preoccupation now. A fourteen-year-old boy needs his father, and I sympathize with you, taking him over at this late date. Got a few ground rules to establish first off, and after that a lot of patrolling to see that they're followed. A full-time job for a few years. From my experience that's not going to be easy. But then, nothing worthwhile is ever easy, is it?"

"No, sir," Christopher agreed with a worried frown.

"The problem of the little lady is quite out of my line," the captain continued. "I wouldn't have the audacity to give you any advice on that matter." He sat, his pipe poised in midair as though he were thinking over something more he wanted to say. Christopher waited. Finally the captain went on, "But in my experience, observing other men, I have noted one thing. Women who are worth their salt aren't going to wait around forever for a fellow to make up his mind.''

"Yes, sir, I've thought about that. In fact I considered proposing to her before I left, but things were so up in the air about my son. And now..." His voice trailed off. The only sound in the room was the drone of the air conditioner, which seemed to have become amplified in Christopher's ears to an annoying buzz. He picked up his glass and gazed down into its contents. "I've been toying with the idea of taking a shore job," he confessed, misery apparent in his tone.

"Is that what you want to do?" the captain asked quietly.

"No, sir. But if I did, I'd be home, and Sarah wouldn't have to take it all on her shoulders."

"I think that would be a big mistake," Captain Loftus said sternly, the amiable smile leaving his face. Leaning forward in his chair, the motions of his pipe emphasized his words. "You're an academy man, Mr. Weaver. You've got salt water in your veins. Your father was a captain. You're slated to make rank, too. Do you think that either your son or Sarah expects you to make that sacrifice?"

"No, sir. I haven't discused it with anyone but you," Christopher said, reddening beneath his deep tan. He knew the captain was as shocked at his words as he had been when Max had told him he was giving up his position. He also knew that if he were to say any more on the subject he might become embarrassingly overconfident.

"Then I'm glad we had this little talk. Sometimes a man gets so embroiled in his problems he considers some desperate alternatives. He can't see the ocean for the waves. But giving up the sea is not on the chart for you." Then softening his tone, he added, "There is one bright light on the horizon."

"What's that, sir?"

"After this leg you have the next two and a half months off. That should give you enough time to get a lot of things squared away."

"I'm sure you're right, sir." Christopher forced a smile as he rose. "Thank you, sir, for listening. You've helped me clarify my thinking. I'm sorry you had to concern yourself with my personal problems."

"Not at all," the older man said, getting to his feet. "I'll be interested to learn how all this works out. You know— Will Sarah say yes? Will Adam settle into his new life? And Christopher," he went on kindly, "we've all had our doubts one time or another whether we were being fair to our families by indulging ourselves in our personal love affair with the sea. Sometimes a chat with a fellow officer helps."

"Thank you, sir."

"I was just going over the yearly rating reports due next month. When I looked at your dossier, I realized I hadn't gotten to know you as well as I should have. You're a fine officer."

"Thank you again, sir," Christopher said, before placing his hat back on his head to go out the cabin door.

The captain's timely words had served to bolster Christopher's conviction that taking a shore job would not get him out of his double bind, but he still couldn't see how he could justify dragging Sarah down with his problems. Yet, how could he stand to lose the woman he loved now that he'd found her?

Checking the double row of clocks mounted on the wall outside the radio room, Christopher saw that it was nearly six o'clock in the morning in Seattle. After talking with the captain he felt an urge to call Sarah. Unlike Max, he rarely used the ship-to-shore communication service, because it offered no privacy. Every word was monitored by the radiomen sending and receiving the satellite-relayed message. In spite of that, he wanted to hear Sarah's voice, wanted her to know that she was on his mind. He'd make it short and sweet. Just a simple call to tell her that he loved her.

LEANING ON THE RAIL of her deck, Sarah watched Erma and Mary Lou at their morning exercise, throwing bread for the flock of sea gulls that circled and squawked overhead. Begging for their daily handout, the gulls were oblivious to Amanda's soprano yaps and Bertha's bass woofs. Erma had devised her own therapy plan for Mary Lou, part of which required that the invalid use only her weaker arm to hurl the day-old slices into the air.

It was amazing to see evidence of the progress Mary Lou had made once she'd decided to try rehabilitation. She no longer looked like the frail old woman to whom Sarah had given Amanda four months earlier. As her muscles developed with therapy and her body filled out from eating Erma's fanciful meals, a growing vitality enlivened her, illuminated her features. The more she took on to do, the more her accomplishments accelerated. Sarah knew Christopher could never imagine the progress his mother was making.

His early-morning call had left her with an unsettled feeling in her heart. It had been the second time, since she'd come to the realization that their relationship was over, that he'd told her that he loved her. She hadn't known how to respond. Fortunately she was sure he'd attributed her reluctance to make a direct reply to the fact that she knew there were people listening in. She did love him...would always love him, and she wished with all her heart she could have told him how she felt. But she knew that she'd never be able to do that now, so she'd held her emotions in check. She felt a wave of guilt wash over her that she hadn't been honest with him before he'd set sail. It hurt to think that he thought they still had a future together.

Stimulated to action by her thoughts, Sarah stuffed her hands in the pockets of her yellow windbreaker and sauntered over to join the busy women next door.

"You're up bright and early," she commented with forced cheerfulness. "Where's that teenager? Still in bed?"

"I called the little critter," Erma answered. The maternal possessiveness in her tone amused Sarah. Adam had arrived in Seattle with only one grandmother to greet him; now, for all intents and purposes, he had two. But to give him credit, he didn't seem to mind Erma's exuberant motherly attentions. "Come have breakfast with us."

"Yes, do," Mary Lou added. "I haven't seen much of you the past few weeks."

"I've been busy," Sarah remarked, struggling to keep her smile steady as she helped Erma wheel Mary Lou into the house. Since the day she'd taken the irreversible step of telling Adam that she had no intention of marrying his father, she'd been living in a daze, willfully keeping part of her brain anesthetized, her deepest and most real emotions numbed. Filling her days with frantic activity, she'd managed to live in the present, moment by moment, suffocating any memories of what had been, refusing to let her mind drift to any dreams of what might be.

Immersing herself in Puppy Power, she'd renewed her contacts with Henry, a retired army sergeant near Erma's age, and the other three volunteers. Together they'd scoured animal shelters in nearby counties for appropriate dogs and had built new cages in her living room for her expanding inventory of animals. Finding new avenues for the placement of her dogs, Sarah had discovered that alleviating others' unhappiness still helped to make her feel less alone and useless.

"Since that sleepyheaded young 'un still isn't down yet, help me git Mary Lou into her chair at the table," Erma requested.

"Of course," Sarah agreed. Following Erma's succinct directions she managed to help Mrs. Weaver from her wheelchair safely into her padded captain's chair at the head of the heavy maple table.

"Now you sit over there, kiddo," Erma directed as she arranged another place setting. "We're havin' flapjacks. Apple flapjacks." She turned and busied herself at the stove.

"You're certainly doing well," Sarah remarked to Mary Lou. "You actually took a step or two while we were helping you. I think you're doing better than any of our other clients."

"Thanks to Erma." Mary Lou turned a fond smile in the cook's direction. "She won't let me rest for a minute. I can stand now with the help of a walker. Monday I'm going to start taking real steps. I can hardly wait."

"No time for lazy bones until you're six feet under, I always say," Erma piped up as she poured them each a cup of coffee.

"Speaking of lazy bones, I don't hear much activity overhead," Sarah said, rising. Going to the foot of the spiral staircase, she called up, "Adam, hit the deck! You'd better hurry if you want to go sailing with Kevin and Dr. Blake this afternoon. We have a list of things to do this morning, remember?" She waited until she heard his feet on the floor.

"Slave driver," he called down good-naturedly as he started for the shower.

Returning to the kitchen, Sarah sat down and sipped at her steaming coffee.

"And Sarah doesn't have a lazy bone in her body, either," Erma remarked with approval, placing a plate of home-made wheat-flour-and-bran doughnuts on the table before taking a seat opposite Sarah. "Whatja up to today, kiddo?"

"Uuum, a whole bunch of things. First of all, Adam and I are going to deliver Bixby to Mr. Langley. I want him to come with me so he can see what happens to a dog he's trained.''

"That the man who lost his wife and took to drink?" Erma asked, her black eyes snapping with interest, a dunked doughnut poised midway to her mouth. "I think it's swell ya got in touch with the AA."

Sarah nodded. "Mr. Langley is exactly the type of referral we're looking for from them. He's not a person with a history of habitual drinking. He just fell into it because of grief and loneliness. I'm sure there are a lot of people in his boat.

"He's as excited as the boys at the ranch were about getting a dog. He's been building a house for Bixby all week at the seniors' center. I wish you both could see it. A real log cabin, with windows, a porch, and even a log chimney. It was so heavy it took six men to lift it into the van. Then we all drove in a procession to Mr. Langley's house to unload it. After we got it in place, I saw some wistful looks on a couple of the other men's faces. I wouldn't be surprised if we got some calls for more dogs from those fellows.''

"That's wonderful," Mary Lou said with a sigh. "And Sarah, I want to thank you for all you've done for Adam. Keeping him busy down at the clinic and teaching him how to train dogs has been so good for him. He's really learning to assume a little responsibility.

"And I especially want to thank you for introducing Adam to that nice boy, Kevin, so that he can go sailing with him and his father on that lovely large boat. I know Christopher will be so pleased."

At the mention of Christopher's name, Sarah felt her cheeks flame and her throat constrict with pain. In every possible way she'd tried to keep from thinking of him, but in this house his presence was so real she couldn't escape.

Struggling to her feet, she was saved a blundering exit by Adam's arrival at the breakfast table.

"Here I am, you lucky women," he announced, as he plopped into his chair. "Where's my breakfast?"

"I've told you a hundred times you don't wear a hat in the house," Erma rebuked. "Take that hat off your head, young man. I'll have your flapjacks ready as soon as you finish your orange juice." She jumped up to open the refrigerator.

"Aw, it took me ten minutes to get it on just right, do I have to? Gram?"

"Do as you're told," Mary Lou said with a laugh.

"I'll be waiting for you next door," Sarah said, solving the argument by lifting the red baseball cap off Adam's head and placing it on her own. Eyeing his blue-and-yellow striped knit shirt and cutoffs, she added, "You'd better bring along your jacket."

"Aren't ya gonna eat?" Erma asked, her disappointment plain.

"Thanks anyway, but the doughnut was enough." She walked toward the door wondering if the deep-fried pastry that sat like a heavy anchor in the pit of her stomach would ever digest.

"Come see me this afternoon," Mary Lou called after her. "We haven't had a talk for a long while, and I miss you."

"I miss you, too," Sarah admitted. "I'm busy this afternoon. Maybe tonight."

Outside, Sarah paused, her eyes resting on the dancing blue water of the lake. A bright yellow seaplane flew overhead in a graceful arc, preparing to land. She'd have to take time to see Mary Lou. It wasn't fair to Mary Lou to stay away because everything in the Weaver home seemed to scream Christopher's name. Until things were settled between Christopher and her, until he understood his true role in Adam's life, she'd have to çontinue to hold up appearances, no matter how painful.

Settling Adam's hat lower on her forehead she thought about how she and the boy had finally become friends. Taking her at her word that she was not a potential threat as a stepmother, he'd allowed her the authority an older sister might have held over him. In the hours they'd spent together the past few weeks, she'd really come to know him. And as he'd confided to her why he'd run away from his mother, she had listened with empathy.

Whether it was true or not, Adam felt that his new stepfather had taken his mother away from him. He could hardly talk about her without crying, and those few times he did cry, he'd let Sarah hold him and soothe him like a small child. There would come a time, and she knew it should come soon, when he would need to see his mother to iron out their differences. The passing of too much time, she was well aware, would make a reconciliation between the boy and his mother difficult, maybe impossible.

Adam pretended indifference to the postcards from Virginia that arrived in every mail. They'd been sent from spots all over Europe. Mrs. Weaver wisely left them on the ledge until, late in the night, they would disappear. A bunch of them had fallen out of Adam's jacket when Sarah had been picking up her living room. No matter how much he wanted to be with his father, his love for his mother, no matter how much it hurt just now, was real.

At other times, when Adam had been abrasive and obstinate, Sarah had patiently discovered that he was worried about his father and whether the man really loved and wanted him. Locked up inside the growing boy was an insecure, pampered child whose world had crumbled around him: a child who needed all the love and constancy a stable home could give him. And although there were occasions when she had to bribe and cajole him into behaving, Adam was beginning to come around. In fact, she thought with a grin, there were even times when they had fun together.

"What's so funny, short stuff?" Adam asked, sneaking up behind her and lifting the hat from her head to settle it back on his.

"I was just thinking what a pain in the neck you used to be," she answered glibly, smoothing down her hair. "I still can't quite believe it, but there are times when you're almost human."

"You'd probably like me better if I was a dog," he scoffed.

Sarah grinned up at him. "Come on, Rover, let's get Bixby and hit the road."

"AND THIS IS WHERE I'll let him take his nap while I take mine," Mr. Langley explained to Adam, showing him the thick throw rug he'd placed by the couch. The gray-haired man's attitude was deferential, as though he sensed he had to win the boy's approval.

"That rug will get a lot of use," Adam replied solemnly. "In my experience, dogs nap about twenty hours out of every twenty-four."

"About my speed," the older man chuckled. "We'll get along fine." He reached down to pet the black spaniel heeling obediently at Adam's side.

"Now," Adam went on with a note of authority in his young voice, "you don't want to overfeed him. Dog food twice a day is enough, and be careful with the table scraps— no small bones. I'll leave you a booklet on dog care and nutrition. One bath a week is what he's used to, and he really likes to swim."

"Swim?" Mr. Langley asked, as though it were a foreign term. He looked stricken as he stared down at the dog.

"Yeah, you know, like, throw a stick in the lake for him to fetch?"

"Oh," the older man said with relief. "I guess I can do that for him. I thought I had to go swimming with him."

"And we'll be by next week to see how things are going." Sarah entered the conversation for the first time since they'd arrived. "Just make a list of any questions that occur to you between now and then.

"Adam, give Mr. Langley the leash. I'm sure he and Bixby would like to make friends."

Sarah noticed the reluctance with which Adam handed the dog over to the man, and, when they were back in Kanga, she asked him why he'd hesitated.

"Doesn't it bother you to give your dogs away?" he asked morosely. "How do you know that old man will take good care of Bix?"

"That's why we'll make a checkup call or two. But I'm sure Mr. Langley is kind and will love Bixby as much as you do."

"Next time you give one away I'm not going with you."

"Why not?"

"I can't stand it. And I don't see how you can, either. You act like you love those dogs. They think you do. Then you just give them away. How can you do it?"

"You have to learn to distance yourself," Sarah answered through stiff lips. "We took those dogs from the pound with the understanding that we would give them to people who would love and care for them."

"Yeah? Well, they don't know that," Adam shot back, his voice quivering with emotion. "How would you like it if someone took you and you thought it was for keeps, then they just gave you away?"

"I know the feeling well," Sarah answered flatly. "I was a foster child for many years." She felt his long stare before he turned back to gaze out the window. "It didn't hurt me, did it?" she asked, forcing a brightness into her voice.

But Adam didn't answer, and her remark did little to lessen the tension in the van. She wasn't surprised when the boy jumped from the vehicle as soon as she parked on the road above the rows of floating homes.

Sarah sat for a few moments, her lower arms resting on the steering wheel. It was ironic that even giving pleasure could sometimes bring pain to the giver. She'd like to help the boy, but there was nothing else she could say. It was a problem Adam would have to work out for himself. Perhaps after a few follow-up visits to Mr. Langley and Bixby he'd see how well the dog had adjusted.

That evening, after she'd walked and fed the dogs, Sarah went over to visit Mrs. Weaver. The first thing she noticed as she entered the house was the abnormal quiet.

"Where's Adam?" she asked, picking up a wriggling Amanda and laying her cheek on the pup's soft head. "I saw him get off the boat when they docked behind my house. Did he go home with the Blakes?"

"He and Erma went to the movies," Mary Lou said, putting down the magazine she'd been reading. "There was some space thriller they both wanted to see. They debated about asking you to join them, but decided that it wasn't quite to your taste. Come in and sit down, dear." She patted the couch beside her.

"I'm glad Adam's not running around with those other boys anymore," Sarah said, placing Amanda on the pillow between them. "No telling what mischief he could have gotten into with them."

"I agree," Adam's grandmother said. "That's one thing to be said for boarding school. In the fall, he'll make many new friends."

"Well, it's nice to see you sitting here," Sarah remarked, not sure how she felt about Adam living away from home part of every week. It may have been fine for Christopher, who had always had a stable home with both a mother and father, but for Adam, she wasn't so sure. Though, she supposed, under the circumstances there wouldn't be much choice. Mary Lou and Erma weren't up to the strain of dealing with the boy day in and day out. Weekends, while Christopher was at sea, would be more than enough for them to handle.

"It's nice to see you sitting here, too," Mary Lou echoed. "Has Adam been such a chore that you haven't had any time for a visit?"

"No," Sarah answered. "I like his company, now that he's settled down and stopped being such a little pill. I guess it's just that Puppy Power is taking up more and more of my time. I'd been neglecting it."

"I don't think that's the problem," Mary Lou said, her eyes, so like Christopher's, holding Sarah's with their perceptive gaze. "What is it, Sarah? You used to be so happy, so sparkling. Now you seem to be worried about something. Is it Adam?"

"No... yes... oh, I don't know," Sarah said, tears springing into her eyes. She looked away, trying to pull herself together. The last thing she wanted was to have Mrs. Weaver feel sorry for her. "He was quite upset having to give Bixby up. I think he needs to have a dog of his own. It would be as therapeutic for him as it was for you. He needs something of his own to love, especially since he isn't sure how his father feels about him."

Mary Lou sighed. "I'm sure you're right, dear. I've been more anxious for Christopher to return than I could tell you. He has some fences to mend with his son. I just hope, for all our sakes, that he knows how."

Knowing she couldn't trust herself to say anything on that subject, and seeing how upset Mary Lou was becoming, Sarah asked, "Do you think Christopher would let Adam keep a dog? He wasn't too keen on Amanda."

"I think my son is outnumbered in the dog department," Mary Lou answered, her hand gently stroking the contented pup at her side. "But, to be honest, I don't think it's worrying about Adam's having a dog that's taken the brightness from your eyes or those pounds off your body. What is it, Sarah?'' Insistent, she repeated her question, her once paralyzed hand slowly moving to cover Sarah's.

That light touch splintered the transparent shell in which Sarah had encased herself from childhood—a shell that had kept her strong and brave, removed from a dangerous and threatening closeness with others. Christopher had weakened the shell, had come closer than she'd ever allowed any other person to come, but Mary Lou's motherly kindness shattered it, leaving Sarah suddenly soft and vulnerable to the terrible pain tearing at her heart.

As though seeking the comfort and solace from a mother she'd long since denied, Sarah pulled her feet up onto the couch and laid her head on Mary Lou's lap, mindless of the fact that she was crowding Amanda away from her coveted spot. The dog whimpered, climbed over Sarah's shoulders and jumped to the floor, scampering up the stairs.

The tears Sarah had been holding back flowed from her eyes as sobs shook her small frame. Mary Lou let her cry, stroking her long hair in sympathy, murmuring, ''That's good. That's fine. Let it all out, dear.''

As her tears lessened, Sarah found herself pouring out her story of frustration and anger... her love for Christopher... her inability to have children... her early life as a foster child... her estrangement from her adoptive family.

Sitting up and drying her tearstained face with the tissue Mary Lou had handed her, Sarah went on in a choked voice, ''I thought that in letting myself love Christopher I was safe. He had a son. He wouldn't be disappointed that I couldn't bear his child. We'd have each other. But now you can see why I have to give him up.''

''No, dear, I don't understand that point.'' A frown of concern furrowed Mrs. Weaver's forehead.

''It's because of Adam.''

"You feel that Adam has come between you?"

"Adam has first claim on his father," Sarah stated emphatically. "When I first started to care for Christopher, I accepted the idea of Adam as an occasional visitor. I believed I could handle that. On the days he was with us, I planned to let him have Christopher all to himself. But now that Adam will be living with his father, there isn't any room for me in Christopher's life. That may sound like I'm jealous of Adam, but that's not it. I just couldn't do to him what happened to me when Melissa, my sister, was born to my adoptive parents, and my mother and father gave her the love they'd given me. I felt as though I'd done something wrong, that I wasn't enough for them. That I'd failed them in a way I couldn't understand."

"Do you think that with Adam and Christopher it's the same thing? Do you think that Christopher's loving you will make Adam feel as though he isn't enough for his father?"

"Yes, I do. I've never felt so lost and alone as I did when Melissa was born. That's when I decided that the only thing I wanted in life was to have my own children, to have a family to love and to love me. That dream was the only thing that kept me going."

"Then you lost that, too," Mary Lou said. Her voice shook with compassion. "Sarah, listen to me. You're a courageous, loving person. A daughter anyone would be fortunate to have. A woman I'd be proud to have as my son's wife—and for my grandson's stepmother. I can't think of anyone I've ever known who gives as much of herself to others. And I hope you don't think what I'm going to say is harsh because I certainly don't mean it that way."

Sarah turned her tearstained face toward the older woman, her round eyes red-rimmed and guileless.

"Dear, is it that you're afraid of coming between Adam and his father, or is it that you're afraid of Adam coming between you and Christopher?"

Sarah looked at the older woman as her words registered on her brain. Hadn't Mary Lou understood any of what she'd told her?

"I'm not thinking of myself," Sarah insisted. "I'm only thinking of Adam!"

"Sarah—" Mary Lou Weaver took her hands "—I think you've been mixed up about a number of things for a very long time. I don't expect you to accept what I have to say, I just want you to think about it. Will you promise to do that for me?"

Sarah nodded.

"Dear, you spoke of Adam having first claim on Christopher. And you mentioned feeling that your sister had displaced you in your family. In a loving family relationship, Sarah, love isn't exclusive. Loving your son doesn't mean you don't love your husband. You simply love them differently—not more, not less. When people truly care for one another, there's enough love to go around."

AT THAT MOMENT, standing on a catwalk, his collar turned up against a brisk wind, Christopher was thinking of Sarah. He'd thought of little else the past thirty days. And the more he mulled over in his mind what losing her would mean to him, the more determined he became to ask her to marry him.

Sarah was a mature independent woman, much as his mother had been when his father had married her. And like his mother Sarah had an ingrained contentment with the things that mattered in life. He felt very lucky there were two such women in the world and that they were both his.

There was a sweetness in Sarah, a power of loving that glowed around her, a dignity and balance that made her both romantic and sexually attractive. His love for her was like a fever in his blood.

They'd work out any problem they had to face together, and together they'd give Adam a good home. Christopher's spirit lifted with a buoyancy he hadn't felt during the long days and nights he'd spent floundering in worry and indecision.

Only five more days and Sarah would be his.

Chapter Twelve

But when Christopher's ship docked on a beautiful clear day in July, it was a strangely quiet Sarah who was there to greet him. At first he chalked up her reticence to her natural unaffected way of letting others have the limelight—and what an exhibition they'd planned for him! Adam ran up the gangplank to meet him halfway, launching into a nonstop account of why he hadn't gone to camp. Before he'd had time to even consider a response, his gaze was caught by the sight of his mother taking a few shaky steps toward the ship, leaning on a walker for support.

The few times he tried to catch Sarah's eye, she seemed so engrossed in all the commotion that he wasn't alerted to the fact that she was deliberately avoiding him. He'd just supposed that she hadn't wanted their reunion to take place under the watchful eyes of such an interested audience. Even later, when Adam rode home with him and Sarah went with his mother's entourage, he hadn't become concerned. She made the maneuver so smoothly he wasn't aware that anything other than her consideration for his son had caused the arrangement.

Keyed-up and excited, Adam kept him occupied with tales of his adventure-filled month during the dinner preparations. Christopher wasn't able to break away to share a single private moment with Sarah, who offered to help Erma in the kitchen.

Using chopsticks provided by the venerable cook, he dutifully downed two helpings of a Japanese meal Erma called her original sukiyaki casserole. He even took a spoonful of a deep-dish concoction of chicken and dumplings she'd thoughtfully provided for the less-adventurous diners. But now that dinner was over, he was certain that something was troubling Sarah. Her smiles in his direction were vaguely impersonal, her answers to his questions far too noncommittal.

He was beginning to wonder if he'd ever escape his son's fond attentions long enough to find out what was bothering her when the phone rang.

"I'll get it," Adam's clear voice rang out, as though he were talking to someone in the next room instead of to the small group sitting at the table.

Seeing Sarah's gaze follow the boy rather than use the opportunity to meet his eyes, Christopher knew he had to do something fast.

"Naw, I can't make it tonight," Adam said, leaning against the wall, the phone caught between his ear and his T-shirted shoulder. "My old man's ship just came in. Yeah, I know I said I really wanted to see that, but—"

"What is it, Adam?" Christopher asked.

The boy covered the receiver with one hand. "It's Kevin. His granddad's gonna take him to the tractor-trailer pull at the Kingdome tonight. He wants me to go. It's gonna be great, but I don't want to leave you—"

"Go ahead, son," Christopher said, trying not to sound too anxious. "I'll be home for the next two and a half months. There's no sense in your missing out."

"His granddad's gonna be there any minute..." Adam said dubiously, looking toward his grandmother who nodded her approval. "And they want me to spend the night, too."

"Just get yer toothbrush and a clean pair of socks, and I'll run ya over to your buddy's house," Erma piped up, grabbing her keys and wallet, heading for the door. "If we git a move on I'll betcha we beat that old man there."

Sarah had intended to help Erma with the dishes, but the unexpected departure for the Blakes' left only Christopher and his mother at the table with her. The anticipation of his arrival home had been such a strain that she didn't think she had the strength left to tell him of her decision tonight.

Standing, she addressed Mrs. Weaver. "If you'll excuse me. I need to walk the dogs."

"I'll go with you," Christopher offered, hastily coming to his feet, placing his napkin on the cluttered table.

"But you shouldn't leave your mother alone," Sarah protested.

"You two go ahead," Mrs. Weaver said. "Sometimes I think Erma's a frustrated race car driver. She'll be back before I can read the front page of the newspaper."

"But you're still in your uniform," Sarah objected as Christopher propelled her out the door to the deck, his hand on her elbow.

"I've kissed you before in my uniform," he said, taking her into his arms, his blue eyes laughing down into her troubled face. "And I intend to do it many, many more times after this."

Tilting her chin for the passionate kiss his lips hungered for, he felt her stiffen and hesitate. Then, before he could pull back to voice a question, she gave a small moan and raised her arms to encircle his neck, her fingers caressing the sensitized flesh above his starched collar, her mouth opening to his like a night-blooming flower.

She'd meant to stay distant, meant to stay indifferent. But the weakness that had hit her knees the second she'd seen him coming down the gangplank had been an ominous warning that his appeal was greater than her resolve.

The evening had been almost unendurable. The perplexity in Christopher's eyes each time her gaze had inadvertently crossed his had been so tormenting, that if Adam hadn't been there, full of hero worship for his father, she knew she would have thrown herself into Christopher's arms and kissed his doubts away.

Now it was happening, the embrace she'd vowed she'd never share...the kiss her heightened senses had almost tasted when, unable to eat, she'd looked across the table at him. As his lips and tongue fiercely demanded the response she was powerless to withhold, she gave herself up to the pure pleasure of being held in his arms again. She loved him. And as long as she was near him she didn't have the strength to deny that love.

His fingers twined into her thick hair, his broad palm cupping the back of her head, his other arm holding her tightly against him, while sensation after sensation pulsed through her quivering body.

Pulling his lips from hers he murmured against their moist fullness, "It's been so long, baby, so very long," before his mouth was again fused to hers. His heat seeped into her flesh, melding her to him as his sensuous assault succeeded in driving her nearly mad with desire.

As though in a trance she felt him lift her into his arms. She clung to his neck, her face resting against the black gabardine of his jacket as he carried her across the boardwalk.

The red sunset was spectacular, coloring the smooth surface of the lake in rosy hues of gold and purple. An old saying she'd always loved flashed through her mind:

Red sky at morning, sailors take warning
Red sky at night, sailors delight.

This time she knew, the omen didn't hold true for the mariner who held her in his arms. The red sky held no promise of a new tomorrow dawning with fair weather and smooth sailing. Tonight would bring the end of their relationship; the only promise the morrow held was heartbreak for them both.

But she wouldn't allow herself to think about that now, as he opened the door of her house, carried her through the living room, past the sleeping dogs, and carefully deposited her on the downy softness of her double bed. She had the moment, and nothing was going to mar her one last precious memory of being truly loved.

It seemed only seconds before he settled his naked length beside her, and his swift fingers completed the task of exposing her writhing body to his touch. Her desire increased, her senses raging as his lips and fingers teased the firm roundness of her breasts and the hardened peaks of her nipples. Then as his maddening touch sought the tender pulsing flesh so close to her core she cried out his name in supplication.

His entry was urgent, strong. Clinging to his heaving body, moving with him, loving him, she was brought to peak after peak of shattering ecstasy by his velvety thrusts. Nothing existed but the man who filled her, intoxicating her with his touch, his scent, his love. Together they reached the delirious height of their shared passion, each calling out to the other in the wonder of their simultaneous release.

He held her closely in the aftermath of their lovemaking, dropping light kisses on her eyelids and cheeks, running his lips along the line where her fabulous hair met the creamy smoothness of her slender neck.

"Sarah," he breathed against her satin skin, "you don't know how much I've missed you. For the last five days the ship seemed to stand still. I wanted to get off the damn thing and push it. See what you do to me, woman?" he teased.

"The next thing you know you'll get a cable telling you I drowned after going overboard to try to jog back to you. How would you like that on your conscience?"

She smiled dreamily, languidly raising a hand to twirl her fingers in his thick, sun-bleached hair. He was so happy, she didn't want to spoil his mood. Maybe she could wait a day or two. How could she tell him now of the anguish she'd suffered as his ship seemed to rush ever nearer during those same days? How, after this ecstatic interval, could she tell him of her decision to give him up?

He looked deeply into her eyes, mesmerized by their golden depths. "Sarah, will you marry me? Will you be my wife? I want to begin again—with you. Have the family only you can give me. I want a chance to do things right this time."

Sarah's hands grasped her abdomen as she curled into a ball, turning her back to the beseeching man. How wrong she'd been to believe she'd been made whole by his love! How wrong she'd been to deceive him!

"I . . . I can never give you children," she whispered. Her fingers clawed at the offensive scar. "I'm barren."

Raising himself on one elbow, Christopher used his other hand to pull Sarah's rigid fingers away. Then slowly he eased her from her tightly curled position onto her back. She covered her face with one arm, still turning her head away from him. Placing his hand on her abdomen he gently rubbed the slightly raised blemish.

"Tell me about it, Sarah," he murmured.

"A horse..." she began in trembling tones, reaching over to turn off the bedside lamp that bathed them in its soft glow. In the darkness where she couldn't see the revulsion she was sure was on his face, or even worse, the pity her story would evoke, she told him of her accident and how it had affected her dreams for the future.

Haltingly she ended, "So you see, I can never be a whole woman. I should never have let myself become involved with you. I should have never let you fall in love with me. It wasn't fair to you."

He gently pulled her arm away from her face and cradled her head against his shoulder. "Sarah, darling little Sarah. It doesn't matter. Don't you know that? It wouldn't have mattered if I'd known right from the start. It wouldn't have stopped me from falling in love with you.

"You're all the woman I could ever want and more. And you and Adam are all the family I need. I would never have brought it up, except I thought you would want them. It took me a while to come around to the idea of having another child, but after I got used to it, a little girl who looked just like you sounded like something I might be able to handle." His fingers were soothing as he stroked her throat and gently raised her face to his.

"A freckled nose—" his lips fluttered along its bridge "—two gorgeous hazel eyes—" they moved to feather her eyelids and brows "—a softly pointed chin..." His tongue flickered along its contours before his lips closed tenderly on hers for a brief kiss. "But all I was thinking of is an extension of you. I don't need that, darling...we don't need that to make our love complete.

"As much as I love him, Adam didn't make my first marriage more fulfilling. In fact, to be brutally honest, disagreements on what our son needed out of life only served to widen the rift between Virginia and me.

"Children are wonderful, Sarah darling. But having or not having them doesn't make or break a marriage. The two of us have Adam, and if you decide you want to have a baby and you want to risk having me for its father, we can adopt."

"Do you really mean that?" she asked in faltering tones. "You won't regret, some time in the future, not having more children of your own?"

"I mean it, believe me," he said with a heartfelt sincerity she couldn't doubt. "I'm thirty-seven years old, in fact nearly thirty-eight. I've never regretted not having more children than Adam before. Besides, I need a chance to make up for the years I haven't been the father to him that I should have been, and I need the rest of my life to show you the wonderful life we can have together. But like I said, if you ever want to take on a new little one—a little girl—I'll do my darnedest to be a good father to her.

"Whether or not we had children of our own was always up to you, as far as I was concerned. And I feel the same way about adopting. Whatever makes you happy, honey, is all I want."

Sarah shut her eyes, hardly able to believe the words she had been sure she'd never hear from a man she loved. Christopher still found her desirable . . . he loved her, he wanted her, he needed her, just the way she was!

Remembering suddenly the obstacle that still stood between them, she whispered, "But Adam doesn't need me and he doesn't want me!" Burying her face in the wiry golden hair on Christopher's hard chest, she began crying softly.

"Sit up, Sarah," he said gently, feeling her hot tears against his skin. "Let's talk. I think I need to know what's been going on here while I've been at sea."

Sniffling, she moved away, snapped on the lamp by the bed and dried her eyes with a tissue before getting up. He watched her as she crossed the small room, opened the closet and pulled on a ruffled, peach-colored wrapper. Disheveled from their lovemaking, she was irresistible. Heated desire surged through him again, but he covered the evidence by wrapping himself in the quilt.

"Come here," he ordered, fluffing up and arranging the ivory-colored pillows against the brass headboard. She joined him. Pulling her into the crook of his arm, he said, "There's nothing for you to worry about. I've got it all planned. Now that my mother is making such great progress, it will work out even better than I'd hoped. I know how fond you are of her, but I didn't like the idea of your thinking you had to take on more responsibility for her when you were my wife.

"We'll get married right away," he continued. "You can quit your job and the three of us—you, Adam and I—will go on a cruise down the California coast. I have the next ten weeks off. In that time I'm sure Adam will get to know you and love you. Who could help loving you?" He nuzzled her neck, nipping lightly at her fragrant flesh.

Sarah straightened, pulling the satin wrapper together where it had fallen open. "Christopher—" she slowly shook her head, biting her lower lip "—you've got a lot to learn about your son."

"I know that," he agreed. "That's why I plan to spend as much time with him as I can. After he's enrolled and settled in at Denton Academy in September, we can take off wherever we like for a couple of weeks—the Bahamas, Tahiti, you name it."

"You don't understand," Sarah said. "It isn't that easy. Adam's too old to be a little pawn, picked up and put down at your convenience. He's becoming a person in his own right, one with fragile feelings and explosive opinions. You can't make decisions about how he's going to spend his time or where he's going to go to school without asking him how he feels. Believe me, it just won't work.

"And it has to work out between the two of you! Adam needs you now more than he ever did. If he's going to develop into the man you expect him to be, he needs a strong role model and you're his idol. There's no way I'm going to come between the two of you. He's already told me how he feels about that.''

"What do you mean?" Christopher asked curtly.

"Right after you left Adam was terrible. Wouldn't do anything I asked him to do. He was surly, sometimes even rude. Finally we had it out and got it settled between us— once he made sure I didn't have any designs on you.''

"Why that little...! It isn't any of his business,'' Christopher said, his mouth twisting in anger.

"It is his business,'' Sarah insisted. "He's only trying to prevent what he feels has destroyed his life with his mother from happening to him again. He's alone, Christopher, and he hasn't any control over his life. That's a terrible feeling. I know.''

"But you wouldn't come between us...'' he protested.

"Adam thinks I would, and that's all that matters. If you love your son, you have to trust me on this.''

"Sarah, darling, you may be reading him wrong. Neither one of us has had any experience raising teenage kids.''

Sarah sighed. "I've avoided telling you my life story, Christopher. I never wanted you to know what it was like for me growing up. I don't want your pity, but I guess you have to know why I'm in a much better position to understand Adam than you are.''

Feeling his gaze on her face, she averted her eyes, staring fixedly at the small peach flowers scattered on the ivory paper covering the far wall. "All the time I was a teenager, like Adam, I was alone. Oh, I lived in a house with other people—people who had been my adoptive parents for four years until they became obsessed with the two babies of their own they were finally able to have. I lied when I told you my parents were dead. I have no idea who they were... who I really am.

"Anyway, with the babies getting all the attention, I had no one to talk to about my feelings, and the changes that

vere happening in my body and to my emotions. I was lost
ind utterly alone until I started to work at the stables
iearby. There, at least, I had the animals to love and care
or, until..." Her hand unconsciously moved to her abdo-
nen.

"Poor darling," Christopher said, moving to bury his
face in her lap.

"Don't get me wrong," she said, absently stroking his
iair. "I was never mistreated—nothing like that. It's just
hat suddenly the whole household revolved around Me-
issa and Stephen. After they were born there just wasn't any
oom for me in my parent's house or hearts. Those babies
came between me and the only real love I'd ever known. I
esented them then, and to this day, I still do." Saying the
words aloud, Sarah felt as though an old wound she'd
hought long healed had opened in her soul.

In a rush she was transported back to the two-story frame
iouse in Hollister, Idaho, that had been the only long-term
childhood home she'd ever had. In her memory she relived
he moment when she'd first known she was no longer
oved. She saw herself running to greet her father as he
oulled in from a long haul, only to have him push past her
with a "Hi, Sarah" and stride into the house, where he
scooped up the new baby and cuddled it against his shoul-
ler. Feeling crushed and humiliated, from that day on she'd
nade sure she'd never been at the door to greet him again.

"I'll never do anything like that to Adam," she declared
vehemently, coming out of her reverie. "It will be hard
enough on him just having you gone six months out of the
year. He'll need all the love you have to give when you are
10me."

Christopher sat up and looked into her implacable face.
"I'll take a port job rather than lose you," he declared. "I'll
be home every night."

"Who do you think you're kidding?" she asked, impaling him with a piercing gaze. "I remember how you felt about Max giving up his chance of promotion for Alani and their children. You didn't consider doing that for Virginia, did you? And last month when Adam came—he'd barely been here a day, but you left anyhow. I know how much your job means to you. You've selfishly put it before everything and everyone all your life. Even if you were serious, I could never allow you to do that!"

"If it's the only way, I'll do it!" he retorted angrily.

Realizing there was an outside chance that if he became too angry he might do something as rash as taking another position just to prove his point, she softened her expression and her words. "If you gave up what means the most to you, you'd become a worthless empty hull like I've been all these years. When I found out that I could never have children, life lost its meaning. Can't you see that the same thing would happen to you if you gave up your dreams of becoming the captain of your own ship? After a while—and it wouldn't take very long—you'd come to hate me for letting you do that out of love for me.

"And it's all beside the point. I can't marry you and come between you and Adam. It's too great a risk. If you lost your only child because of me, I could never give you another."

"Sarah, Sarah, that's not going to happen! I won't let it!"

"It can happen," she said in emotionless tones, "and it would. I couldn't face the time when you'd come to see me as an interloper. Adam would never be happy, and knowing that, you couldn't be, either. You'd come to realize I wasn't worth the sacrifices you'd made to make room for me in your lives. I couldn't bear to have your love for me turn to ashes like my parents' love did when they had children of their own."

Christopher could see that he'd get nowhere by arguing urther with her tonight. She was adamant in her refusal to narry him, and her reasoning tore at his heart. She had had ll this bottled up inside her, waiting to let it out for Lord knew how long. She needed time to recover, if only from the ordeal of telling her story. He was beginning to see that she vas more deeply scarred by her childhood experiences than by the blow from the horse's hoof, that she was convinced here was a parallel between her own blighted teenage years and Adam's. It would take more than just a few hours of alking to convince her that she wasn't a menace to his son's future.

Caring for her even more than he'd thought possible, he lidn't want to prolong her agony. There was no need, while he was in this highly volatile state, to drag up additional letails of her disturbing past that would serve only to multiply her doubts concerning the bright future he offered.

"I love you, Sarah. And the offer—all, or any part of it—till stands. I want you for my wife, and I'm not going to ive up on that! We'll talk about it more tomorrow night—I have to oversee the unloading of the ship in the morning. Meanwhile, you get some sleep." Throwing his legs over the ide of the bed, he stood and carefully tucked the quilt around her, before heading for the shower.

He could see that it would take all of his powers of persuasion to convince Sarah—and Adam—that the three of hem could make a life together. Physically his son was nearly grown, but he was still a child when it came to understanding that he had to take others' wants and needs into account. The boy had to come to understand that it wasn't necessary for the world to revolve around Adam Weaver in order for him to be happy.

Growing up as a pampered only child, Adam wasn't used o compromise, but he'd learn. Christopher would never abandon the boy, but he had no intention of sacrificing

Sarah to his son's childish whim, any more than Virginia had put aside her marriage to Greg. Adam was being unreasonable, and he'd have to come around.

The harder task, he suspected, would be convincing Sarah. He wouldn't even try, he decided, until he'd had the matter out with his son. The first thing he'd do when he got off cargo watch the following afternoon would be to pick up Adam and take the boy to dinner somewhere where they could talk.

Sarah lay still while Christopher showered and dressed, pretending to have fallen asleep when his lips lightly brushed her forehead. Too numb to feel the pain she knew would engulf her as soon as he was gone, she could only think of how nearly he had been hers.

Chapter Thirteen

The next morning Sarah stayed in bed, counting on his work to prevent Christopher from stopping by, counting on his thinking that she'd be too emotionally depleted to have risen early. Once she was sure he'd left for the ship, she got up and pulled a large battered suitcase from behind the water heater. Staring at the brown plaid cardboard monstrosity, she wished she had something else to use. She'd purchased it at a thrift shop in Hollister years ago, when she'd finally made up her mind that she was leaving home. All she could see was her mother's white face when she'd come into her cheerful bedroom that long-ago afternoon and found her packing.

Shaking her head to clear away memories she'd suppressed until now, she began throwing her clothes into the musty suitcase, putting into action the plan her feverish brain had devised during her sleepless hours. She was leaving. She didn't know where she was going, and it really didn't matter. Right now it was enough to know that she was removing herself from being the problem that would ruin the homecoming Adam had anticipated with such joy and hope.

After leaving a message with Dr. Blake's answering service that she'd been called away on an emergency and would be in touch with him soon, she waited until she heard Erma take Amanda and Bertha for their morning walk, before she hurried over to the Weaver house.

"Mary Lou?" she called softly at the open door.

"In here, dear." The answer came from the living room.

Going in, Sarah clenched her fists and gritted her teeth. No tears, she promised herself.

"I'm leaving for a few days," Sarah stated bluntly.

"You're white as a sheet. Has something happened?" Mary Lou asked, looking up at her in alarm.

"Nothing for you to be upset about," Sarah hastened to say, resting one denim-clad knee on the arm of the couch. She needed a little support, but she didn't want to risk sitting down, knowing the act had a sense of permanence that might give the older woman the impression she wanted to be talked out of her plan. "It only concerns me."

"Anything that concerns you enough to make you leave concerns me, too," the older woman said.

"I have to go away until after Christopher and Adam leave on their trip. I don't want to become an issue between them."

"Oh, is that it. But where will you go, child?"

Sarah shook her head. "I have no idea. I just wanted you to know I'm going so that you can explain that I didn't mysteriously disappear. And I don't want anyone looking for me."

"That's very considerate, but have you thought how your leaving will affect all of us?"

Sarah looked up at the ceiling, biting her lower lip to keep from crying. "I know it seems selfish and immature, but please trust me. I know what I'm doing."

"I'm sure you do, dear, and I won't pry into your reasons."

Looking down into Christopher's mother's faded blue eyes, she knew she owed this patient woman an explanation even though she would never demand one.

"You see, Christopher asked me to marry him last night, and I can't do that to Adam. He ran away from his mother because of a stepfather. I don't think he could handle it if he felt he'd lost his father, too. I don't want to hurt him the way—" She stopped suddenly. The last thing she needed right now was pity.

"The way you feel your family hurt you?" Mary Lou finished for her.

Sarah lifted her chin, gazing out the window beyond them, unable to meet the white-haired woman's eyes.

"Sarah, I've done a lot of thinking about you since you told me about your past with your family, and dear, I think it's a good thing that you're leaving."

Sarah's mouth dropped open with shock.

"I'll see to it that Adam takes care of your dogs until he leaves on his little trip with Christopher, and Erma can take over for a few days after that," the older woman went on calmly. "Now, don't stand there looking like I've lost my mind. Come around here and sit down." She patted the coral cushion beside her.

Sarah obeyed, dropping to the couch in bewilderment.

"What's the name of that town in Idaho where you came from?"

"Hollister."

"Oh yes, Hollister. I've been trying to remember it for several days. Well, I think you should go back to Hollister."

"Why?" Sarah asked, searching Mary Lou's impassive face for some clue as to why Christopher's mother wanted her gone. Had Mrs. Weaver reconsidered her feelings about Sarah's being a suitable wife for her son, now that she'd had time to consider her potential daughter-in-law's unknown heritage and rootless beginnings?

"I don't think you've faced the truth about yourself, Sarah," Mary Lou said kindly. "Your infertility isn't the

source of your unhappiness, dear, but your estrangemen
from your family is. Until you go back home and settle you
differences with them, you won't ever be whole again.''

But no matter what I do, I never will be! Sarah wanted t
shout. Instead, forcing herself to imitate Mary Lou's calr
tones, she said, ''I cut myself off from Hollister long age
My past there is dead. I'll never go near the place again.''

''You may think it's dead, but you're still being haunte
by its ghosts who need laying to rest. Sarah, go home. Se
your family. Now that you're a mature woman, mayb
you'll be able to look at things with different eyes.''

''I doubt that my family wants to see me any more than
want to see them,'' Sarah said, suddenly assailed by uncer
tainty. She knew they didn't want to see her, had most likely
forgotten all about her by now. She'd left because they n
longer cared about her, hadn't she? What Mary Lou wa
suggesting went against everything she'd believed for th
past nine years. Still, something kept her from arguing an
caused her to stay where she was, listening.

''Your adoptive parents loved you—you told me s
yourself. You said that the first years after you were adoptec
were the happiest of your life. Isn't that true?''

Sarah nodded mutely.

''I can't believe their love for you ended so abruptly. An
if it did, perhaps they realize their mistake by now an
blame themselves. Go home. Show them what a lovely an
loving woman you've become.''

''I . . . I can't,'' Sarah stammered. ''It's too late.''

''It's never too late. Remember? Those were your ow
words to me, and I believed you. Because of your faith I'n
learning to walk again. Now I think you're the one in th
invalid chair, waiting to die. Only it's worse for you. You'v
never really lived, and yet you have a great many mor
lonely years to suffer through than I—unless somethin,
happens to turn you around.

"Sarah, go home," she repeated. "Find out if you're suffering needlessly. You may discover your parents need your love and understanding as much as you need theirs. Do you think Virginia will find any peace until she and her son are reconciled?"

"No," Sarah agreed, "of course not. Adam's too much a part of her life. I'm sure she loves him every bit as much as he loves her."

"I'm sure, too. Can't you see it may be the same for you and your parents? And if it's not, you'll at least have the satisfaction of knowing, once and for all, that it's over between you and them. You thought you cut your ties when you left, dear, but you didn't. You still have unfinished business that has to be resolved one way or the other before you can go on with your life."

Sarah sat silent for a long while. Hollister was the last place in the world she wanted to go, but now that the idea had been posed, now that the old wound had started to fester, she wondered if Mary Lou could be right. Was there any chance that going there would put an end to the incessant pain that throbbed in her mind and soul?

"I don't know if old Kanga can make it that far, the way she's been drinking oil lately..." she said at last, weakened by old and new doubts tearing at her raw emotions.

"You can try," Mary Lou said with heartfelt warmth. "You can try."

SARAH ATTEMPTED to keep her mind as empty as her rattling van, as she traveled down the vacationer-filled interstate freeway toward Portland. If she thought too much about what she was doing, she knew she'd turn back. Nevertheless, it was easier and far less distracting to think of Hollister and what she might find there than of Seattle and what she'd left behind.

Melissa and Stephen had been five and four when she'd left nine years ago. Simple arithmetic told her they were now fourteen and thirteen. Adam's age. Good Lord, she thought with a start, I wouldn't know them if I passed them on the street. As ridiculous as it seemed, in her mind's eye they'd stayed suspended in childhood, never changing from the young children they'd been when she'd last seen them.

And her mother. How would she look? Still the slim youthful woman she'd thought so beautiful? Sarah remembered how proud she'd been to be able to point out Joan Mitchell to her classmates as her mother when parents had come to school on special days.

Suddenly, a dam burst in her brain, allowing memories she'd kept from her consciousness to flood out, inundating her mind with pictures so vivid, so real, she gasped at their pungency. Time had dimmed nothing. It was all there, just as though it were yesterday. From the joyous day her adoption papers had been finalized, through the blissful days when she'd been an only child, to the bitterly poignant, distressful days when she'd gradually lost the certainty of a love she'd come to believe was to be hers alone forever.

Crossing the wide bridge over the mighty Columbia into Oregon, she headed east along the river, pushing ever nearer to the town in Idaho that she still feared could offer only more heartbreak. Yet, as she traveled along, hope began to grow in her heart. She felt as if she were caught up in an arduous quest. Exactly what she was seeking, she hadn't quite fathomed, but seized by a strange exhilaration, she drove on and on through the late northern evening as though in pursuit of a wondrous prize.

By nightfall she could hardly keep her eyes open and began to worry about falling asleep at the wheel. Pulling off the main road to slowly drive through small towns, she found that motels had long since been filled with holiday travelers. It wasn't until after midnight, just short of the

Idaho state border, that her bleary eyes spied a neon vacancy sign. She gratefully pulled an overheated Kanga into a parking space beside a row of vehicles. The motel was old and tawdry, obviously not a popular stopover, but Sarah didn't care. As long as she could sleep for a while and have a shower when she awoke, her surroundings didn't matter.

In the early morning she was off again, stopping at a truck stop after she'd crossed into Idaho for a cup of coffee, a tank of gas and two quarts of oil—Kanga was swilling the stuff like a parched laborer working in the dry Idaho fields would gulp down water once the sun had risen in the sky. Studying her map, mentally adding up the tiny confusing red numbers that were scattered haphazardly along the lines representing roads, she figured she had a little more than two hundred miles to go—give or take ten or twenty, she thought wryly.

Her hands shook as she wrapped them both around the heavy crockery cup. How often had her father stopped his truck here on his long drives to the coast? How many of the men sitting at the tables around her would know his name if she asked? Disturbed by the realization that Jim Mitchell could walk through the door even as she sat on the counter stool, she quickly finished off the rest of her coffee and hurried out to her van.

Traffic picked up around Boise, but thinned out greatly as she started the long lonely stretch toward Mountain Home. Glens Ferry, Bliss, Hagerman, Buhl, then Filer.... She recited aloud the names of the towns that she'd pass through on the way to Hollister. She'd stop in Filer for another fill-up. Funny, she hadn't thought of those towns in years, but there they were in her memory as fresh as they had been in the days when she'd gone on shopping sprees to the "city" with her family.

As she traveled through each small familiar community, butterflies fluttered in her stomach. Her palms grew damp, and her T-shirt and shorts stuck to the patched Naugahyde of the seat as the scorching summer sun rose higher over the rolling arid rangeland. Kanga wasn't air-conditioned and the air was stifling, burning her throat as it roared in through the open windows.

She considered calling ahead to let someone know she was on her way. But when she stopped for a cola at a crossroads grocery and went to the outside phone booth, she couldn't make herself go that far. Hollister was her destination, but what she'd do when she got there she hadn't yet decided.

Kanga's lurching and bucking into a service station on the outskirts of Filer decided matters for her. She'd nursed the ailing van along for the last five miles praying it wouldn't break down before she was within walking distance of help. When the engine died, she managed to coast the last few yards before coming to a stop at the pumps.

"Your bearings are seized up," the middle-aged mechanic informed her, dismally shaking his head after lifting the hood to inspect the motor. "Stiff as a dead mule. When's the last time you put oil in this contraption?"

"Just outside Boise," Sarah said, staring with utter frustration at the smoking engine.

"Then you must've left a trail of the stuff from there to here on the highway. Dry as a bone."

"Can you fix it?" she asked with a grimace, sure she wouldn't want to hear the answer.

"No, ma'am. You're going to need a complete overhaul job. Your engine's frozen up tight as a drum—probably wouldn't be worth the money it'd cost you, either," he added skeptically, giving the dusty utility van a quick once-over. "Where you bound for?" he asked.

"Hollister."

"Got folks there?" he asked, squinting into her face as though he ought to recognize her.

"Yes," she admitted. "Jim and Joan Mitchell." It was the first time she'd spoken their names in years. Suddenly she wondered if they still lived in Hollister. In nine years anything could have happened to them. Stricken, she felt anxious concern replace the burden of anger, which had lessened as she'd driven the long miles through the harsh yet beautiful landscape.

"Yeah," he said, taking off his greasy baseball cap and scratching his thinning hair before settling it back on his head. "I know Jim. Drives a big rig. Comes in here for a fill-up once in a while. Matter of fact, he drove by day before yesterday on his way home. Always honks his horn at me. Nice fella."

Relief swept over Sarah like an incoming tide.

"Look, you go on into the station and put in a call to him. I'll get the boys to push this buggy over there to the side. It's not goin' anywheres for a while. You can leave it here while you decide what you're gonna do with it.

"There's a scrapyard in Twin Falls that might give you a few bucks for it," he called after her as she started toward the building.

Staring at the phone, Sarah hesitated. Could she take this last step? Could she handle the Mitchells' cool refusal to have anything to do with her? Uncertain, she wondered if she could face the finality of a total break with the only family she had ever known, if that's what the next few moments brought. Then she remembered Mary Lou's words: "You can try, Sarah. You can try." Strengthened by the older woman's indomitable courage, Sarah picked up the phone and dialed the number, which sprang readily into her mind.

A girlish voice answered. Melissa, Sarah thought as she asked for Joan Mitchell.

"Who's calling, please?"

For a long moment she groped for an answer, wondering if Melissa would even know who she was. Finally she managed to say, "It's...it's Sarah."

"Mom! Mom! It's Sarah!" Hearing the high-pitched shout, Sarah's stomach churned and her hand tightened on the receiver.

In seconds the unmistakable voice of her mother came through the wire. "Sarah? My baby? Is it really you?"

"Yes, Mom," she answered. Tears welling in her eyes, she turned and lifted her arm, resting her palm against the station's dusty window for support.

"Where are you? Are you all right?"

"I'm in Filer...at the Shell station...my van broke down. I was on my way to see you." It was hard to talk over the lump rising in her throat.

Her mother's words came rapid-fire. "Stay right where you are. Don't you move an inch. We'll be there to get you as fast as we can. Oh, darling, you don't know how I've prayed for this day!"

"Me, too, Mom," Sarah said, and as sweet relief washed away the last vestiges of anger and doubt, she realized it was true.

After she hung up, she went into the women's rest room to bathe her face, but her tears kept flowing as she held on to the sides of the rust-stained white basin, washing out and cleansing the cankerous wound that would finally have a chance to heal.

SEATED AT THE BREAKFAST TABLE long after the hearty morning meal was finished and her brother and sister had gone off to a day of tennis and swimming with their friends, Sarah and her parents caught up on the years that had passed.

"We always knew where you were," Joan Mitchell confessed. "We hired a detective to find you right after you left.

It was our only comfort. Whenever Jim was in Seattle he'd go by and check up on you to see if you were all right or if you needed us."

Sarah's eyes widened with surprise. "Mom...Dad...I'm really sorry I put you through all that. If only we could have talked or—"

"No apologies," her father quickly put in. "We weren't all that great shakes as parents to a budding teenager—we know that now, after what we're going through with these two kids. We never figured out exactly what went wrong between you and us until long after you were gone. Even then we were afraid to approach you, afraid you might not be ready and that we'd drive you off for good."

"Every Christmas, when we wrapped the packages and did the cards," her mother added, "we could hardly keep from sending something off to you."

"And your birthday was the same way," Jim Mitchell added. He sighed as if weighted down by memories. "We just kept saying our prayers that someday you'd come home. And thank God, they were finally answered.

"Sarah, honey," he continued, his deep voice at once earnest and comforting, "we decided long ago that if you ever came back to us, we'd forget about the past and go on from there. I hope you can do the same thing. We never stopped loving you...not for one minute."

He chuckled and the lines around his mouth deepened in his weather-beaten face. "You gave us a little scare a few months ago when I went by to look at your houseboat and it wasn't there. Took me a few days to locate you again. Let me show you something."

Taking his wallet from the back pocket of his well-worn jeans, he unfolded a string of plastic enclosures, producing a series of pictures. All of them, Sarah realized with a start, were of her. The one that caught her eye showed her and Christopher working on the Weaver houseboat. Seattle seemed so far away from this lovely old frame house, standing against the winds of time in the middle of its own five acres. Christopher Weaver had become a dull ache somewhere in her overflowing heart.

"Took that one from a seaplane," her father admitted. "I never knew what a telescopic lens was until after I started keeping track of you."

Emotion-choked, Sarah reached across the table to take his callused hand in hers. It was almost more than she could grasp. All through the years when she'd felt herself alone, and entirely dependent on her ability to make it on her own, her parents had been keeping careful watch over her. Reassured by their silent devotion, Sarah felt a renewed bond grow between them, stronger and more real than before.

As the days of her homecoming progressed, Sarah began to build a relationship with Melissa and Stephen. Though a year apart in age, the tall slim teenagers looked enough alike to be twins. The overtures on both sides were tentative at first, but before long she fell into an easy camaraderie with them, much like the one she and Adam had enjoyed. The morning after Melissa had shyly asked if she could spend the night with her—keeping her awake until three o'clock in the morning with her questions and concerns—Sarah awoke with a grin on her face, popcorn and candy wrappers in her bed, pinned down to the pillow by a newfound baby sister who had thrown one arm across her neck in the deep sleep of innocence.

Secure as she had never been, Sarah became aware of a new sense of self that gave her a confidence she'd never had. Completely sure now of her family's love, her past no longer haunted her. With the demons laid to rest, she was fortified with a new inner strength and resiliency.

Exactly a week after her arrival, as they sat over second cups of steaming coffee in the pleasant country kitchen with ts western exposure, Sarah confided to her mother, "I painted my kitchen this same color."

"And your house is the same gray trimmed in white," Joan added. The scent of honeysuckle wafted on the breeze that lifted the ruffled Priscilla curtains.

Sarah nodded. "Except for a few touches of brass, my bedroom is decorated all peach and ivory, just like my room here. I guess subconsciously I wanted my house to be as nearly home as I could make it."

"Do you feel comfortable here now, honey?"

"Yes, I do," Sarah answered, smiling into her dark-haired mother's unlined face. The threads of silver woven through her thick brown hair did nothing to detract from the fifty-two-year-old's inherent good looks. It gave Sarah pleasure to find that the years had been kind to Joan and Jim Mitchell. The couple was more active than ever, and she knew anyone who met the two wouldn't find it odd that they had children as young as Melissa and Stephen.

"I heard you ask that doctor you work for for a long leave of absence. Does that mean you'll stay with us?" The hopeful note in her mother's voice caused Sarah to look down at her cup.

"I don't know... I'm so confused. I guess I'm up to my old tricks again—running away." A rueful grimace pulled down the corners of her mouth.

"From what, Sarah?" Joan asked.

"From a man who wants to marry me. Christopher Weaver." Suddenly his image cut through the blanket of loving security which the nostalgic atmosphere of the house had wrapped around her, insulating and shielding her from the outside world. So effective had been its comforting cushion that for a solid week she'd been successful in hiding herself from her other cares. Her eyes widened as a jolt of emotion tore through her like a bolt of lightning.

"Do you love him?"

Stunned, she heard her mother's question as if it came from a great distance.

"He has a son Melissa's age." Her own voice seemed detached, bodiless.

"That's wonderful, especially since..." Joan's enthusiastic reply faded off.

Sarah felt herself float back to reality as the words permeated her consciousness. "Since I can't have children of my own? You can finish your sentence, Mom. I don't know if I'll come to accept the idea—ever—but at least I think I'm beginning to learn to live with it. Christopher claims it doesn't matter to him, so that's not the problem. It's just that Adam needs his father now, and I'm afraid I'd be in the way."

"Sarah, tell me about Adam and Christopher," Joan said quietly.

So Sarah told the story of her love. Not as she'd choked it out in tearful sobs of despair to Mary Lou, but rather as a confident person would disclose the details of her life to a good friend. Joan listened intently, nodding with understanding, her grave intelligent eyes fixed upon her daughter's face. And as Sarah revealed her feelings about Adam, drawing a parallel between his life and hers, her newfound security allowed her to see that what Mary Lou had suggested had been correct. She had envisioned the boy as a threat to her own happiness—a selfish and self-seeking happiness that she'd wanted only for herself. A flush spread over her skin as she realized she'd been every bit as selfish and self-centered as she'd accused Christopher of being.

"I can see you love this man very much," Joan said when her daughter had finished. "If he feels the same way, and from what you've told me I'm certain he must, your problems don't have to be insurmountable. It's a mistake for you to project and imagine too many parallels between your life and Adam's. That boy may not be the problem you seem to think he is, honey. There's no reason why you should feel you have to take his mother's place. The child is fortunate to have so many people love him. Remember that day he told you to jump in the lake?"

Sarah nodded, vividly recalling the scene. "I'll never forget it." Her house of cards had fallen down around her, scattering her hopes like the blossoms drifting over the water from nearby flowering trees.

"He was only striking out at you in a flash of justifiable anger—anger with his mother for marrying, and anger with his father for leaving him just as he'd arrived in Seattle. You just happened to be the only target he could hit."

Joan sighed and a note of sadness entered her voice. "Teenagers are so volatile. So emotional. So changeable. I wish I'd known how to deal with your problems and your insecurities better. If I had, I know we'd never have spent these terrible years apart."

"Don't blame yourself, Mom," Sarah said, reaching out to cover the older woman's hand where it rested on the table.

"I do, though, Sarah," she said, a tear trickling down her smooth cheek. "You were my first baby and you came to me with those big wide eyes of yours that had already seen too much unhappiness. Your life hadn't been good before we got you, and I loved you like my own. I wanted to make everything right for you. But I let you down. I got so wrapped up in the babies when they came along, that you felt I didn't love you. You slipped away from me without my realizing it. I had no idea you were so withdrawn from us until the day you left.

"What makes it all the worse—" her dark eyes clouded with pain "—was that Jim and I always felt that the babies were a gift from you. We think—and the doctor agrees—that if you hadn't come into our lives, I would have never been relaxed and happy enough to get pregnant. And when you had your accident..." Unable to go on, Joan Mitchell broke into an anguished sob.

"Don't, Mom, please," Sarah pleaded, her own eyes spilling out hot tears of regret.

"I couldn't cope, Sarah. I just couldn't handle it. I love you so much it was worse than if it had happened to me." She broke off. Pulling her hand free she buried her face in her folded arms, her slim body racked with heaving sobs.

Grateful for the hard-won maturity that let her accept and understand her mother's words, Sarah's heart filled with loving compassion. She gathered the suffering woman up into a loving embrace. They stood in the sunlight, holding one another, weeping, tied together with the indestructible ribbon of love between mother and daughter.

At that moment, Sarah knew she didn't have to give Christopher up because of Adam. Mary Lou had been right. When people really loved one another, that love wasn't exclusive. She'd give Christopher this time alone with his son to resolve the problems they had, and then she'd be ready to go back to Seattle to see if his offer still held. If it didn't...if by any chance he'd changed his mind, she was now strong enough to make him see that they were made for each other. Well on the way to reestablishing her bonds with her family—bonds she was sure would never be broken again—she was ready to take on new relationships and commitments in a way she'd never been before. The part of her heart that had always been full of doubts that she could never seem to put to rest, was at last quiet and still, filled with a serene new joy.

When, after several long moments they separated, Joan dried her tears with the edge of her apron, and reached up to gently wipe the moisture from her daughter's cheeks. "What would your father think if he came in here and found us crying like babies?" she asked, a trembling smile on her lips. "He'd never understand."

"You're right, Mom," Sarah said, with an answering smile. "He probably wouldn't, but I finally do. Thank you."

"Now, where were we?" Joan asked briskly as though to cover her embarrassment at having broken down. Seating herself at the sturdy oak table her great-grandparents had brought west on the Oregon Trail, she freshened their coffee from a waiting pot.

"We were discussing Adam," Sarah said, resting her elbows on the yellow-and-white checkered tablecloth. "I can't see how he and I can ever come to an understanding about this."

"Don't be so sure, Sarah. I've learned a lot about teenagers since that dreadful day nine years ago. I've made a point of it. I'd be willing to bet that if you asked him today, Adam'd deny he ever told you to jump in the lake and he'd believe it wholeheartedly."

"Do you really think so?" Sarah asked, her voice at once hopeful and wistful.

Chapter Fourteen

Seated in front of a crackling driftwood fire, Christopher leaned back on his elbows and stretched out his long legs. Though he'd wiped his feet at the door, the edges of his cowboy boots were caked with the mud he'd sloshed through to bring in the load of dry wood Adam and he had collected and stacked in the lean-to the summer before. A steady gray rain fell outside, blurring the outlines of the sailboat moored to a buoy in the small cove in front of the cabin.

They'd sailed out of Seattle in drizzling rain, and ever since they'd arrived at their cabin on Whidbey Island they'd been hit with one deluge after another. Jeans, jackets, flannel shirts and socks hung around the cabin in various stages of drying, giving mute evidence to miserable efforts to enjoy the out-of-doors. Even rain slickers hadn't kept Adam and Christopher dry the times they'd ventured out on a hike.

The bleak weather suited Christopher's mood, but he knew his young son was going stir-crazy. For the boy's sake, he'd considered heading back home, but the wind that had accompanied the rain had led to small-craft advisories, and almost as important, he'd needed the near solitude to think.

Stirring himself from his lethargy in an effort to be companionable, he asked the restless boy lounging beside him on the braided rug, "How about a game of cribbage?"

"Penny a point," Adam declared with enthusiasm, jumping up to get the board and cards. "You owe me more than five bucks already."

Christopher's mouth tilted in a wan smile. He rose to his feet and seated himself at the round pine table. With Sarah's image ever before him, it was difficult to concentrate on anything, let alone a card game. Each time he and the boy had walked to the grocery store two miles down the road for fresh provisions, he'd been tempted to call her, but he'd refrained, knowing that he wasn't yet ready to counter her logic by addressing each of her accusations and premises.

However, no matter how painful the past two weeks of introspection had been for him and how boring for Adam, the time had been well spent. He'd learned more about himself than all the previous years of his lifetime had ever taught him.

"Come on, Dad, it's your turn to deal," Adam said, exasperation plain on his freckled face.

"Sorry, son," Chris apologized, his large hand scooping up the cards on the table and absentmindedly shuffling them. "I was just thinking."

"That's all you've been doing," Adam said, picking up each card as it was dealt to him and arranging it in his hand. "What's the weighty problem? Or is it some big secret? Look, I'm not a little kid anymore, Dad. If you're thinking about what to do with me, I gotta be in on it."

Looking up from his hand, Christopher saw the anxiety in his son's eyes. "I've been thinking about all of us—you, me...and Sarah."

"What about Sarah?" Adam asked pointedly, folding the fan of cards in his hand and laying it facedown on the table, his dark eyes alive with interest.

Christopher's first impulse was to give some vague response, preferring not to share his unformed thoughts until he'd completely reasoned them through and decided upon a satisfactory course of action. Then, remembering what an impact any decision he made about Sarah would have upon his son's life, he laid down his own uninspected hand and spoke. "I'm in love with Sarah. I want her to be my wife." He waited for Adam's reaction, but his son's gaze was steady and his facial expression didn't change.

"I figured that one out," the boy said after a prolonged pause. "I wondered how come she went to Idaho instead of coming here with us, but with the look on your face lately didn't dare ask." He gave a snort.

"How do you feel about Sarah?" Christopher asked as casually as he could manage, suspecting his whole future rested on the fourteen-year-old's reply.

Dropping his gaze, Adam gave an indifferent shrug, his fingers reaching out to stir the six cards before him.

For a moment Christopher regretted starting the conversation. It was the first time he remembered asking the boy how he felt about anything, and maybe it hadn't been such a hot idea. Adam was too young to make decisions that could affect all their lives. But he did want to know his son's feelings, and he couldn't just drop the subject now that he'd opened it.

"She says that she can't marry me because of you." The second the words were out of his mouth he mentally kicked himself. *Terrific,* he thought. *Get the kid on the defensive and blame the whole mess on him right off the bat! Great going, Weaver,* he told himself sarcastically. *Nothing like blowing your first honest attempt at parenting.*

"Geez, what'd I do now?" Adam asked sullenly, turning his back and flinging one arm over the top of the wooden chair.

"It wasn't fair of me to say that," Christopher said, self-reproach rising like bile in his throat. Choosing his words, he explained, "What Sarah meant was that she couldn't marry me because of her concern for you. She thinks you need me more right now than she and I need each other. She's afraid of coming between us. Can you understand that?"

"Yeah, I sure can," the boy answered, still not turning to face his father.

Standing, Christopher put one hand in his jeans pocket and rubbed the back of his neck with the other. No wonder he'd shied away from any deep talks with his son. He had no idea what was going on under that red baseball cap and mop of bleached curls. But he couldn't back out now. "Can you understand that I love you both and need you both?"

Another shrug was his only answer.

"Look, Adam," he said, walking around the table to face the boy. "Sarah said that I was selfish—that I'd always been selfish. When she first hit me with that accusation, I tried to chalk it up to her being upset. But the more I thought about it, the more I began to realize she was right.

"I'm trying hard to change, son. I'm trying to think in terms of what's best for all of us, not just what's best for me. Right now I'm not sure how Sarah's doing, but I'd be willing to bet she's as miserable as we are."

Walking across the small room he stood before the large window, leaning his heated forehead against the rain-cooled glass. "I'm sorry I haven't been better company, but I've been preoccupied, wrestling with this problem by myself. I should have asked for your help and advice long before this. But when you're my age, you'll understand how hard it is to change the habits of half a lifetime. But I know it can be done, if you want to badly enough. And you're looking at a man who seriously wants to shake some bad habits.

"I need to talk with you, Adam," he said, going back to the table. He turned his chair and straddled it, gratified when his son did the same. Folding his arms on the chair back, he stared into the flickering firelight that played its dancing shadows upon his chiseled face.

"I need your help and I need your advice. Like I said, I'm ready to admit I've been selfish. But I don't have to tell you that. You know that better than anyone else in the world. I love you, Adam, and I hope to God you know it, because I've been a rotten father to you.

"I wonder now just how many times you wanted me in Lincoln for something special." Feeling a lump in his throat, he swallowed hard. "Your sixth-grade play, the time you won the city basketball shoot, and other times that I can think of through the years. I was in port. I don't know why I didn't catch a flight to be there for you instead of settling for programs and lousy newspaper clippings. I missed the boat—" he gave a humorless laugh at his pun "—I can see that now. I don't know why I didn't long before this." His voice softened. "I guess it was because I didn't have Sarah to help me see it. She told me I'd been using you like a pawn, moving you in and out of my life to suit my schedule. Picking you up and putting you down whenever it was convenient for me—not necessarily when it was important to you."

He drew in a deep reflexive breath. "There's no way around it, pal. Up to this point I've put my career first every step of the way. I've been a slave to my ambition, and I didn't give much thought to who got hurt along the way. I haven't even been the son to your grandmother that I should have been. Sure—" he shrugged his plaid-shirted shoulders "—I've been doing all the right things for her, but for the wrong reasons. I've only been concerned with keeping her comfortable so that I could set sail without any worries. She deserves better than that. If I'd taken an extended leave of absence and stayed with her and worked with her for six months after her stroke, she might not have spent the last three years as an invalid."

He glanced toward Adam. The boy's eyes were fixed upon him. "Now, maybe in wanting Sarah I'm even being more selfish. She's been great with your gram. She'd never be out of that wheelchair if it weren't for Sarah and that little mutt, Amanda. Sarah's shown she can handle you, too, and that she cares a lot about you. And I like having her there when I come home. She's a very special person."

Sighing, he rested his stubbled cheek on his folded arms. "But what do I have to offer her?" he went on as if to himself. "A husband who's gone six months out of the year? A teenage son and an invalid mother? Is it right to tie her down to that?"

"Don't ask me," Adam said flippantly. "Ask her."

"I did ask her." Christopher struggled to keep the annoyance he felt out of his voice. He'd bared his soul to this kid, and in return he'd expected more than a smart-aleck reply. Suddenly he realized he was doing it again—expecting his son to follow his agenda. What else could he expect from a teenage boy than for him to cover his true feelings with a flippant reply? "Now I'm asking you how you feel about her."

"She's okay, I guess," Adam said, only a little grudgingly. "We'd sure be having a better time if she was here. At least you wouldn't be moping around all the time."

"Adam—" Christopher rose and walked around the table to put his hands on the boy's bony shoulders "—you're my only child. I love you as I love no one else. My loving Sarah doesn't change that one bit. And if you honestly feel that our getting married will harm you in any way, we need to talk about it, so that I can understand where you're coming from. You and Sarah are the most important people in the world to me, and I just can't let this drop. Son, I'm sure that she isn't going to wait for me until you're grown up.''

He looked into Adam's clear open face, searching his eyes for any trace of the boy's true feelings.

"I like her, too, Dad," the boy finally admitted. "I guess she wouldn't get in my hair too much. She treats me like a real person, not like a little kid the way Mom does. And believe me—" his young voice turned scornful "—Sarah's nothing like Greg. She makes everything better, and he makes everything worse.''

Christopher moved his hands to the sides of Adam's face and looked long into the boy's bright brown eyes. Adam was going to need help adjusting to his stepfather. He'd have to talk with Virginia to see what they could work out. Jealousy was the likely culprit, but then again there might be some basis for Adam's feelings about Greg. Whatever, he felt confident that if they all pulled together they could work it out. He had too much regard for Virginia to want to see her estranged from their son. Bending down, he kissed the boy's smooth forehead before moving back to stand before the window.

"Another thing I've been thinking about is giving up my place on the ship. Taking a shore job so that I'd be home every night with you."

"That's a bunch of bull!" Adam shouted, jumping up so quickly his chair toppled over. "That's the last thing in the world I want from you."

Christopher swung around to face the angry man-child striding toward him.

"I told all my friends how you were going to be captain of your own ship just like Grandpop was. The only reason I try to get good grades in school is so I can go to the academy like you did when I graduate. Half the reason of why I came to live with you was to be near salt water. How could I learn to be a sailor in Nebraska? If you do anything stupid like that I'll never forgive you!'' Tears swam in his dark eyes.

Opening his arms, Christopher pulled the tall boy to his chest. Holding him close for a moment, he patted him reassuringly on the back before releasing him. Keeping one arm around Adam's shoulders, he said with a chuckle, ''That's about the same violent reaction I got from Sarah. I guess it wasn't such a hot idea.''

Adam shook his head. ''You got that right!'' His arm encircled his father's waist. ''Dad?''

''What, son?''

''Let's go get her. Let's get Sarah.''

Christopher smiled down into his son's knowing eyes, giving his shoulders an affectionate squeeze. ''Good idea. I was kind of thinking the same thing myself.''

''Yeah,'' Adam said, moving out of his father's range, a mischievous look in his eyes. ''She's a better cook and a better cribbage player than you are!''

Christopher groaned, bending at the middle in mock pain. ''That hurt!''

''WHERE ARE YOU?'' Sarah nearly shrieked into the phone, her hands trembling as she held the receiver to her ear. She had pencil in hand to take a message, expecting the call to be the nearly two hundredth one she'd answered that morning for Melissa and Stephen. Her brother and sister, surely Hollister's most popular teenagers, had been streaking in and out of the house like greased lightning, on their way to or just returned from who knows where, with whatever friend wasn't calling at any given moment.

The shock of hearing Christopher's deep voice was causing all sorts of strange things to happen to her. Her knees felt like the plum jelly she'd been helping her mother put up, her throat went as dry as the plowed-under potato patch, and her eyes turned misty. Her heart pounded in her chest loud enough, she was sure, for him to hear.

"We're at the county airport outside of Twin Falls," he answered calmly as if he'd been expected. "I'd rent a car, but there doesn't seem to be any available here."

"Kanga died in Filer," Sarah said, frantically pulling out the rubber band that held her hair in an old-fashioned ponytail, heedless of the silky threads that went with it, "but I'll take my mother's car and be right there to get you."

"Good," Christopher answered. She could hear the smile in his baritone voice. "At least now I know what to buy for a wedding gift."

"Who's getting married?" Sarah asked in breathless tones. Feeling her heart thump in her ears, she wondered briefly if anyone had ever keeled over from pure excitement.

"We are, love. My son's finally given his consent!"

SARAH NEVER REMEMBERED the drive to the airport that day. It was as if she had been transported there on a flying carpet that her overstimulated mind had conjured up. One minute she'd been talking to Christopher on the phone, the next she was wrapped tightly in his arms and being thoroughly kissed, much to the amusement of the mechanics and clerks standing in the small airport terminal.

As she drove her two men home, she listened to their tale of how they'd both decided that Sarah was the only woman for them. Later, when she thought about it, she was grateful for the lack of traffic signals between Twin Falls and Hollister. Her magic carpet had stuck around for the trip back, only this time Christopher and Adam had joined her for the ride.

Sarah proudly introduced the Weaver men to her mother and her attractive siblings, who'd come home for lunch to find themselves corralled and ordered to spruce up to meet their guests. She was delighted to see her mother and the man she loved reach an immediate rapport. When Joan Mitchell explained that her husband had just taken his rig to the truck terminal for its monthly inspection, saying that she was certainly glad he wasn't off on a trip, Christopher was his most charming self. He nodded his head in understanding, drawing a parallel between Jim's life on the road and his at sea.

Adam stood a little to the side, a wary look on his face, his fingers hooked over the tops of his pockets, until Joan suggested that her son take him into the kitchen where the two of them could help themselves to the food she'd put out on the counter for lunch.

As the two boys left the room, with Adam remarking on the heat and Stephen suggesting that they take a swim later on, Sarah realized her sister was motioning her toward the guest bathroom. Seeing her mother and Christopher engrossed in easy conversation, she excused herself to dutifully follow Melissa, who shut the door to the small room behind them.

"What's up, 'Lissa?" Sarah asked, her hazel eyes puzzled.

"You've been holding out on me," the teenager accused.

"I don't know what you're talking about," Sarah said. Teenagers! And she'd thought things were going so well between her and Melissa.

"I thought we were best friends!"

"We are," Sarah agreed. That fact had been settled the night of their pajama party.

"Then why didn't you tell me about that gorgeous hunk you have wrapped around your little finger? I don't usually go for older men, but for him I could make an exception." Melissa rapidly raised and lowered her dark eyebrows two or three times to emphasize her point. "Mom filled me in about him while you were gone to the airport. I'll bet he looks fantastic in his uniform.''

Sarah laughed, affectionately hugging the slender girl, who at fourteen was as tall as she was.

"And his son!" Melissa exclaimed, pulling back to look her big sis in the face. "He's somethin' else, too. I've never seen a boy with hair the color of his except in movie magazines—"

At that Sarah broke into the laughter she'd suppressed when Christopher had remarked, upon seeing Adam for the first time with his shock of bleached curls, that it seemed odd the boy's hair had lightened in just that one spot. Trying to stifle her peals of laughter in her mother's best guest towel, she collapsed on the side of the tub, too weak from the release of her pent-up emotions to stand.

"What did I say?" the dark-haired girl asked, looking down at Sarah, her face screwed up in astonishment.

As soon as they'd finished a lunch of fresh fruit and homemade wheat-bread sandwiches stuffed with thick slabs of honey-cured ham, Adam happily went off with Melissa and Stephen, who were anxious to show off their newfound friend.

Taking a refreshing swallow of cider, Christopher placed his glass on the table and announced, "We're getting married right here. I'm not taking any chances of losing you again."

"But it takes time to plan a wedding," Sarah objected. "I don't even have a dress."

"Yes, you do, darling," her mother put in, happy tears swimming in her eyes. "I've saved my wedding gown for you. A few simple alterations and I'm sure it will be perfect. I'll get it out of the storage closet and we can get started right away. I'll just call Tom's bakery, Loretta down at the flower shop, Reverend Williams and..." She paused. "Just what day did you have in mind?" she asked Christopher.

"Tomorrow," he answered without hesitation, reaching over to cover Sarah's hand with his.

"Tomorrow?" Sarah squealed. "Have you lost your senses?"

"No," he drawled, with a slow grin that sent familiar tingles creeping deliriously up her spine, "I've just recently found them."

"Well," Joan said a little unsteadily at first, and then with growing excitement, "if you two run on down to City Hall right now and get your license, we might just make it." She rose. "Now, I just have to make sure your father's suit is pressed, and call Georgia, the church secretary. She can arrange for the ladies to bring the food, and whoever she can't get hold of, the kids can spread the word to tonight. Good thing tomorrow's Saturday. The whole town'll turn out— Your father! I've got to get hold of him. I don't want him to hear this from anyone else..." She hurried from the room, never stopping her monologue.

"Your mother's a lot like you," Christopher said approvingly. "She knows how to get things moving."

"But Mary Lou and Erma," Sarah wailed. "We can't get married without them."

"I'm here with their blessing," Christopher said, rising and pulling her to her feet. Standing just a heartbeat away, his blue eyes seemed to radiate a warmth as mesmerizing and appealing as flames leaping from a camp fire on a cool summer's night. "They're waiting with packed bags by the phone for our call," Christopher said. "All you have to do is say yes, and they'll be out here on the next plane."

"But the dogs!" Sarah protested. "Who's going to take care of them?"

"Erma and Henry have placed all but two, and Henry's going to house-sit until they get back. You know, I think that old guy has a thing for Erma."

"Really? Erma's never mentioned that to me. Do you think she knows?"

"I'm sure she does," he said with a wide grin. "Why else would he jump each time she calls? Come here, woman."

As he enfolded her in his embrace and his lips closed upon hers, Sarah knew the ecstasy of promise fulfilled. He was her man and she was his woman. She knew, as certainly as Mrs. Weaver had known of his father, that no matter what distances separated them Christopher would always return to her.

After sharing a wondrous kiss sweeter than any she had ever known, he pulled his lips from hers to murmur against her heated cheek, "Sarah, will you marry me?"

"Yes, oh yes, my darling," she said, her hands reaching up to turn his face to hers for still another kiss, delirious in the knowledge that this man would indeed be hers.

LATER THAT NIGHT in the motel room Christopher had taken, Sarah lay cuddled against Christopher's chest. Her fingers slowly caressed his skin languidly revitalizing her memory of every inch of his powerful body.

His deep voice echoed resonantly in his trim torso as he talked. "Far from coming between Adam and me, you've made the bonds between us stronger. After I took him into my confidence it was as if an invisible barrier between us was gone. We've had some terrific talks. I know him better than I ever did. He's ready to see his mom now. He's a great kid."

"I know what you mean," Sarah said dreamily, thinking of the lines of communication that had opened between her family and her. "It's so important for him to be able to talk to someone who loves him."

"And I have been selfish, Sarah," he admitted, bowing to kiss the part in her fragrant tawny hair. "I know that now. I haven't been willing to share my thoughts with anyone. I promise you I will change. I won't make decisions without consulting everyone involved." Then tilting up her face, he reverently feathered kisses from her forehead to her chin.

"I have it all planned out," he said, his eyes alight with boyish excitement. "We'll buy a farm up near Bothell where you can set up a regular kennel for your dogs. You can quit your job and devote all the time you'd like to Puppy Power. Even go into breeding if you wish."

Sarah smiled. This man she loved still had a lot to learn. "Issaquah," she corrected him. "And no dog breeding for me. I'm more interested in strays."

"Fine. Issaquah," Christopher agreed. "After we move, my mother and Erma can stay on Lake Union on the houseboat. I can't imagine my mother wanting to leave here."

"We'll have to ask them about that, won't we?" Sarah said sweetly, twining her fingers in the springy hair on his chest. "Perhaps they'd like to have a little place built on the farm near us."

"Sure," he consented, "that's no problem. And Adam can go to Denton during the week . . ."

"I think he might be happier at the local high school, and I'd like having him around when you're gone. But that's for him to decide, isn't it?"

"Yeah, well, I guess that's up to you and him," Christopher agreed. "He wants to go on from here to Nebraska for a week or so. So I thought we could take a quick honeymoon in Hawaii. I want to mend my fences with Max and Alani. I need some time to talk with Max, and I want you to get to know Alani as she really is. You'll like her."

"I'll go along with that one," Sarah agreed. "No correc tions there." Tilting her head back, she rewarded him with a soft smile.

Rolling his eyes toward the ceiling, Christopher let out a groan before meeting her amused gaze. "I'm at it again aren't I? Planning everyone's life for them. I guess I'm going to be a slow learner."

"That's all right, darling," she whispered, seductively reaching up to wrap her fingers in the sun-bleached thatch of hair that she had come to love as no other shade. "We've both got a lot to learn, but we have the rest of our lives to do it."

Harlequin Regency Romance™

Romance the way it was *always* meant to be!

The time is 1811, when a Regent Prince rules the empire. The place is London, the glittering capital where rakish dukes and dazzling debutantes scheme and flirt in a dangerously exciting game. Where marriage is the passport to wealth and power, yet every girl hopes secretly for love....

Welcome to Harlequin Regency Romance where reading is an adventure and romance is *not* just a thing of the past! Two delightful books a month, beginning May '89.

Available wherever Harlequin Books are sold.

Have You Ever Wondered If You Could Write A Harlequin Novel?

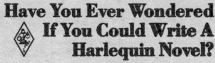

Here's great news—Harlequin is offering a series of cassette tapes to help you do just that. Written by Harlequin editors, these tapes give practical advice on how to make your characters—and your story—come alive. There's a tape for each contemporary romance series Harlequin publishes.

Mail order only

All sales final

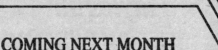

Harlequin American Romance®

COMING NEXT MONTH

COMING IN MARCH FROM

Harlequin *Superromance*

**Book Two of the
Merriman County Trilogy
AFTER ALL THESE YEARS
the sizzle of Eve Gladstone's
One Hot Summer continues!**

Sarah Crewes is at it again, throwing Merriman County
into a tailspin with her archival diggings. In *One Hot
Summer* (September 1988) she discovered that the town
of Ramsey Falls was celebrating its tricentennial one
year too early.

Now she's found that Riveredge, the Creweses'
ancestral home and property, does not rightfully belong
to her family. Worse, the legitimate heir to Riveredge
may be none other than the disquieting Australian,
Tyler Lassiter.

Sarah's not sure why Tyler's in town, but she suspects
he is out to right some old wrongs—and some new
ones!

The unforgettable characters of *One Hot Summer* and
After All These Years will continue to delight you in
book three of the trilogy. Watch for *Wouldn't It Be
Lovely* in November 1989.

SR349-1